PI
DRIVE

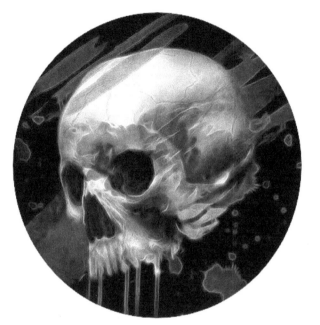

WRATH
JAMES WHITE

deadite press

DEADITE PRESS
P.O. BOX 10065
PORTLAND, OR 97296
www.DEADITEPRESS.com

AN ERASERHEAD PRESS COMPANY
www.ERASERHEADPRESS.com

ISBN: 978-1-62105-308-8

Prey Drive copyright © 2013, 2019 by Wrath James White

Cover design by Deadite Press

Printed in the USA.

For Mom

PROLOGUE

The prosecutor was a thin, fastidious man with narrow, rectangular glasses behind which his green eyes appeared enormous. He wore a dark gray suit and a pink shirt and tie that he was continually readjusting, looking as if the thing was on the verge of strangling him. His head was shaved bald and it turned a livid red when he spoke passionately, which he did frequently when describing Joseph's crimes to the jury. Earlier that day, the young district attorney had painted a picture of Joseph Miles that made the accused murderer sound like the biggest threat to the safety of mankind since the invention of the atomic bomb.

His shoulders rolled inward and his chest was sunken in as if he had received a tremendous blow to the upper torso and feared subsequent blows, avoiding them by remaining in that cowed posture. Contrary to the rest of him, his jaw was strong and square, his chin tilted high in the air, looking almost aristocratic.

He stood just barely more than five feet, five inches tall and was anemically thin. When he spoke the heavy bass timbre of his voice was almost comical issuing from such a diminutive man. His eyes challenged Joe from across the courtroom, focusing on him throughout the cross-examination of the prosecutor's expert psychologist by Joe's court-appointed attorney.

The judge, a large black woman with long dreadlocks salted with gray and pulled back into a ponytail, nodded to Joe's lawyer. "You may continue with your cross-examination, Mr. Leyendecker."

"Doctor, do you think it's possible for anyone, including

5

the defendant Joseph Miles, to have an irresistible impulse to rape, murder, and cannibalize fellow human beings?"

Dr. Sabine, an Indian man with bushy eyebrows and piercing eyes and an unsmiling face that appeared to have been hewn from stone, cleared his throat and took a sip of water before he spoke in tight, clipped sentences, trying hard to suppress his accent. "It is certainly possible, yes."

"Would you say it was probable in the case of the defendant, Joseph Miles?"

"Objection," the prosecutor interrupted.

Joe's attorney nodded his assent before the judge had even sustained the prosecutor's objection. Joe couldn't imagine what had been said that was out of order, but everyone else seemed to understand and accept that the attorney had somehow overstepped his bounds in the questioning of the prosecutor's psychologist.

Mr. Leyendecker began again. "Is there a distinct line between neurosis and psychosis, or are they the same?"

"Those terms are used to differentiate between degrees of mental illness. What differentiates between the two is the person's ability to perceive and react to reality in a true sense."

"And would you say that someone who believed he was turning into a werewolf was reacting to reality in a true sense?"

"Objection!"

"Withdrawn. What exactly differentiates between these two terms, doctor?"

"It's sometimes difficult to make a clear distinction. It's not black and white. There's some gray area. A psychotic person does not perceive reality as we do. A milder psychotic condition might mistakenly be interpreted as neurotic. Very severe neurosis may likewise be mistaken for psychosis. We can generally differentiate between them, although the lines do blur and there's some overlapping. Generally speaking, a psychotic person perceives the world incorrectly and a neurotic person sees the world correctly but reacts incorrectly, overreacts."

"Is the defendant, Joseph Miles, neurotic?"

"Yes, in my professional opinion, he is."

"Earlier in your testimony, you said the defendant had a tendency toward paranoid delusions. Would that indicate Joseph Miles may suffer from psychosis?"

"Objection," the prosecutor said. He was still staring at Joseph Miles and only watching the proceedings from the corner of his eye. He turned to face the judge, only to object before returning to stare at Joe. He seemed more interested in how Joe was reacting to the psychologist's testimony than to the testimony itself.

Joe felt uncomfortable in his chair. It was too small for his massive frame and the crowded courtroom distracted him. The aroma of flesh, sweat, perfume, aftershave, menstrual fluid, soap, shampoo, semen, and fear—delicious, intoxicating fear—formed a luxuriant miasma that enflamed his olfactory senses and kicked his salivary glands into overdrive along with his libido. Joe had to swallow several times to keep from drooling.

There was another scent in the air that Joe recognized all too well. It was the scent of female arousal. It was the smell of vaginal fluids moistening the walls of the female sex, preparing it for the intrusion of a stiff cock. Some of the women seated in the gallery were getting off on this.

The urge to turn toward the gallery and hunt through the crowd for the source of each scent, to follow each delectable human fragrance to its origin and taste it, devour it, and make it part of him was overwhelming. Joe shifted uncomfortably in his chair. He closed his eyes and inhaled deeply, but the instant his eyelids descended and darkness rushed in, carnal images of violence and passion succeeded the soothing blackness and the monster came roaring awake, pressing hard and insistent against the buttons of his orange jumpsuit, commanding him to feed.

With a shudder of unsatisfied desire, Joe struggled to regain control of his passions, succeeding with great effort that etched itself across his features in lines of anguish. Joe looked back in the direction of the district attorney and saw the man studying Joe's expression with his eyebrows knitted in concentration. Joe had the distinct impression the man was trying to read his mind. He turned back to watch his semi-competent lawyer do his worst.

The judge had overruled the DA's objection and Mr. Leyendecker had resumed his questioning of Dr. Sabine.

"Would you please answer the question, Dr. Sabine? Could the anxiety symptoms you described to the court earlier, the paranoid delusions you said Mr. Joseph Miles exhibited, result in deviant and abnormal behavior?"

"No, I'm afraid I cannot. I don't quite understand what you mean by 'deviant and abnormal.'"

"Eating other humans is certainly deviant and abnormal, wouldn't you agree?"

"Objection!"

"Sustained."

"Is it possible, in the defendant's case, that his normal impulse control was lower because of these paranoid delusions and he was not capable of controlling the irresistible impulse toward cannibalism and sadism?"

"Objection!"

"Objection sustained."

"Dr. Sabine, would you consider psychoneurosis a mental defect?"

"I would consider it a mental disorder."

"Not a defect?"

"Defect is not a psychological term."

"It is a disorder then?"

"Yes."

"Did your examination show this mental disorder in the defendant, Joseph Miles?"

"Yes."

"Would you say the cannibalistic tendencies the defendant has are a mental disorder?"

"Objection," the prosecutor said wearily. This time he didn't even turn his head from his study of Joseph Miles.

"Sustained."

"If the evidence were to justify the prosecutor's belief that over a period of three to four days, the defendant vivisected and consumed the flesh of the deceased and that while doing so, the defendant believed himself to be under the influence of a communicable disease that he says turns people into monsters, like lycanthropy or vampirism. If it were to be proven that during the torture and mutilation of Alicia Rosado, the decedent, the defendant not only disclosed no remorse but actually derived sexual enjoyment up to the point of orgasm, would that behavior pattern suggest that he was insane?"

"Objection."

"The objection is sustained."

"Do you think the defendant is afflicted with any mental disease whatsoever either now or at the time of his crimes in December of 2008?"

"Yes, I would say it was a neurotic delusion."

"Not a psychotic delusion?"

"Objection. Asked and answered."

"Sustained," the judge replied, waving her hand dismissively. She appeared riveted by the testimony and annoyed at the interruptions, however valid.

The defense attorney turned his back on Dr. Sabine and paced over to the jury, locking his eyes on each juror one by one as if directing his question to them rather than to the witness.

"Please indulge me for one final question, Dr. Sabine. I would like your professional opinion based on your evaluation of my client, the defendant, Joseph Miles. Seeing the pictures of the victim's remains"—he gestured to a television screen, upon which was the image of Alicia's corpse. It was just a pile of gnawed bones stripped of flesh, some of them cracked open with the marrow sucked out— "and your testimony here in the courtroom today, do you believe that his meeting with Alicia Rosado at that sex club in the South of Market district of San Francisco and her subsequently accompanying him back to his apartment could have ended any other way?"

Joe stared at the photos of Alicia's remains, remembering the succulent taste of her, how her soul had burned in his belly after he had consumed it. He remembered the expression of profound love on Alicia's lovely face as her spirit went the way of her flesh, devoured bit by bit to be merged with his own.

"Objection!" the DA shouted. He stood up in his chair and held out his arms as if pleading with the judge to intervene. It was the first time he had taken his eyes off Joe for any length of time.

"Withdrawn, your honor. I'm done with this witness."

Joe sat through several more days of testimony, including testimony from his former professor, Dr. John Locke.

"Dr. Locke, please state your credentials for the court."

"I have a doctorate in criminal psychology and a master's degree in psychotherapy. I worked for the Federal Bureau of Investigation for fifteen years in the behavioral science department where I interviewed close to thirty convicted serial killers. I currently teach abnormal psychology at the state university."

"You were the defendant's teacher for an entire semester, correct?"

"Yes."

"At any time during your acquaintance with my client, have you had cause to examine him?"

"Yes, I have."

"And what did you conclude from this examination? Would you agree with Dr. Sabine's testimony that Joseph Miles suffers from a neurosis rather than a psychosis?"

"No. I would not agree. Joseph is incapable of distinguishing between his delusion and reality. He believes himself to be powerless before a disease. In his mind, unless he finds the source of this disease, the first cause of the infection, he will forever be a slave to it. That's what he was doing when he murdered Damon Trent at the state hospital. That's what he was doing when he murdered his father. Both crimes which he has already been found not guilty by reason of insanity. He was trying to cure himself the only way he knew how, by destroying the source of the infection. He was trying to cure himself before this overwhelming homicidal impulse caused him to kill the woman he loved, Alicia Rosado," Professor Locke said.

Joe felt a slight tinge of betrayal listening to the professor's testimony. He was saying Joe was crazy, that his disease was a mental one rather than a physical virus. While Joe knew the professor had to say these things in order to save his life, he couldn't help but wonder if his mentor really believed what he was saying.

"Does this psychosis inform every decision the defendant makes? Does it affect every aspect of his life?"

"I can't say with absolute certainty. It would not necessarily have to."

"It would not necessarily have to, but it might?"

"It might."

"Do you have any personal interest in the outcome of this trial, Dr. Locke?"

"A personal interest? No. My interests are strictly professional. I wish to study the defendant."

"And whether he is convicted or not doesn't matter because you would still have access to study him either way?"

"That is correct."

"So then your opinion could be considered completely objective and would be based solely on your knowledge of psychology, your experience with signature sex murderers during your years as an FBI profiler, and your examination of my client?"

"That is correct."

Mr. Leyendecker began to pace again.

"The defendant is charged here with the offense of first degree murder in the death of Alicia Rosado. Doctor, have you formed an opinion as to whether the defendant was sane or insane at the time he committed the crimes for which he is being indicted?"

"Yes, I have."

"What is that opinion, may I ask?"

"In my opinion, he was insane when he murdered that woman."

Mr. Leyendecker again locked eyes with the jury as he asked his final question.

"And, Doctor, have you an opinion as to whether he is sane or insane at the present time?"

"In my opinion, Joseph Miles is completely insane."

The gallery erupted and the judge pounded her gavel to silence them. Joe was hardly aware he had been masturbating in open court until he let out a roar as the orgasm jerked his body like a ragdoll in the mouth of a vicious dog and he ejaculated onto the defendant's table. The bailiffs rushed in to restrain him as the judge banged her gavel again, harder this time, breaking the head off.

"Get this pervert out of my courtroom!" she yelled, pointing at Joe with the handle of her gavel, seeming to want to stab it through his heart. Joe's erection jutted forth from his unbuttoned jumpsuit, pearlescent droplets of semen still glistening on the engorged head of his massive cock.

Even as he was dragged from the courtroom, Joe could

not tear his eyes away from the picture on the screen of Alicia's skull, cracked open, the brainpan licked clean. He remembered the taste of his lover's thoughts. It had been the deepest ecstasy he'd ever known. One he longed to know again.

"Get him out of here! Now! Court is adjourned!"

Over the next few days the jury heard closing arguments from both the district attorney and Joe's defense attorney. Both sides acquitted themselves well and Joe had to retract his previous assessment of his attorney as barely competent. His defense rebuttal was brilliant. It took less than an hour before the jury returned a verdict of not guilty by reason of insanity and Joseph Miles was committed to the state hospital for the criminally insane. Four years later, he was declared legally sane and transferred to state prison, super maximum security.

PART ONE

Raw Fillipino Kinilaw

5 cloves of garlic minced
2 pieces of siling mahaba chopped
1 medium sized yellow, red, or white onion sliced into rings
1 scallion chopped
4 stalks of green onion chopped
1 small piece of ginger root minced
½ cup coconut vinegar
2 medium-sized cherry tomatoes chopped
Salt and pepper to taste
One large circumcised penis, skinned and chopped
Two testicles skinned and thinly sliced

Marinade chopped man meat in coconut vinegar for at least 30mins to an hour, Drain, then combine with all ingredients. Let stand refrigerated for another 30mins to an hour. Serve chilled with your favorite drink.

1

Dear Lana,

   I know you must think me a monster for what I did to your beautiful sister. Your continued silence confirms this and I can hardly blame you. It must be as difficult for you to understand what I did as it is for me to explain, but I'll try. I owe you that.

   The hardest thing about being what I am is that no one recognizes it as a disease. To most, I'm simply evil. But that explanation could not satisfy you. Evil is not a reason any sane human understands. My curse (and a curse it is) defies all the normal fetters of morality and civilization. It confounds the reasonable mind. I have puzzled for years over my nature and my conclusions sound irrational, even to me, though every experience, every urging, every lust confirms my prognosis.

   I have a disease and it has made me a monster. It has made me a creature far removed from the society of men, a pariah. I'm as hopelessly addicted to the consumption of human flesh as an addict is to his next shot of heroin. Yet the drunk, the junkie, the coke fiend, and even the glutton inspire more sympathy and compassion than I could ever hope for because their compulsions do not disfigure or destroy others. Their obsessions leave only themselves and their own loved ones in tears. It destroys their own friends and families, their own lives. I could only hope for such a benign addiction. I would gladly trade my curse for theirs.

The addiction that tortures me is like the terrific thirst of a vampire combined with the rapacious hunger of a werewolf and I'm convinced the curses are one and the same. That's why I was judged insane and sentenced to life behind bars instead of put to death, because no one understands this thing inside me and no one will listen! They do not believe this monstrous thing that I am has little choice or freewill involved in it, except for the choice whether or not to indulge it, which, for me, would be like choosing not to drink when my throat is parched or eat when my stomach churns with hunger pains. That is hardly a choice. This thing that has led me to such loathsome crimes is a disease that was passed to me. It does not describe my character. I'm a naturally mild person. I would not willfully harm the tiniest flea were I not compelled to do so by this terrible curse.

The man I see when I look in the mirror is not the man I once was, not the man I aspired to be. It is not the man who first met Alicia and, I believe, not the man I would have been had I never been accosted by my own homicidal fiend, Damon Trent, or had I not been born of the seed of a malevolent father, a sadistic pederast far worse than Damon Trent. I know how this must sound to you, like I'm avoiding responsibility for my actions, but make no mistake. I know I'm responsible. The lives I took haunt me, even those who were not so innocent. I'm a predator who grieves his prey and my immense remorse is the only proof I have that I'm still human. I mourn Alicia every day. I miss her as you could never imagine. She is the only woman, besides my mother, who ever truly loved me. I loved her too, more than I could ever express. My desire for her brought out the monster within me and I failed us both by letting it overcome me and then her.

I'm sorry for what I've done. Please find it in your heart to forgive me.

Sincerely,
Joseph Miles

Joe folded the letter and placed it in the envelope. He knew the language sounded oddly stiff and formal, antiquated. He couldn't help it. The longer he remained behind walls of steel and concrete, the more he forgot how real people spoke to one another. All he had for reference were books by Mary Shelley, Bram Stoker, Leo Tolstoy, and Charles Dickens. They, along with a host of other grand figures of historic literature, were his only friends now. He thought it was better he sounded like them than like one of his fellow convicts or the coarse prison guards.

The next time he saw his lawyer, Joe planned to give the letter to him with instructions to mail it to Lana like he'd done with the rest of them. He didn't want to know where she lived. He didn't trust himself. If he ever managed to leave this hellhole, he didn't believe he could resist the urge to pay the woman a visit. The idea that she might resemble his beloved Alicia in any way would be an irresistible temptation. If she wrote him back, her return address would be on the envelope. Joe knew himself well enough to know he'd take it as an invitation. He'd made a promise to himself to destroy the envelope if she ever returned one of his letters. Joe had been writing her a letter a week since he'd been incarcerated. They had all gone unanswered so far.

Joe placed the envelope on the lone metal shelf bolted to the wall of his cell opposite his bed. Then he wrapped a towel around the shelf, stuck his legs out straight, and began the first of ten sets of twenty pull-ups. The shelf shuddered and buckled under his weight, but it held.

He'd begun his second-to-last set, biceps and lats burning with lactic acid, when the guard in the control tower called his inmate number. He had a visitor. Joe washed his face and armpits in the sink and quickly rubbed deodorant under his arms. In the super maximum (supermax) security wing of the prison, visitors were received from behind bulletproof glass. Still, Joe wanted to look and smell his best. Hygiene was his only remaining connection to his former life, his life before the monster had taken over.

***

Lionel Ray Miles had been a cruel and vicious man in whom the milk of human kindness had curdled long ago. He was dead inside long before his son had torn off his head. Few people who knew the man were surprised by the manner of his death. Violent men came to violent ends. The little good there was in him he'd passed on to his son, Joseph, but then Lionel Ray corrupted that as well, turning Joseph into a monster. Few who knew the family were surprised by Joseph's crimes. His mother least of all.

Agatha Miles was the picture of matronly love and concern as she walked into the visiting room of the state prison's supermax security wing. Joe hadn't seen his mother in years. She'd left his father soon after Joe left for college. He always felt the separation had been calculated, like she'd been planning for years to leave his father but hadn't wanted to break up the family, but then figured it was okay once her son was a man and out on his own.

She took a seat behind the glass partition, fiddling with the leather-bound Bible in her lap and looking far older than Joe remembered. Her hair was almost completely gray and a web of wrinkles fanned out from the corners of each eye. There were hard lines around her mouth and she seemed to have lost a lot of weight. She was no longer the plump, rosy-cheeked woman with the perpetually sunny disposition he recalled from his youth, smiling at him through tears on the day she said goodbye. She looked pale and thin. Her skin looked as if it had been draped over a skeleton. Every movement she made, however slight, seemed capable of injuring her, fracturing her brittle bones.

She raised the telephone receiver from its cradle and even that seemed like a strain. Joe had left her alone without a husband or a lover to take care of her and the effect had been catastrophic. She seemed mere seconds from the grave. She reached out for Joe and her fingers encountered the glass partition and remained there, pressed hard against the barrier. Joe placed his hand against the glass, dwarfing his mom's birdlike digits with his massive fingers. He kept his hand there, willing his atoms to pass through the barrier to merge with hers. Whether he succeeded, he couldn't tell. He couldn't feel her, couldn't smell her. He imagined her spirit a smoky charcoal gray, the embers of a fire long ago snuffed out, with dim, infrequent flashes of electric blue appearing

23

here and there like lightning through a storm cloud that eventually dissipates without once losing its bolts from the heavens. He imagined that if he could smell her, her scent would not be the scent of electricity, blood, and the nectar of fruit that he smelled wafting maddeningly from the skin of the young people at his former college. It would be the scent of something dead and turned to dust.

His mother removed her hand and Joe eventually did the same, sighing over his failure to connect with her.

"My poor Joey. I should have taken you away from that man. I loved him though. I know you can't understand that, but I loved your father."

Joseph Miles never once mourned his father's death. Seeing his mother weep over her murdered husband was disconcerting.

"He was a killer, Mom. He murdered children."

"And you murdered him and those other people. Should I turn my back on you, Joey?"

"Maybe you should, Mom."

His mother shook her head, and for a moment he could see the strength she'd once had. "Your father was sick. He had a weakness inside him, an illness like the one you have. You don't know all the things he went through as a child. I don't even know all of it, but what Damon Trent did to you, terrible as it was, was nothing compared to what your father went through. We tried to protect you, Joey. We never wanted you to turn out like him. He never wanted that. If it wasn't for that Damon Trent …" She shook her head and wiped a tear from her eye with a handkerchief.

Joe's thoughts paused, stuck on what his mother had just confessed.

"You knew what Dad was? You knew?"

"I suspected. I knew he had a mean streak and I was sure he'd killed people before. I just never knew it was children. I thought maybe he'd killed guys in bar fights or maybe even evening ladies. That's why I left him. I thought he might have been buying whores and hurting them. Men do that sometimes. I never knew it was children."

Joe stared at his mother, seeing her through different eyes. *Men do that sometimes.* She made killing prostitutes seem as natural to man as leaving the toilet seat up. Maybe she wasn't the innocent, clueless victim he'd made her out to be. Maybe she wasn't exactly a saint herself.

How far did the corruption in his bloodline go? Joseph wondered.

"He was proud that you went off to college. You know that? He was always talkin' about his big college boy. We thought you were going to do great things. He called me when he saw on the news that a woman was murdered at your school. I didn't even know he knew how to find me. He knew it was you who did it. I don't know how he knew, but he did."

Joe smiled weakly and shook his head. Looking at his mother, hearing how she'd known or at least suspected what his father had been up to all those years—yet had done nothing—had continued to love him, Joe realized he'd never had a chance. He'd been cursed from the womb. Furthermore, he wondered if perhaps he'd been following the wrong bloodline. Perhaps the curse had not begun with his father but with his mother. He chased the thought from his mind, not liking the conclusion it inevitably led to or the actions that conclusion would necessitate.

"I love you, Mom. Goodbye."

Joe stood to his full, hulking, six feet, six inches and summoned the guard. He never looked back once as he left the visitation room, even knowing he probably wouldn't see her again until her funeral.

"Goodbye."

The guard took Joseph Miles back to his cell. Joe waited until he heard their footsteps echo down the hall before he allowed himself to weep.

2

It was dark. The air was moist with Joseph's sweat, and every surface within reach was hard and cold, metal and concrete. He breathed in his own musky funk and breathed it out in a steaming cloud of halitosis. The guards had taken away his toothbrush and he hadn't showered since they'd placed him completely naked in solitary confinement in a "strip cell." His "crime" had been refusing to leave his cell for a shower. That had been enough.

The idea of solitary confinement was ridiculous in supermax because every day was solitary. He was locked up twenty-three hours a day. The only thing they'd taken away by throwing him into solitary was his hour-a-day trip to the exercise yard and his thrice weekly showers.

Joe held his hand up in front of him and couldn't see his fingers. In addition to his own rank, animal scent, the room smelled of urine with the slight hint of old blood. It roared in Joe's nostrils and singed his nose hairs, causing his eyes to water. This was the first time in days Joe could remember the lights being off. The guards had made a habit of leaving them on all day and night. It was another form of subtle torture, the screws trying to mindfuck him. He hugged himself and rubbed down the goose bumps on his arms and shoulders. The temperature was just a few degrees above freezing.

He heard footsteps approach his cell door. There were several of them, at least three people. The door opened and one of the guards shined a light in on him. Joe winced. He sat naked on the floor, holding up a hand to shield his eyes from the light. He'd worked out to the point of exhaustion and now knelt in a pool of his own sweat. Bringing himself to the point of absolute physical fatigue was the only way he could force himself to sleep surrounded by the screams and shouts of the damned.

"Look at this crazy son of a bitch. He looks like a wet dog. Damn, it stinks in here!" one of the guards said.

There were two corrections officers standing in the doorway, shining a flashlight in on him. Between them stood a large shadow. A man easily as big as Joe himself if not bigger.

"You got a visitor, Joe. A new cellmate."

There was mirth in the guard's voice. Joe knew what he was up to. It wasn't his first rodeo.

"There's already someone in there!" The voice was high-pitched, feminine, with a slight lisp. As Joe's vision adjusted to the sudden intrusion of light, he could make out more of the man's features. He was naked, like Joseph. His cock was massive and hung almost to mid-thigh. The man was heavily muscled, black, with long braided hair that hung down past his shoulders. He couldn't make out the man's face, but he could tell by his posture that he wasn't happy. The officers removed the visitor's handcuffs and leg shackles.

"This is the only strip-cell available. You two are going to have to double-up."

The guard's voice was familiar. Joseph could picture the fat corrections officer's ruddy jowls and bloated belly, his crew-cut, so short he was almost bald, and the long scar on his scalp that ran down to his forehead, a reminder of when he'd been attacked by an inmate who'd made a shiv from a sharpened toothbrush. He worked in the control booth at night and was responsible for everything from locking and unlocking the cells to turning on and off the lights to what TV programs they got to watch.

"You two go ahead and get cozy. We'll be back for one of you in the morning."

27

There was no mistaking the guard's intentions. In supermax they called it "cockfighting." The guards would take two convicts with a history of unprovoked violence, strip them down, and put them in the same cell. It was done to get rid of problem inmates, as a form of discipline, and for simple amusement. He'd even heard that the guards bet on the fights. It wasn't Joseph's first experience with cockfighting. As one of the prison's more high-profile and dangerous offenders, he'd seen the worst the institution had to offer. Most of the corrections officers hated and feared him, so they routinely did things to try to break him, such as leaving the lights on twenty-four hours a day for weeks at a time, leaving the TV on, the volume up, tuned to a televangelist station for hours or even days, and putting him in the occasional cockfight. He wondered what his new cellmate had done to warrant the CO's ire.

The cell door slammed and locked. Joseph rose to his feet. He could feel the monster rising, stiffening, lengthening, the bloodlust swelling within him, tingling at the root of him. As usual his killing instinct was nearly indistinguishable from sexual passion. It was like a separate being living inside him, a parasite that was always hungry, always demanding to be fed. Ever since he'd been locked up, his thoughts and fantasies had become increasingly animalistic, reduced to the most base impulses; fuck, eat, kill—and not usually in that order. The terrible hunger he'd been living with for months had now become a persistent, maddening ache. The guards were going to get a show this time. They were going to get more than they ever bargained for.

The big man with the high-pitched voice and the long braids shambled forward in the dark. "Where are you? We don't have to fight, you know? Just because those fucking assholes stuck us in here hoping we'd kill each other doesn't mean we have to."

Joe was silent, listening to the man's heavy, nervous breathing, letting his eyes readjust to the darkness. The man smelled like sweat, semen, and perfume. The scent was maddening. Joe's stomach growled.

"What's your name? Who are you?" the stranger asked.

Joe walked closer to the man until he was standing just out of reach. "Joseph. Joseph Miles."

He heard the man's breath quicken. *Good*, Joseph thought. *He knows who I am. Knows what I can do.*

"J-Joseph Miles? The … the serial killer? The guy who eats people?" the large black man whispered. There was panic in the stranger's voice now. His high-pitched squeal was little more than a hoarse squeak.

"Yes." Joe stepped closer and the man retreated. Now Joe could smell blood and feces on the man in addition to the sweat and semen. He knew that unique combination of smells very well. It reminded him of his first night with Alicia. It was the scent of violent sex.

"You stay away from me, motherfucker! I swear, I'll whoop your ass and rape you! I like white boys. If I lose, I just get my ass kicked, but if you lose, you get your ass taken! I promise you that!"

A prison rapist. That explained why the guards had brought him. They wanted Joe to teach the guy a lesson. Joe stepped even closer.

The big rapist retreated further until his back was against the door he'd come through. Joe's erection was a spear stabbing the air in front of him. The monster was hungry. It was time to feed.

"If you lose, your ass will get eaten," Joe warned, "and not the way you like it eaten. The way I like it."

The man turned and began banging on the cell door. "Let me out of here, motherfuckers! You sick bastards! You locked me in here with a fucking psycho! Let me out!"

Joe was right on top of the man now.

The guy turned and punched the air, inches from Joseph's nose. "Get back! Get away from me!"

"No." Joe charged forward. He kicked the rapist in the stomach, expecting the blow to knock the wind out of him and double him over, allowing Joe to slip behind him and put him in a rear choke. But the guy was strong. He took the kick well. The blow drove him back but didn't seem to have hurt him. Suddenly the lights came on, blinding Joe. It was another trick the guards liked to pull. Leave them in absolute darkness for hours at a time and then suddenly turn on the lights in the middle of a fight. It kept things interesting for them.

A punch landed on Joe's jaw, and then another and another. Flashes of light went off in his head and everything began to fade, becoming gray and foggy. He knew he was about to pass out. Then Joe felt the man's thick arms encircle his throat and begin to squeeze. Obviously, the rapist had the same fight plan Joe had.

"My name's Luscious , you sick sonuvabitch. You feel that? It's going right up your tight little ass as soon as I put you to sleep. I warned you, didn't I? I told you what I would do if you fucked with me!"

Joe could feel Luscious's (pronounced Loo-shuss) enormous cock stiffening against the crack of his ass, parting his butt cheeks and probing at his anus. Joe grabbed one of Luscious's arms with both hands, the one locked around Joe's throat, and pulled down on it, giving himself room to breathe. He tucked his chin down between Luscious's forearm and his own throat to create more space and keep the big man from choking him unconscious. With one hand, he reached over and grabbed one of the big rapist's fingers, the middle finger, and jerked it back, snapping it. Luscious howled in pain. He let out a high-pitched shriek like a scream queen in a horror movie. At the same time, Joe bit into Luscious's forearm with teeth he'd filed into sharp points. He bit deep and jerked his head back and forth like a shark in the midst of a feeding frenzy, ripping through muscle and sinew, feeling the splash of warm blood as it flooded his mouth. The monster swelled, lengthened, throbbed. The taste of blood had awakened all the old desires.

He tore out a huge chunk of flesh from Luscious's forearm, swallowed it without chewing, and then seized his arm again. Luscious let go of Joe, but Joe didn't let go of him. That taste of flesh had sent the monster into a frenzy. His hardened cock pulsated between his legs, tingling on the brink of orgasm, hungry for more flesh.

"Ahhhhh! Aaaaaaaaaaaahhhhhhhhhhhh! You bit me! You fucking bit me! Let go! Let me tha-fuck GOOOooo! Heeeeeelllllp! HEEEEEELLLLLP! Guards! GUARDS!"

Joe jerked his head again and tore another huge avulsion in the big rapist's forearm. He took a punch to the temple from Luscious's free hand, causing him to release his lock on the man's arm as he staggered backward. The room wobbled and tilted and Joe almost collapsed. His balance quickly returned as Luscious charged again. This time the big rapist had his head down, his bleeding arm cradled in one hand, as he dove forward in a clumsy football tackle. Joe shot his legs out to avoid having them yanked out from under him and landing with Luscious on top of him. Joe had little doubt the man was still dangerous, even when injured. He sprawled on top of the large black man, driving him face-first into the floor. This time he was able to scramble around to take Luscious's back, but instead of choking him, he bit into the side of his neck, chewing through Luscious's carotid artery, tearing off and swallowing piece after piece of the man's neck as his would-be-rapist struggled beneath him, trying to escape Joe's savage onslaught.

Joe heard footsteps hurrying down the long tier. The guards were coming. Joe wasn't done yet. It had been so long since he'd tasted human flesh. He wanted to savor the moment, to make the most of it. He rolled Luscious onto his back. The big rapist was already trembling and hyperventilating in shock. This was the first time he'd been able to clearly see the man's face and Joe was surprised to see a handsome man wearing garish prison cosmetics, red Koolaid on his lips for lipstick and purple eye-shadow applied with a wet, purple Skittle. He had long eyelashes, high cheekbones, and full, bow-shaped lips. He was a transvestite and a beautiful one at that, though his muscular physique was anything but feminine. Joe yanked open the man's legs just as he heard the guard's voices outside the door.

"Open cell six! Open cell six! Back away from that convict, Joe! Get away from him! Put your hands on the wall!"

Joe ignored their commands. He lowered his head between the big transvestite's thighs and seized Luscious's cock and testicles in his jaws. He bit deep and pulled, stretching the foreskin and the wrinkled sack of Luscious's testes. Joe jerked his head violently, tearing the delicate flesh of Luscious's genitals as the man screamed in anguish. They tore free from the man's body—penis, testicles, and all—with a wet, sticky, ripping sound. Luscious's screams reached an octave that would have made a castrati tenor envious. The cell door opened and Joe put his hands behind his head, kneeling in Luscious's blood as he continued to chew. The familiar euphoria flooded over him as meat and blood filled his belly. Luscious's testes exploded in Joe's mouth as he chewed, bathing his taste buds with the succulent flavor of semen and blood. Joe let out a long growling moan as an orgasm ripped through him. The monster erupted, shooting a long stream of warm, white liquid onto Luscious's thighs and belly, mixing his seed with the rapist's blood.

"I told you to back away from the damn prisoner!" one of the SORT team guards yelled as he charged in behind a riot shield, swinging a baton at Joe's head. There were five other guards dressed similarly behind him.

The odds were against Joe. He ducked the first swing and then brought his arms up to defend his head from subsequent blows. But there were just too many of them, and punches, kicks, and baton strikes rained down on Joe in an avalanche of pulverizing pain. They wouldn't stop until Joe was unconscious. He knew that from experience. So Joe allowed himself to slump to the floor, going limp and pretending to have lost consciousness while still keeping his hands over his head to protect himself from the more life-threatening strikes. One of the guards straddled him and wrenched his arms away from his head. A few punches were landed to his face even after the officers thought he was unconscious, along with a kick from one of the officers standing above him. Joe didn't mind the punches and kicks; a baton to the head was far more likely to cause permanent brain damage.

Finally, Joe was handcuffed, very nearly hogtied, bent backward with his wrists cuffed to his ankles. One of the officers spit on him and the others laughed. They left him like that for more than an hour before they finally came back and took him to an isolation cell. Joe knew he wasn't being punished for ripping off the big transvestite's testicles. The guards had enjoyed every minute of the fight. He was being punished for defying them and not stopping when they told him to, and for that he would spend the weekend immobilized in a cell even smaller than his normal cage and his stay in supermax would be extended.

3

Strapped to a concrete bed, the overhead lights glaring down on him, a televangelist whipping his flock into a frenzy on the TV, Joe retreated into his head. He relived the salacious ecstasy of consuming human flesh again after months of abstinence. It had been glorious! Fighting for it, battling another predator for the prize, had somehow made it sweeter. And the blood! That sweet nectar of life. Its taste had been absolutely intoxicating, but it hadn't sated his hunger. It had only increased it, enflamed Joe's desire for murder and mayhem. He was like a caged wolf and the sheep were his captors.

Joe was naked again. The guards had shackled him and almost beat him to death trying to get the transvestite's masticated penis out of Joe's mouth before he could swallow it. They had been unsuccessful and they were punishing Joe for their failure. They had hogtied him, chained his handcuffs to his ankle cuffs, and then dragged him into this room and strapped him to a cold concrete slab. Then they left him there. Alone. Naked in the dark. Joe wondered if they would throw another inmate in with him now that he was helpless. He would not have been at all surprised.

As he lay immobilized, Joe had time to analyze his predicament. He'd become exactly what he'd feared becoming since the moment his violent urges began. He was an animal, a ravenous beast, and now he had been chained and caged. Somewhere, out there, was the one responsible for the monster that had blossomed inside him. Joe remained convinced that the disease taking over his mind, warping his personality, had been passed on to him, transmitted through blood, semen, or saliva. But after murdering the child killer who'd abducted him when he was a boy and then killing his own father with no result, Joe was forced to consider the possibility that his transformation was a genetic flaw passed onto him from his murderous father, an immutable part of his essence.

In jail, he learned that the police had found the deteriorated and decomposed remains of more than thirty boys on his father's property. He knew his dad was the one who'd made Damon Trent the murderous pederast that he'd become. Maybe his father's killing genes, his psychotic spirit, had been passed on to Joe.

Maybe there's no cure for what I am and this cage is the best place for me, Joseph wondered. But something inside him revolted at that idea. He was reminded of Quasimodo, limping through the darkened halls of Notre Dame shouting, "I'm a man!"

"I'm a man," Joseph whispered. "I'm not a monster. I'm a man."

But he wasn't so certain.

4

One week later ...

Professor John Locke walked the long, sterile white hall accompanied by a prison guard who looked like he'd been weaned on a cocktail of testosterone and human growth hormone. The corrections officer had the size and stature of an NFL lineman and the professor suspected the hyper-muscular guard once held those very aspirations. The man probably still played for a league on weekends. He wore weightlifting gloves on his stubby fingers and there were sweat stains in the armpits of his uniform, as if he'd just worked out in it. The officer walked bowlegged, like a gunslinger. His face held a perpetual frown that appeared to be a deliberate affectation, a warning to others to stay away.

"So you really think you can cure this guy?" the guard asked.

"I wouldn't be here if I didn't," Professor Locke responded.

The officer shook his head.

Professor John Locke was the polar opposite of the corrections officer who accompanied him. He was tall and slender with gray hair cut short and neat. Since his association with the serial murderer Joseph Miles had begun, he'd lost more than twenty pounds and still found it difficult to eat more than the occasional salad or fruit cocktail. He was now a vegan due to circumstances rather than design. He now found it impossible to stomach meat. The professor had wrinkles at the corners of his mouth and eyes and hard lines in his forehead from years of worry. His teeth appeared too small for his mouth and his lips were almost nonexistent. His mouth was little more than a thin gash in his face, just above his square chin. He wore a plain brown suit and thin, wire-framed glasses that were appropriately professorial.

"Why bother fixing this freak? He's already killed folks. He should be on death row right now by all rights."

The professor shook his head and sighed heavily. This type of attitude was what had retarded the study of the sociopathic disorder that led to signature sex crimes for decades. Finding live subjects to study who were this far advanced was difficult. What they didn't know about serial murderers could fill volumes, entire libraries.

"You'll have to take my word for it that he's of far more value to society alive than dead. Alive we can study him and use him to find a cure for his disorder."

"Fuck curing these bastards. There ain't no cure for crazy. There ain't no remedy for evil."

The professor nodded. There was no sense arguing with the officer. Nothing in his demeanor indicated he could be swayed. His disposition was unusually dour, unusual even for this place, as if he could find nothing to enjoy in his chosen occupation. The professor could understand. He didn't know how anyone but a psychologist like himself could enjoy spending his days surrounded by murderous psychopaths. Even he often found it taxing despite his intellectual curiosity and his thirst for recognition and fame.

Most of the COs on this end of Seattle's supermax prison were large, burly types who looked as hardened and dangerous as the convicts they guarded. The criminals they housed in this cellblock were completely insane, guilty of crimes that confounded all rational explanation. This was where they kept the "mental cases," the most violent and deranged inmates. A large percentage of them should have been in mental hospitals. Instead, they got their antipsychotics and antidepressants prescribed by prison doctors and administered by prison guards who were less than sympathetic.

In this cell block, there was a guy who locked families in their houses before he torched them, watching as they burned alive in their own homes; a guy who chopped the arms and legs off prostitutes and kept their torsos in his basement; a child molester who dissolved his victims alive in acid once he'd had his way with them; a guy who kidnapped old women and forced them to eat his feces—and then there was Joseph Miles. Joe kidnapped, raped, murdered, and cannibalized—and not always in that order—more than half a dozen victims. All the convicts were crazy, but the violent nature of their crimes had ensured they would never win an insanity plea. No judge wanted to let guys who raped, murdered, and mutilated go to a mental hospital. The public outrage would have been immense. Americans wanted them locked up or put down permanently like you would a rabid animal. So they brought them to supermax prisons where they were locked down for twenty-three hours a day and given no rehabilitation. What did it matter? None of them were ever going to be released.

The CO led Professor Locke past dozens of locked steel doors. Screams and shouts echoed down the hallway. Curses, prayers, catcalls, ranting gibberish, sobbing, pleas for rescue and salvation, and baleful stares followed them as they passed cell after cell. The sounds of madness and desperation. The familiar smells of blood, feces, and urine accompanied the cacophony. The psychologist wondered how anyone could smell that malefic stench and not realize they were amongst the insane. To him, this was the smell of a shattered mind. He'd smelled it at every mental institution he'd ever visited, even beneath the overpowering odor of bleach and ammonia. There was no masking it.

Every other cell they passed contained someone screaming biblical rhetoric, political conspiracies, or about aliens or demons infecting their minds. Professor Locke considered it a travesty of justice that any of these men had ever been declared legally sane, though he suspected that more than a few of them had gone mad during their incarceration. That too was not uncommon.

They stopped in front of one of the only quiet cells on that tier. The CO gestured toward the narrow window in the door, and the professor peered beyond the locked steel hatch into the cell beyond. Joseph Miles lay face down on the floor, pushing himself up and down on his knuckles, pistoning out pushups with machine-like repetitiveness. His face was tensed in concentration, teeth clenched, forehead furrowed, sweat dripping from his brow. The muscles in his shoulders and triceps bulged as if ready to burst through the skin. Veins and pulsing capillaries roped their way down his arms like night crawlers. He looked every bit as dangerous as he had the day they brought him in. His muscles were not as large as they had been. Since he'd been transferred to supermax following the episode with the model, he'd had no access to exercise equipment, but he'd obviously been improvising. His body was leaner now, harder, like something chiseled from the steel and concrete walls that surrounded him.

Joseph stared straight ahead as he continued a seemingly endless set of pushups. He stared through the steel door, through the professor and the guard, not appearing to even notice their presence. The professor shuddered. Joseph looked crazier now than ever. He'd thought they'd been making progress in the treatment of Joseph's disorder, but he couldn't help but question that. The man sweating and straining on the other side of that door looked anything but peaceful and well-adjusted. He looked like he was preparing for war.

"How long has he been doing that?"

The guard shrugged. "A half hour. Maybe longer. He was doing squats for about half an hour before that and before that he was doing crunches and before that some kind of pull-ups with a sheet tied to that metal shelf on the wall. He'll keep going for hours."

The professor nodded, narrowing his eyes and stroking the whiskers on his chin, trying his best to hide his unease. "And this has been going on for how long?" he asked.

"Ever since they transferred him here from the state mental hospital four years ago."

Ever since that lunatic whore from his art class cut her nipple off and fed it to him, the professor thought.

Professor Locke looked into the small windowless cell. There was a lidless stainless-steel toilet with a sink attached, a stool bolted to the floor, built in metal shelves, a cot bolted to the wall with a sheet and a pillow on it, and a TV with no controls. Other than that, the only furnishings or decorations the room contained were several paintings Joe had created using dissolved candy for watercolors and nearly a dozen shoeboxes tied with twine. The boxes were filled with fan mail. The corrections officers intercepted most of his mail and edited the ones they could. The ones that couldn't be edited into anything suitable for an inmate with his mental abnormalities were destroyed. For every letter they delivered to Joseph, they destroyed five. Most of the letters were from men and women declaring their love for him, asking Joseph to marry them, impregnate them, and even to eat them alive. Professor Locke had built his career studying the peculiar pathologies of deranged killers. Still, even he was shocked by how much our culture not only bred and nurtured these monsters but celebrated them. If he thought too long about how deranged the world was, he would wind up in one of those cells himself.

"I'm not taking him out of there by myself. I need to call another guard," the big CO said, displaying genuine fear. Not for the first time, Professor Locke wondered if his own fearlessness in regard to Joseph Miles was due to his objective observations of the man's behavior and his overall clinical detachment, or just plain foolishness.

5

Supermax was hell, even for a super-predator. Joe paused for a moment, dripping with sweat. Every muscle in his body burned with lactic acid. He studied each muscle as it contracted and relaxed. He knew he'd lost quite a bit of muscle mass, but he felt somehow deadlier with his leaner, harder physique. Like a large feline predator, a jungle cat. The stronger he felt, the more testosterone built up in his body, the stronger the urge to fuck and kill grew. Only the daily dosages of serotonin inhibitors kept him from total madness.

The sensation of his own body was his only comfort. If he could not have contact with other human beings, he would lose himself in the carnal physicality of his own flesh. He licked the sweat from his arms and remembered the sweaty, meaty taste of a woman's breasts after love making. He bit into his forearm and tasted the blood trickle onto his taste buds, setting them aflame with memories of those he'd consumed.

Joseph had spent the first week following his transfer in the strip cell. The guards removed all of his clothing and kept him in a windowless room with the heat turned down to fifty degrees and the light on twenty-four hours a day. There he had begun his new workout regimen. He'd started by doing six hundred pushups and crunches a day. That number had gradually increased to a thousand and then to two thousand. Then he'd added squats and pushups against the wall from a handstand position. Not only did the exercises keep him warm, they got him more in tune with his body. When he wasn't working out he masturbated, reliving every moment he'd spent with Alicia. He'd stroked his cock raw on several occasions. He'd even ejaculated blood once. That earned him a trip to the infirmary and his last night in the strip cell. But his new cell was no better than the strip cell.

Unlike the normal maximum security prison he'd been housed in or even the state mental hospital, in supermax there were no group activities. No sports, no therapy sessions, no religious meetings. No work and no opportunity to finish his education and get a degree online or through the mail. The inmates ate isolated in their cells. The only time they were allowed out was for an hour of exercise every day in a room with high concrete walls and a chin-up bar. Joe was allowed a ten-minute shower three times a week.

Joe spent his daily hour of exercise on the chin-up bar. Like his pushups, he was now able to do a thousand chin-ups in an hour. He was twenty pounds lighter than he was when he committed the crimes he was convicted of, but Joe's endurance was now off the charts. He felt quicker, more agile, and a hundred times more lethal than he had even a week ago when he'd killed the big transvestite. His hulking, sculptured physique was like a piece of iron, forged in the furnace of his murderous will.

For hours at a time he ran escape scenarios in his head, murdering guards, taking others hostage, and forcing them to open some doors and lock others to give him an unobstructed exit. He fantasized about all the ways there were to kill a man and pantomimed the murders as the very guards he was plotting against watched him on camera. Joseph ripped out imaginary throats, gouged imaginary eyes, and imagined his fingers piercing through to temporal lobes. He cracked skulls, hammering them into misshapen pulps with his elbows and knees. Ripped off testicles and bit through jugulars and carotid arteries. Then he imagined the feast, devouring the spoils of battle and ingesting the essences of the fallen, absorbing their power.

He remembered the taste of every muscle, every organ, and put new faces to them. The meaty biceps now wore the face of the guard who brought him his meals in the morning. The quadriceps belonged to the guard who walked him the five hundred yards to the shower and back. The brain bore the countenance of the officer in the control booth, and the heart came from the tortured visage of the lawyer who'd been trying to get him transferred to a psychiatric hospital. The breasts and ass, those still bore Alicia's face. They probably always would. But the hips, labia, clitoris, and nipples now accompanied the memory of the young model, Selene Cassaro, and her extraordinary gift. Joseph wanted more, so much more.

Ever since his fight with the transvestite, the lust for human flesh had become a raging tempest inside him that was thankfully quelled somewhat by the serotonin inhibitors Professor Locke had placed him on. But he'd been needing larger and larger doses lately, doses that left him dazed and disoriented, made it difficult to focus his thoughts. As much as he wanted to cooperate with the experiments, he needed a clear head if he was ever going to escape imprisonment.

Seeing Selene again was now almost impossible. She'd been banned from visiting him, and even if she did, in supermax, visitations were strictly "no contact," with visitors sitting behind a Plexiglas window and speaking through a phone. For Joseph, seeing her without being able to touch her would be even more maddening than not seeing her at all. Phone calls were also limited and heavily monitored. Even Joseph's conversations with his lawyer were now conducted through a Plexiglas window. The only one who'd been allowed to come into physical contact with Joe other than the guards was Professor Locke. Somehow he had been allowed to continue his research and treatment even while Joe was locked down, which allowed him a few extra hours a day out of his cell for therapy sessions consisting of the professor questioning him, taking blood and urine samples, and performing MRIs and PET scans in the prison hospital. Grant money raised by Professor Locke had purchased the equipment, which was likely one of the reasons he was allowed such access.

Even books and magazines were denied in supermax unless approved by the COs. The televisions inside the cells were controlled by the guards and were invariably tuned to institutional programs and religious services. It was not unusual to have the TV come on unexpectedly, broadcasting a "worship and praise" marathon by some televangelist well into the night. It was another form of subtle, insidious torture the guards employed.

Personal privacy was nonexistent in supermax. Guards monitored Joe's movements by video cameras around the clock, and communication between prisoners and control booth officers was mostly through speakers and microphones. The lights and door locks were all controlled electronically in the control booth. If the officer in the booth was pissed off, he'd leave the light in Joe's cell on all night.

The cells themselves were eight-by-ten concrete dungeons with all sensory input limited to concrete, steel, the bare seventy-five-watt bulb in a cage on the ceiling, and the television on the wall that came on periodically to broadcast messages of hope and redemption.

Joe was just about to begin his crunches when he noticed the professor standing at his door. A voice from the control booth ordered him to stand and place his hands on the wall in the back of the cell.

"You know the drill, Joe. We need to get you shackled for transport."

Joe did as commanded, rising and walking to the rear of his cell where he knelt and placed his hands on the wall. The guards rushed in and efficiently cuffed his wrists and ankles, and then helped him to his feet.

"How have you been, Joseph?" the professor asked, smiling warmly. He put a hand on Joe's shoulder and patted lightly as the guards led the enormous man out of the cell. Even with all the weight he'd lost, Joe knew he still struck an imposing figure. Professor Locke tried to insinuate himself into Joe's life as some sort of surrogate paternal figure, but Joe knew the man was secretly terrified of him. Joe's real dad had never been scared of him. Not even when he'd ripped the man's throat out with his teeth.

"I've been fine, Professor."

"And how are your urges?"

"Still strong, but manageable, sir." Joe saw no reason to lie. He'd never denied what he was, not even at his trial. Everyone in the room knew that he'd murder any one of them if left alone with them long enough. There were no secrets here.

"That's good, Joseph. We're going to try a new drug this week. It's designed to treat patients with bipolar disorder, but I think it can help you as well. I need to do another scan of your brain first to see how the serotonin inhibitors are working."

"Okay, Professor."

They began walking out of the cell and down the hall. Joe was staring at the floor as they walked the long corridor. The reality of spending the rest of his life in this cold, lifeless dungeon was increasingly affecting him. He didn't see how he could possibly survive another year in this place, least of all the rest of his life.

"Professor?"

"Yes, Joseph?"

"Do you think I'll ever be cured? Do you think I'll ever be able to leave this place?"

"I don't know, Joseph. Even if I cure your pathology, there are still the crimes you committed. You killed a lot of people. I don't think the state is going to forgive that. Let's just concentrate on making you well, okay?"

Joe nodded and looked back down at the floor. Lately he wasn't so sure he would ever be normal again, and if Professor Locke didn't have the solution to his disease then he would have to find it himself. And he couldn't do that behind bars.

6

Joseph was led from his cell to the PET scan room in handcuffs, belly chains, and leg shackles.

"You're going to have to take those off him."

"No way," the guard said. He was a large man, six feet, three inches and well over two hundred and fifty pounds. He looked nervous, terrified. "This guy eats people. There's no fuckin' way I'm taking these off him. He just bit the nuts off another inmate a week ago!"

Professor Locke lowered his glasses and looked over them at the big corrections officer. "That inmate never should have been anywhere near Joseph. That was either a careless mistake or deliberate malfeasance on the part of one or more of your fellow officers."

The CO's eyes went wild. His face turned bright red. He stepped forward so that his face was mere inches from the professor's. "You saying that one of us set that guy up so Joseph could mutilate him? Is that what you're saying?"

Professor Locke held his ground, meeting the angry officer's gaze calmly, unperturbed by his blustering outburst. "I'm saying it's a genuine possibility."

"That's bullshit!" The officer exploded.

Spittle sprayed from his lips and dotted the professor's glasses. Professor Locke calmly removed them and wiped them with a handkerchief he produced from his back pocket.

"Well, that may be. It's irrelevant in any case. What's done is done. So long as it doesn't happen again."

Joseph's prior good behavior during transport had led to his being "promoted" from a Level I inmate to a Level II, which meant he no longer needed two guards to transport

47

him from place to place, but he was still considered a danger to other inmates and was not allowed to leave his cell on his own or without restraints.

Professor Locke looked down at Joseph's handcuffs and ankle cuffs and shook his head. "I can't have any metal near the PET scan. He shouldn't even be in this room with those on. The warden promised me full cooperation."

The guard folded his massive arms across his chest and stared straight ahead, immovable. His arms were even bigger than Joseph's. Still, it was obvious at a glance that Joseph was the more dangerous of the two.

The doctor sighed. "If I drug him, will you remove the cuffs?"

"I will if he's out cold."

"If he's out cold the test won't work. Don't you have any of those plastic cuffs?"

The guard nodded. "I got 'em, but I don't think they'd hold this monster."

"Don't call him that. For Christ's sake."

"But that's what he is, isn't he? He's a fucking monster, a psycho killer."

"He's sick and he needs my help.'

"He should be on death row."

Joe watched the exchange between the professor and the guard with mild interest. Neither was desirable to him. Professor Locke was too old. His meat smelled stale and full of medications. Killing him would have been a mercy, culling the herd. The risk would not be worth the reward. Besides, he needed the professor. While there was even a glimmer of hope that he could be cured, he had to keep the professor alive.

The guard, on the other hand, was young and strong. His life force was like a furnace bristling with raw power. The smell of the man was thick and musky, full of male pheromones. The blood, sweat, meat, and adrenaline were intoxicating. But there was danger there. He was strong and aggressive, and Joseph was in chains. Besides, Joseph preferred women, though he was not picky when the hunger was upon him. Lately the hunger had not been as strong. The Prozac they'd been giving him in higher and higher doses dulled his appetite for flesh … slightly. It had made his hunger less urgent, less insistent. That left him free to be more selective, and right now he could not get his mind off the model.

She'd brought him her flesh. Her nipple. And since he'd tasted her, he couldn't think of anything else. She was sweet, delicious, and willing, eager to be consumed by him. Even with the letters heavily edited, cut to Swiss cheese by the guards who censored all his communication by excising any controversial words, the subtext was clear. She wanted him. She was offering herself to him.

. Even though she'd been permanently banned from the visitors' list and had been fined and jailed for passing him that succulent morsel of herself, she still sent him pictures. The guards didn't censor those. However, Joseph suspected they kept the more erotic ones for themselves and passed along those that were slightly less provocative, though even the ones he received were fully nude.

She had been fattening herself for him. Her hips, ass, thighs, and breasts were thicker, rounder. He wanted her so badly he could still taste her flesh on his tongue. He wanted to fuck her while he devoured the rest of her lovely breasts. He wanted to make love to her bleeding carcass as he consumed it. He imagined ripping large chunks from her breasts, arms, thighs, ass, tearing out her beating heart and swallowing it. Feeling the warmth of her flesh and her wild, uninhibited spirit, spreading through him, filling him. He wanted to express his love for her luscious physique, his appreciation for the skin, muscle, fat, and organs that comprised her, to marry it to his own.

Joseph closed his eyes and let out a low moan of soul-deep desire.

The professor misinterpreted it. "Are you okay, Joseph? Are you feeling poorly?"

"I'm okay, Professor. The shackles just hurt my wrists."

Professor Locke finally won his battle with the officer and Joseph was given a sedative. He watched with mild interest as he was injected. The professor waited for several minutes for the drug to take effect before asking the guard to remove the restraints.

"It doesn't look like he's sedated to me. He looks the same."

Joseph could smell the fear wafting from the CO's pores. The man was so full of adrenaline he was like a meth addict on a binge. Joseph had little doubt the man would order the SORT team to gun him down at the slightest provocation.

"I'll give him a stronger dose."

The professor made eye contact with Joseph. He didn't say a word. His expression didn't change in the least. Still, Joseph knew what the professor wanted him to do. This time, when he was injected, Joseph let his eyes droop and his body slump.

"There. Happy now? Can we get these manacles off him now?"

"Sure, but I'm calling some more guards in here first. Just in case he decides to get squirrelly."

Joseph didn't know why the doctor hadn't given him a real sedative. He suspected it was just what the doctor said. A real sedative would have screwed up the tests. And the tests were all that mattered to the professor. That gave Joseph an idea. He let his eyes slump further until they were mere slits, and then he began to drool for added effect.

"He doesn't look so dangerous now, does he?" the big CO said.

There were four more guards in the room now, SORT

officers in riot gear, the penitentiary version of SWAT. They looked eager for a fight, like fighting dogs tugging at their leashes. Joseph knew he couldn't take them. Those guys were trained to be quick and efficient. When Joseph killed, it was messy, sloppy, crimes of passion. He would stand no chance against them. Still, he continued his act. It may not help him this day, but one day Joseph knew that letting them think he was helpless would give him the element of surprise, and that might be all he needed.

Joseph stumbled along as he was led over to the PET scan and laid on his back. He was given a pillow and a blanket, and then what looked like virtual reality goggles were placed over his eyes.

"I'm going to be showing you some pictures," the professor explained. "I don't want you to say anything. I just want you to look at each picture while I take a scan of your brain. Do you understand?"

Joseph nodded.

"It'll just take the scanner a few minutes to warm up."

The professor pressed a button and the big machine began making a series of loud hums and clicks. A few minutes later, the professor pressed another button next to the platform upon which Joseph lay and it slid inside the big machine. Joseph felt his shoulders roll inward as he slid into the long cylindrical machine. It was almost too small for him and the walls of the machine pressed tight against his sides. In moments, pictures began to flash in front of him.

At first the images were simple. A baby smiling, a kitten playing with a toy, a puppy, a fireman, then a woman with large breasts in a bikini, then a naked woman, then a dead woman who'd been eviscerated, breasts cut off, abdomen cut open, then a piece of bloody meat, then a woman in red lingerie, then a woman's headless torso, and then a woman bound and gagged, and on and on. Joseph watched with interest. He was just as intrigued to discover what aroused him, what repulsed him, and what elicited no response at all. He was learning more and more about himself, but he knew none of this would cure him.

The image of a voluptuous woman with breasts like beach balls flashed on to the screen and Joseph thought immediately of Alicia. He missed her, but her memory never brought him sadness. Quite the opposite. Remembering the beautiful zaftig Spanish woman who'd traveled with him to Seattle in search of a cure for his curse, the woman he'd eaten alive over the course of several hours and then completely consumed in a matter of days, always aroused him, and now was no exception. He reached into his loose-fitting, prison-issued pants and began to stroke his hardening penis, mindless of the officers and the professor watching him.

More images of large naked women and dismembered corpses flashed before his eyes. Joseph jerked and tugged on his turgid flesh, licking his palm and rubbing the swollen head of his cock, feeling the orgasm build slowly within him. Then the images changed.

The next photo was of the librarian, his first victim. It was a picture of her at a party wearing a low cut dress. The next photo was of charred bones on an autopsy table. He could only guess that they were the librarian's remains. The next photo was of Frank, the masochistic homosexual Joseph kidnapped and dragged with him halfway to Tacoma to use as a snack. It was a crime scene photo of Frank's body, still smoldering, still on the spit where Joseph had left him after devouring his meatiest parts. Joseph continued to masturbate, aroused by the memories the photos were allowing him to relive.

Next was a picture of the transvestite prostitute and her pimp Joe had murdered at that rundown motel in Washington. After that came an image of the orderly he'd murdered to gain access to Damon Trent. This one did nothing for him.

That had been a crime of necessity, passionless. Then Damon Trent's corpse flashed on to the screen and he felt a surge of white-hot rage sear through his mind. His teeth clenched and his muscles tightened. He was surprised by how much hatred he still had for the man. Even knowing the fat pedophile hadn't been the one who'd made him into a monster, he still hated the man for what he'd done to him.

Next came another crime scene photo. This one was of Joe's father, a stake through his heart, mouth filled with garlic and Bible pages. Joe's anger came roaring back. If Damon hadn't been responsible for the disease that had made Joe a murderous cannibal, then it was congenital, inherited from his father. Before Joe's anger reached its limit, a new image flashed before his eyes. He gasped. His erection swelled anew and a warm smile softened his features. It was a picture of Alicia.

The photo had been taken long ago, before Joseph had ever met her. She was wearing a black lace negligee, cut low to reveal her massive cleavage. Her breasts were almost falling out of it and Joe thought he could make out one of her nipples peeking from the top of the garment. Her hair had been straightened and her long black locks spilled out over her shoulders and down her chest, framing her breasts. Her bow-shaped lips, painted dark red, were pursed as if she were preparing to blow a kiss. Her makeup was dark, almost sinister. She looked every bit the sultry vixen he'd followed around the sex club, desperate to meet. He began stroking himself again as he took in Alicia's long thick legs and voluptuous hips and remembered how they'd felt and how they'd tasted.

Then the next photo flashed onto the screen. It was a picture of Alicia taken the day she'd been admitted to the hospital, after Joseph had eaten her breasts down to the ribcage, unable to control himself. Next came a photo taken at Alicia's home. It was of her skeleton, picked clean, not an ounce of flesh remaining. Joseph stared at it and stroked himself more vigorously, tugging at his hardened flesh, remembering every moment of his last days with Alicia, how she'd begged him to eat every morsel of her flesh. She said she'd wanted to be part of him forever. He closed his eyes and recalled Alicia's drowsy smile just before she succumbed to the drugs and the blood loss and the trauma of being slowly cannibalized. Her eyes had looked so peaceful. So beautiful. Joe wished she was here with him now … so he could fuck and eat her all over again.

7

"Hey! He's jacking off in there! That sick fuck! Pull him out of there!" the CO said. He was in the booth with the professor and the SORT guys behind lead-lined glass to protect them from the sterilizing radiation from the PET scan.

"No! The experiment is not finished," the professor answered.

"He's getting off on this shit! What kind of experiment is it? Are you showing this sicko porn movies?" the CO asked.

"In a sense."

"What? You trying to see what turns this twisted fucker on?"

"Yes, in a way, that's exactly what I'm doing."

The large corrections officer's jaw dropped and his eyes bulged like they were ready to pop. "Y- you're doing what? Does the warden know about this shit?"

The professor sighed. "Officer?"

"Belton."

"Officer Belton, do you have any idea how much it costs to house a federal inmate?"

The burly corrections officer shook his head.

"It costs between twenty-seven and thirty-five thousand dollars a year. Now, do you know how much I'm paying the state of Washington for access to Joseph Miles? We have received hundreds of thousands in grant money and most of that is going directly to you guys. I'm paying your salary right now as we speak and if I don't get what I want I'll use all my influence to have Joseph transferred to another facility where the officers are more accommodating. My grant money will leave with me. It would then be your duty to explain my departure to the warden."

The professor never raised his voice. His tone remained calm and non-threatening, but there was no doubt that he had just issued a very pointed threat.

"You win, Doc. You and your psycho can have your little peepshow. But I'm telling the warden about it."

"Be my guest, Officer Belton."

Inside the big computerized tomography scanner, Joe smiled.

8

Back in his cell, Joe watched a guard slide mail through the slot in his door. It was a small stack of ten letters. There were fewer and fewer letters every day as Joe's name faded from the headlines. At one time he'd received fifty or sixty letters a day from the curious. Most he never answered. Joe felt uncomfortable being a celebrity and found the idea of gaining fans by eating the woman he loved more perverse than the act itself. There were a few he answered, like Selene, the nude model who'd visited him in jail and fed him her nipple; a few "long pigs" he'd recognized from the now defunct long pig message board—long pig being the slang for human flesh (Joe often wondered what made these people tick … what made someone volunteer to be someone else's dinner?); and several doctors, scientists, and professors—including Professor Theodore Acker, a psychologist from one of the big Ivy League colleges in Boston who was a rival of Dr. Locke—who were interested in his theories about what turned people into serial killers. There was even a celebrity sushi chef in San Francisco who sent him new recipes for the preparation of human flesh for consumption. The recipes all sounded delicious and inspired many fantasies. As the months passed, however, the communiqués dwindled. Now only his most hardcore fans wrote to him.

There was a letter from Selene in the stack. He smelled it. She'd sprayed it with perfume, but she'd also saturated it in her vaginal fluids and speckled it with her blood. It was a way to send Joe a message the guards could not understand or censor: *I'm yours. Take me.* He shuffled it to the bottom

of the pile, saving it for later, wanting to savor it. He opened
the next letter. It was from his younger cousin, Dirk. Dirk
was one of those kids who was obsessed with serial killers,
horror movies, and Goth music. The kid had been delighted
to discover a famous serial killer in his own family, unlike
the rest of Joe's family who'd promptly disowned him. Dirk
was now Joe's only link to the rest of his family. Recently,
Joe had been inquiring about his grandparents.

```
Yo, Cuz,
    I asked my dad about Grandpa and you
wouldn't believe the crazy shit he told
me. Your dad was adopted! From what they
told me, Grandpa's brother, Mike, went
to prison for (get this shit) attempted
murder! He tried to murder his own damn
wife. She took off after the trial and
Grandpa took you in. Your dad was Mike's
kid. Your dad and my dad had different
moms and dads. They don't know what
happened to your real grandfather, this
Mike dude. He never came back after he
was released. Ain't that a trip, Cuz?
    Anyway, I just thought you'd like to
know. I know everyone else in the family
is kind of trippin' about you killing
your dad, but I understand. That fool
was evil! All those kids he killed. He
had it coming. Don't worry, Cuz. I'm
behind you 100 percent. You just let me
know what I can do to help.
    By the way, I'm saving up the cash for
a bus ticket to come see you again. As
soon as I get a car I'll be coming up
every weekend.
```

Talk to you soon, Cuz!
Luv,
Dirk

Joe smiled. The first time Dirk came to see him, Joe had given the kid a message for Selene, something he couldn't put in a letter, something he didn't want the guards to read. He was happy to hear the message had been passed along. He couldn't wait to read Selene's letter now, but he knew the guards were watching. They were always watching. Instead, he took the letter and rubbed it beneath his nose. He'd never made love to Selene in real life, but he did so now in his fantasies.

He reached into his pants and freed the monster. It was already hardening. It only took a few strokes to bring it to full mast. If the guards were watching him now, they would get a nice show.

In Joe's mind Selene was in his bed, in his old apartment in downtown San Francisco. She was naked and she'd put on several pounds. Her hips, thighs, ass, and breasts were round and full. She cupped her breasts in her hands and lifted one up to her mouth, licking the nipple and then biting and sucking it as Joe stood above her, removing his clothes. She let one hand slide down between her thighs and began flicking her middle finger rapidly across her clitoris, which had swollen to the size of a grape. She rolled over onto her back and the most voluptuous ass Joe had ever seen wobbled into view. It was perfectly round, perched high on her back, and it was familiar. It was Alicia's ass on Selene's body. He lay on top of her and began kissing Selene's neck, shoulders, all the way down her spine to the voluptuous cream-colored mounds of her buttocks.

Joe rubbed his cheek across the two corpulent globes of muscle and adipose tissue, delighting in the way the smooth flesh jiggled against his skin. He kissed and sucked each cheek and then flicked his tongue across the crack. Selene quivered and moaned. Joe kissed them again. He bit down hard on one of her buttocks, drawing blood, and then sucked it until it bruised. Selene screamed. It sounded like ecstasy. Joe licked the cleft between her buttocks, which sent another shiver through her, and then he wriggled his tongue deep into her clenched anus.

He could feel her tense and then begin to shake and thrash. Her body went wild as he fucked her tight ass with his tongue and then with a cock the length and girth of an infant's arm. He bit down on the back of Selene's neck like a mating lion as he thrust deep inside her, slow and easy at first and then with increasing force and urgency, racing toward orgasm. Joe ejaculated silently— alone—in his cell. His seed shot up onto his stomach and chest. He still gripped Selene's letter in his hand, unopened. As he lay panting on the bed with his back pressed against the hard concrete wall, he marveled at the fact that he was able to reach orgasm without a single violent thought. Perhaps the professor's treatments were working after all.

He picked up a few sheets of loose leaf from a stack on the floor by his bed and used them to wipe the semen from his hard, striated abdominal muscles and then placed each sheet on the floor to dry. He would use those to write her back.

There was no delaying it any longer now. It was time to read Selene's letter. If the perverted guards were still watching after he'd masturbated, at least they wouldn't think that it was something in the letter that was getting him off. If they ever thought that, Joe was certain the letters would suddenly stop coming.

Joe ripped open the pink, perfume-and-pussy-scented envelope. Selene's neat, elegant handwriting greeted him. Joe was aware that his isolation from the rest of the world was affecting his perspective. He was aware that he was grateful for any contact with a woman and writing letters to someone you couldn't see or touch was different than having a conversation with someone sitting in front of you. Letters could be rewritten a dozen times to get just the right wording. In real life, people were rarely so thoughtful and eloquent. In real life, there were myriad distractions— work, friends, family, and other women. Locked up, there was no one for Joe to think about but Selene. She had his undivided attention. As a result, the amorous emotions he was developing toward her were highly suspect though no less profound. He had to work hard to suppress them, but it was getting harder and harder each day.

This was why so many lonely women wrote to men in prison. An inmate was a captive audience. There was no competition for an inmate's affections. Beggars couldn't be choosers. Despite Joe's attempts at caution, he sucked in a deep breath and his chest and face flushed with warmth when he read the first words of the letter.

Dear Joseph,
 I LOVE YOU!!! I know we haven't spent much time together, but I feel like I've known you for a lifetime. I still have the painting you did for me when we first met at the university and all the sketches you've done since (including the naughty ones. Tee hee!) You are such an amazing artist. So full of passion! It still blows me away that I could inspire that in someone. I wish it had been me (redacted). I would want nothing more than to feed your tremendous appetite.
 I had a dream about you the other day. In the dream, I was lain out on a table and you were—(redacted)

I have been thinking hard about your request and I would LOVE to help. It's funny, because I'd been trying hard to think of ways for us to be together and everything I could imagine was just … well … extreme. I've hired a lawyer to help. I never told you, but my family has a bit of money. That's how I was able to come see you before they banned me. My dad gave me the money for the plane ticket. I just work as a model because I think I should make my own money. You want to know something funny? I have been getting more modeling jobs since I gained the weight. Beautiful plus-sized models are in high demand right now.

Anyway, my lawyer will be filing a motion for a new trial based on your public defender's incompetence. That should hasten our reunion. I can't wait to (redacted). You're all I can think about. You're my very own cannibal Casanova. I love you sooo much!

Love,
Selene

Joe read the letter three times. As much as it pissed him off that the guards had cut out so much of the letter, he could fill in the blanks. He grabbed the loose leaf paper he'd set aside to dry and began writing his response. He was hopeful for the first time since his incarceration. Freedom now seemed more than possible. It seemed inevitable. Even if he had to die to do it, he'd be free one way or the other. He began the letter with his usual sappy, overly romantic flourish. He'd always been a fan of Lord Byron and the longer he was incarcerated, the more he lost touch with reality and imagined himself as a Byronesque romantic hero.

```
My Luscious Dream Girl,
    I miss you so much. The taste of you
haunts my dreams. Every waking moment
is spent dreaming of holding you in my
arms and making you feel like the most
desirable woman in the world. You are my
universe now, my only connection with the
world. You are my only hope for normalcy
in a world of madness and chaos. No one
understands me but you. I knew you were
the one from the moment I painted your
picture. The passion you inspired in me
then, the hunger you inspire in me now,
is every bit as powerful as what I felt
for Alicia.
    I can't wait to see you again. I cannot
wait. Even if the world stands between
us, I will find my way to you. With your
help, we will be together again.
    Sincerely,
    Your Cannibal Casanova,
    Joseph Miles.
```

Cannibal Casanova sounded so ridiculous that Joe was happy he was writing it rather than trying to force the words out past his lips. He'd never be able to say it with a straight face. But he knew enough about women to know that Selene would be delighted he'd adopted her little pet-name for him, silly and embarrassing as it was. Joe needed her now, so he was willing to say or do whatever it took to further endear her to him. Besides, his emotions were out of control. He didn't know what he felt. Isolation had made him needy, dependent, every bit the sappy romantic he was pretending to be. Selene elicited a confusion of emotions within him from lust to love to raw, carnal hunger. He didn't know if he wanted to eat her, fuck her, or marry her. Worst of all, he still missed Alicia.

As long as Joe remained in supermax, his chances for escape remained hopeless, but if Selene's lawyers could get him transferred to general population, he'd have many chances. The problem was his record for violence. Getting him transferred was going to be tricky.

PART TWO

Braised Buttocks in Wine Sauce

*2 ¼ pounds of gluteus maximus (buttocks), trimmed
and skinned (female preferred)
1 ½ cups dry white wine
2 celery stalks, finely chopped
1 carrot, peeled and chopped
1 white onion, coarsely chopped
1/3 orange with peel intact, thickly sliced
4 whole star anise
1 tablespoon whole black peppercorns
2 tablespoons olive oil
2 cups veal stock
Kosher salt and freshly ground black pepper to taste
2 tablespoons unsalted butter
1 tablespoon sherry vinegar*

*Place buttocks in a large bowl and toss with the
wine, celery, carrots, onions, orange, star anise,
and black peppercorns, making sure that the meat
is coated in the wine. Cover and refrigerate for at
least 8 hours.*

*Remove the buttocks from the marinade, pat
dry with a paper towel, and set aside. Strain the
marinade into a small bowl and reserve.*

*Warm the olive oil in a large heavy-bottomed
saucepan over medium heat. Add the buttocks and
sear for 2 to 3 minutes on each side, or until evenly
browned. Add the marinating liquid and bring to
a boil. Reduce heat and simmer for 10 minutes or*

until the liquid has reduced by half. Add veal stock; season with salt and pepper to taste. Bring to a boil once more, then reduce the heat to low and cover the saucepan. Gently simmer for 2 hours, or until buttocks are very tender throughout. Long slow cooking gives the meat an unctuous quality and rich succulent taste. Stir in sherry vinegar. Serve drizzled with sauce.

9

There was an announcement over the PA system. "Inmate number 177252! Miles! You've got a visitor!"

It wasn't lost on Joe that his prison number was the same as the late Jeffrey Dahmer's. It was an inside joke between the inmates and the COs. Minutes after the announcement, Joe heard the sound of boots on the tier, heading toward his cell. There were only three people on Joe's visitors list: Selene, his lawyer, and his cousin. Between the three of them, Selene was the only one he would have been excited to see. But getting out of his cell for even half an hour was reason for excitement.

"On your knees! Hands against the wall, Joe. You're coming out."

Joe did as he was instructed. He knelt down with his hands against the bare concrete wall. Two guards walked in and cuffed his wrists and ankles. One of the guards, a big, muscular black officer named Officer Belton was the same one who usually took him to see Professor Locke. He delivered Joe's mail, brought him his meals, and took him for his thrice weekly showers and hour-a-day trips to what could loosely be called an exercise yard. In supermax, the guards did everything. There were no trustees to clean floors, hand out mail and library books, or bring the inmates their meals. The COs did that and they resented it. They often complained that they felt like servants to the inmates. Piss one of them off though, and you might not get your mail or a library book for days, and you might even miss trips to the exercise yard or even a few meals. Joe had seen inmates die in their cells because a CO refused to take them to see

69

a doctor, tired of hearing them bitch and moan. The guards were your only lifeline and they could pinch it off at any moment and leave you in your cell to rot.

Joe felt Belton's disgust and disdain radiating like heat from his skin. He hated the idea of doing anything for a serial killer. He believed in the Old Testament law "an eye for an eye" and Joe knew the man thought he should have been put to death for his crimes, not locked up and treated like a celebrity. Joe agreed with him; he should have been executed. This was much, much worse.

The other officer who walked in with Belton was a woman Joe hadn't seen before. She was older than Joe by at least ten years and had a sad look about her, like she expected the world to hurt her. She reminded Joe of the school librarian from the college he used to attend, the one who had become his first victim, in spirit if not in appearance. She was pear-shaped with large hips and a plump ass, but breasts that were just barely discernible through her uniform. Not Joe's usual type, but something about her triggered his appetite. He couldn't stop staring at her. She had big, brown eyes that looked sad and wounded. Her skin was so pale it was almost the color of milk, but there was not a blemish on it except for a scar on her chin and one on her forehead that Joe assumed she'd gotten from fights with inmates. She had thick brown hair pulled back into a French braid and she wore glasses. Joe looked her over from head to toe, slowly, wanting her to see that he was appraising her. When he saw her watching him, he licked his lips and winked. When she blushed and averted her eyes, he knew there was something there.

"You've got a visitor, Joe," Officer Belton said bitterly. His tone was filled with regret, as if he lamented the fact that Joe had any human contact outside of the guards.

"My lawyer?"

"No. A woman. Two women, actually."

Selene? Joe wondered. Had they lifted the ban and

allowed her to visit him again? It seemed unlikely, but Joe could not stop himself from hoping. Maybe her lawyers had worked some magic to get the restrictions lifted.

"Are you new?" Joe asked the female officer.

"Huh? Umm, yeah. I just got transferred in." She was blushing again.

"From where?"

"Pelican Bay. I just moved to Seattle."

"Welcome. We can use a pretty face around here to brighten the mood." Joe found himself easily slipping into predator mode, saying all the right things, luring his prey. He smiled and she smiled back. He was in. It was well-known that female guards were much more likely to fraternize with male inmates than male guards were with female inmates. Rumors of female corrections officers having affairs with inmates were common. Forty-seven percent of all sexual abuse cases in prison involved women employees and male inmates. Joe was well aware of the statistics. A lot of women are drawn to dangerous men. There's a strong correlation between fear and sexual arousal. That correlation accounted for most of Joe's fan mail. It also explained why many women were drawn to the job. Many of the women who worked in prison were lonely thrill-seekers and Joe knew that, if nothing else, he was pretty damn thrilling.

Officer Belton caught the exchange between Joe and the guard and cut it off quickly. "You shut the fuck up, Miles. Unless you want to wind up in a strip cell instead of seeing your visitors. You give Officer Addison the same respect you give me. You hear?"

"Yes, sir." Joe nodded and turned his gaze away from Officer Addison, but not before giving her another smile. She smiled back sheepishly and giggled a little.

Officer Belton looked like he wanted to commit murder. He clearly did not approve of the flirtation. "Move!"

Joe shuffled forward with Officer Addison on one side

and Officer Belton on the other. They reached a locked metal door at the end of the tier. Officer Belton pressed the intercom button and was buzzed through without saying a word. There were cameras everywhere and the officer in the control booth could already see who was at the door. Joe was led down a hallway into an elevator.

As he stood in the elevator beside the two officers, Joe allowed his eyes to roam again. The mousy new corrections officer was not bad looking. She wasn't gorgeous by any stretch of the imagination, but she did have the sort of round, plump rear he liked. Her breasts, however, were a disappointment. She was barely a B-cup. Joe kept staring at them as if he could will them to grow. Beneath her diminutive breasts was the swell of a belly likely enlarged from childbirth. Even her pelvis bulged outward like a second stomach. She had well-rounded hips and thick thighs, but paradoxically, her arms and shoulders were thin. The one thing that almost tipped her over into beautiful were those big, sad, watery eyes, puppy-dog eyes. They were the eyes of a victim, the eyes of prey. A cologne of misery filled the air around her. It was obvious she'd been hurt before, probably many times.

Joe inhaled deeply of the pheromones wafting from Officer Addison. He could smell the sweat beneath her arms mixed with antiperspirant and rose-scented perfume, the moistness between her thighs, and something deeper, more primal, elemental, the scent of her soul. Her spirit was an echo of power, the faded remnants of some chaotic force like the smoldering embers after a forest fire with the potential to reignite into an inferno. The monster surged, roaring and raging to be fed. Joe wondered if the new officer was really as attractive as she seemed to him now or if it was just the long months of confinement without seeing a single female. Absence makes the heart grow fonder, but that's nothing compared to what it did to the sex drive … or the prey drive.

Officer Addison's lips were thin and pink. She wore

no makeup and needed none. She had chubby cheeks and when she smiled, dimples erupted on both sides of her face. Staring at her, Joe couldn't help but smile, and this time, there was nothing manipulative behind the expression. The guard was "cute." That was the best way to describe her. She was practically adorable. Her obvious bashfulness only made her more endearing. Joe knew he had to win her over. If Selene's lawyers failed, she could be his ticket to freedom. He only hoped he wouldn't have to kill her when it was over. His conscience was still struggling with Alicia's death. He didn't want any more regrets.

The elevator doors opened and Joe was led down two more long halls and through three more doors before finally being led into a room to be strip searched. He was walked through a metal detector and then Belton patted him down and waved a wand over him before handing him off to a slender, pockmarked older officer Joe didn't know. They usually had a CO from another cellblock do the strip search. COs and inmates often got too familiar and the warden didn't want a CO letting something slip or getting paid off to ignore a piece of contraband. If the guards and the inmates didn't know each other, that type of collusion was a lot less likely.

Both Officer Belton and Officer Addison remained in the room as Joe was ordered to strip.

"Normally, there's only two of us in here for this. But since this is your first day, I didn't want to throw you to the wolves so soon. And this motherfucker right here is the goddamn wolfman! Don't let him fool you. He'd rip your goddamn throat out if he could. He's in here for eating a woman alive along with three other folks. Did you know that? They said there was nothing left of her but bones when he was done with her," Belton said, watching the new officer for a reaction.

Joe turned to see her reaction too. She shivered and rubbed her arms like she was trying to rub away goose bumps.

73

"I've got it from here," the pockmarked old CO said as he donned plastic gloves. "All right, Mr. Miles, you know the drill. Everything off."

Belton unshackled him so Joe could remove his shoes, shirt, pants, and underwear. Joe folded them neatly and placed them on a metal cot. He made eye contact with Officer Addison while the old pockmarked CO checked under his tongue, in his hair, under his arms, beneath his ball sack. He saw her appraise his striated chest muscles, chiseled triceps and biceps, pronounced six-pack that was nearly an eight-pack, the thick trapezius and deltoid muscles in his shoulders, his huge quadriceps and calf muscles, and the impressive length and girth of his sexual organ, which was thickening and hardening as he stared at her. She inhaled sharply and managed, with obvious effort, to pull her eyes away from his groin.

"Touch your toes, son."

Joe bent over and the officer checked his rectum with a flashlight before probing it with his fingers.

"He don't look so tough now, do he? Huh? He still look sexy with a fist in his ass?" Belton asked Officer Addison, glaring at her in disgust.

"Okay, he's good."

"Get dressed, Miles. Your visitors await," Belton said gleefully.

There was something different in the way Belton spoke to him now. There was a smirk on his face. Earlier he seemed incensed at the idea of anyone coming to visit him, especially two women. Now he seemed to be delighted by the idea.

"Who are they?"

Belton waved toward the visiting room. "See for yourself."

Joe hurried back into his prison clothes and the two officers walked with him into the visiting room. Seated on the opposite side of a thick glass partition was a voluptuous

Spanish woman with long, black, curly hair, pudgy cheeks with deep dimples, full bow-shaped lips, and large, timid eyes with heavy eyelashes. She was young, barely twenty, and painfully pretty. Even through the conservative, high-necked blouse she was wearing, it was obvious that her breasts were larger than average.

Joe paused in the doorway of the visitor's room and staggered backward a few steps. "No. It can't be."

"What's wrong, Joseph? You see a ghost?"

Behind the Spanish girl was a woman in her forties with the same long curly hair, the same dimpled cheeks and bow-shaped lips, the same voluptuous bosom, the same fiery, explosive aura. It was evidently the girl's mother and she looked familiar. Joe remembered seeing her at the trial. She was Alicia's mother. He shuffled forward as if in a daze, pulled out the metal folding chair, and sat down. With trembling hands, he picked up the phone and the woman on the other end did the same.

"A-Alicia?"

The woman shook her head slowly. Her eyes filled with tears and her bottom lip trembled. "No, you piece of shit. I'm her sister. Lana."

Joe turned to look at the older woman. She snatched the phone from Lana's hand and hissed between clenched teeth. "Alicia was my daughter. You murdered her! I just want to know why. Why! At the trial, you said you loved her. How could you say you love her and do … do what you did to my baby?"

The tears cascaded from her eyes. Her face creased and pinched in a grimace of pain, mouth snarled, brow furrowed.

Joe looked away from her, and at Lana.

Lana scowled in contempt and took the phone back from her mother.

"Did you read my letters?" he asked.

"No! I don't want to read some bullshit you spent nights

perfecting, picking just the rights words to make yourself sound better! I want you to tell me right here and right now. How the fuck could you do that to my sister?"

Joe dropped his head and his lip trembled. A tear spilled from his eye and he quickly wiped it away. He took a deep breath, raised his head to look Lana in her eyes, and spoke. "I-I did love her. I was sick. It wasn't my fault. I couldn't help myself. I loved her so much. You have to believe me. I still think about her."

"We don't want to hear about you fantasizing about Alicia. You murdered and ate her. We just wanted to ask you why. We want to be able to find closure, to forgive you so we can move on. But we can't do that until we know why you did it."

Joe struggled with the words. He could see Alicia so clearly in Lana's face. Her voice even sounded similar. Her expression, full of pain and anger and fear, marred by his betrayal, was almost identical to the expression Alicia had worn when he began to cannibalize her breasts. Even with all the guilt and remorse Joe felt now, he couldn't stop himself from staring at Lana's breasts. He began to salivate and the monster awakened, hungry and mean.

"She was just so beautiful, so sweet, so … so tragic," Joe said.

Lana dropped her head and cast a look toward her mother at the word "tragic." The older woman nodded with her eyes down. They both knew what he meant by tragic. He was referring to Alicia's late father and why he'd killed himself.

"I fell in love with her the moment I saw her. She was going to help me fight this thing inside of me. She was going to help find a cure, but the longer I stayed with her, the harder these … urges were to resist. She was the most flawless, the most perfect woman I'd ever seen. I never wanted to hurt her."

Lana's voice was softer now, less combative. "But you did. You did hurt her. You killed her. You fucking ate her alive, you sick fuck!"

"She asked me to," Joe replied.

"What?" Lana and her mother asked in unison. Joe hadn't testified on his own behalf at the trial. He'd sat sullenly beside his lawyer as expert after expert, including Professor Locke, testified to his mental state. This was the first time he'd spoken about Alicia to anyone other than the professor.

"She asked me to eat her. She said she wanted to be part of me. "

Lana's mother gasped and let out a moan like she'd lost her child all over again. She looked heavenward and clasped her hands in a position of prayer against her forehead. Tears wept from her eyes. Lana's eyes blazed brilliant with rage.

"No! I don't believe that. You're fucking lying!"

"She loved me too, Lana. She understood me."

"*Bullshit!* You murdered her! She trusted you and you betrayed her. You're a sick, perverted bastard and you deserve to be locked up forever!"

Joseph nodded. "You're right. I'm a sick bastard and I do deserve to be locked up, but you're wrong about Alicia. We loved each other and now we are one. I still feel her inside of me, in my blood. I'll always love her. She's part of me forever." Tears welled in Joe's eyes and spilled down his cheeks.

For a moment, as she watched the big cannibal weep in obvious pain, Lana's expression softened. For just a moment Joe could tell she believed him, that she wanted to believe him. Because the way he described Alicia's death almost beautiful, poetic, not like the horrific photographs they'd shown at his trial. And Joe knew Lana needed to believe Alicia had died happy, loved, rather than screaming in pain, afraid, and alone, helpless in the grip of a sadistic serial killer. Thinking about her sister dying that way had obviously been tearing her and her mother up inside. Joe's story offered her another interpretation, one that might allow them both to sleep at night.

Then, as abruptly as it had come the expression was gone and Lana's dark, beautiful eyes hardened once more.

"No one could ever love you, Joseph Miles. You're a fucking *monster*! No one could ever love you!"

Joe nodded in agreement. The tears flowed without relent now. "I am a monster. You're right. And you should never forgive me. I took her away from you. I took her from the world. It was selfish of me … of both of us. I'm sorry. I couldn't help it. I tried. I'm sorry."

Joe hung up the phone and stood. Lana and her mother stared at him, hugging each other for support. Hatred burned in Lana's eyes. Joe had never seen such raw, naked aggression in a woman's eyes before. Lana looked so much like Alicia it was breaking Joe's heart to look at her. She could have been Alicia's twin. It hurt him to see that expression on a face so beautiful, a face he had once loved, that he still loved. He turned and knocked on the door.

The new CO, Officer Addison, opened the door and Joe held out his hands for the shackles. The officer's hands trembled as she secured the cuffs around his wrists. Joe was weeping openly now. His body jerked and hitched, wracked by the force of his sorrow. He couldn't get Lana's face, those eyes filled with rage and sorrow, out of his mind. Her words followed him out of the room.

"No one could ever love you, Joseph Miles. You're a fucking MONSTER! No one could ever love you!"

She was right. This thing he had become had robbed him of any chance he had of giving and receiving love. Anyone or anything he got close to he destroyed. Joe continued to weep unselfconsciously. Beyond Officer Addison, standing in the hallway, Officer Belton smiled.

10

Officer Cindy Addison didn't know what to think of the giant serial killer weeping and moaning the name Alicia over and over again as he lumbered along beside her, shackled at the wrists and ankles. There was something so painfully tragic about him. He'd looked so dangerous and intimidating when they'd come to remove him from his cell, so arrogant, powerful, even sexy. But now he looked perfectly pathetic. He'd been almost hysterical with grief ever since she'd escorted him from the visitor's room, and she could tell by Belton's demeanor that he had known this would happen.

Immediately after Joe went into the room, Belton had told Cindy that Joe's visitors were the mother and sister of one of his victims. The warden had granted their request to visit Joseph even though they weren't on his visitor's list. The warden had made an exception and Cindy wondered if it had only been to help the two women get whatever closure they had come seeking or if it had also been done to further torture Joseph, to punish him for his crimes, to break him. Obviously, Joseph Miles wasn't the remorseless sadist the tabloids and talk shows had made him out to be. And that confused Cindy. She'd read quite a bit about serial killers. It was a bit of a hobby. They were sociopaths, incapable of guilt or empathy or remorse. That didn't fit at all with Joseph Miles' reaction to confronting the family of his victims. If it was an act, it was damn convincing and he was staying in character long after the curtain had fallen.

Before she knew what she was doing, Cindy's maternal instincts took over. She reached out and patted Joe on the back, consoling him. He turned to look at her, eyes red from crying, and nodded, acknowledging her moment of compassion. Belton jabbed the big cannibal in the small of his back with the baton, ushering him forward.

"Keep your ass movin', Miles! We ain't got all damn day!"

Joe nodded and continued shuffling along the tier toward his cell.

"Cryin' like a little bitch! I bet you wasn't cryin' when you was eatin' that woman's daughter. How much you think your victims' loved ones are crying now? Fuck your bitch-ass tears!"

Cindy saw the look that passed over Joe's face when he locked eyes with Belton. There was no remorse in it now, no mercy, no forgiveness. They didn't waver and he didn't blink once. His eyes looked completely empty, cold, like the eyes of a snake. He smiled, revealing a mouthful of teeth that had been filed to points. For a moment she was afraid the big inmate was going to lunge for her new partner, and despite his restraints, she wasn't sure either of them could have stopped him before Joseph Miles tore Belton's throat out.

Belton's mouth dropped open and his eyes got big and watery. He could sense it too, his own fragile mortality confronted by a force of merciless savagery.

Then Joe turned and continued shuffling forward toward his cell.

Cindy and Belton swallowed hard. They didn't relax again until Joseph Miles was once again safe in his cell.

As Cindy uncuffed his wrists and ankles and then turned and slowly closed the door, Joseph Miles turned to her with a bashful, wounded look, staring at the ground before slowly raising his tear-filled, ice blue eyes to hers. "I want to thank you for … your kindness. This entire ordeal has been so hard on me. Professor Locke has been the only one who understands my illness, the only one trying to help me. I don't want to hurt people. I want to get better. Anyway, thanks."

Cindy stood in the doorway, the cell door partially open, speechless. Her bottom lip hung open and her mouth worked soundlessly. "Um ... yeah ... uh ... you're welcome." She gave him a small nod and started to close the door again.

His next words stopped her cold and made the blood rush to her face and her loins. "You're very beautiful, you know? You're one of the most beautiful women I've seen since my Alicia. I just thought you should know that. Most women don't hear that enough. Men can be jerks sometimes when it comes to giving a lady compliments," he said, still maintaining eye-contact with his deep blue eyes, dark hair, high cheekbones, and strong, dimpled chin. He had the looks of a matinee idol, a leading man, like an action star or a superhero. He looked almost like a young Christopher Reeve with much, much more muscle.

He was working her. She knew it. But he was right. No one had told her she was beautiful since her first year of marriage, no one except inmates who hadn't seen a woman in years. Two kids and one divorce later, hearing a compliment like that from someone who looked like Joe was more than just rare, it was like hearing the voice of God.

She'd allowed herself to get too close to inmates before. It was an occupational hazard. She'd had an affair with a drug dealer in Pelican Bay that lasted more than a year. He was a huge black man with biceps as big as her head, a shaved scalp, and a way with words that had made her melt. His name was Frank White and he'd been a major cocaine dealer who was rumored to have murdered more than a dozen people, rival drug dealers, on the streets of Oakland. She used to let him out of his cell at night and have sex with him in stairwells, in the shower, the exercise room, the kitchen, the library, the laundry, wherever they could find a moment's peace. They'd fucked in almost every corner of the prison that the surveillance cameras didn't reach. Luckily she knew the location of them all. Once rumors of her affair had begun to spread throughout the prison and the other COs had begun whispering about her behind her back, she put in for a transfer. Besides, Frank had gotten greedy and had started asking her to smuggle him things into the prison. Little things at first, like chewing gum, his favorite cupcakes, special pens that had good ink for making prison tattoos. Cindy wasn't completely stupid though. She knew where it was headed. Soon he would have been asking her to help him smuggle drugs into the prison. It was time to get out. Fucking an inmate was one thing; getting caught with a balloon full of China White in her cunt and winding up an inmate? That was something else entirely. So she'd left. Out of the frying pan and into the fiery gaze of Joseph Miles.

"Uh, th-thank you," she stammered, slamming the door and hurrying off down the tier before Belton could see how deeply she was blushing. As soon as possible, she would have to get her shift changed. As long as she was working with Belton, he would be watching her, scrutinizing her every move, and she wanted to talk to Joseph Miles more. She wanted to find out more about him, why he'd done the horrible things he'd been convicted of and, most of all, she wanted him to look at her like that again, like she was the most desirable creature on Earth and she wanted to hear his sweet compliments. She needed to hear them. The prisons had long been the only place where men seemed to still find her attractive, and every woman needed to feel attractive.

She caught up with Officer Belton, who had stormed off down the tier like she had done him some personal affront by pausing to talk to the big serial killer. "Who's Professor Locke?"

Belton stopped and looked her up and down, not disguising his disdain for her, going out of his way to make it clear. "You'll meet him soon enough. He's another idiot who's been fooled by that animal in there."

11

Joe's mind was working overtime. For the first time in months he had options. Now he had to figure out what his next steps would be, how to turn these new developments into advantages, and what he would do when he finally got out. There was no doubt in his mind now. He would get out.

If he could seduce Officer Addison, get her to fall in love with him, convince her that his disease was real and there was a cure out there somewhere and he knew how to get to it, then he might be able talk her into smuggling him out of here.

Joe reached out until his fingertips touched the walls of his 6x12 cell. These walls had been the totality of his world for the last several months. The idea of being outside them, away from the concrete and steel, the chains, psychotropic drugs, and scratchy wool blankets, the screams and cries of the deranged and the condemned consumed his thoughts. Outside these walls was flesh. There were women who loved him. Women who would do anything for him. There was Selene, but she seemed so far away, farther away now, after seeing Lana, than she had an hour ago.

"Lana." Joe spoke the name aloud and smiled. He tried to imagine Alicia, but now her face had been supplanted by the fierce and lovely visage of her younger sister, Lana. Lana's furious, tear-filled eyes haunted him. Joe made a mental note to find her if he ever made it out of prison. Just knowing she was out there made it harder for him to accept his incarceration. He knew that she was not Alicia, yet some part of him could not help but think of her as Alicia reborn and rejuvenated. They shared the same blood, the same wickedly curvaceous figure, the same heartbreakingly pretty face. Joe closed his eyes and imagined himself kissing Lana's luscious, bow-shaped lips. He imagined squeezing her hips, running his fingertips over her thighs, her belly, the swell of her bosom, each nipple, her collarbones, her jawline. He moaned deeply as he remembered his first night with Alicia and replayed it in his mind, only this time with Lana. He imagined licking her in places no other man had. He imagined what her face would look like at the moment of orgasm and in his mind he saw Lana's bottom lip quiver, her brow knit in an expression of rage and ecstasy, a scream, like a war cry tearing from her throat as her body bucked and jerked.

"Lana." Joe said her name again in a breathless whisper as he took himself in hand and began to stroke his engorged sex organ. "Lana," he said again. Licking his palm before rubbing the head of his cock, he imagined it was Lana's sweet vagina surrounding his manhood rather than his own calloused palm.

"Lana!" he gasped, tugging furiously at himself as he imagined bending her over and entering her from behind just as he had Alicia. Then he imagined Officer Addison bent over on all fours. His mind filled in the blanks for the parts of her he'd not yet glimpsed. He imagined her voluptuous posterior without those ridiculous uniform pants. He imagined those tiny breasts barely filling his hands. He imagined her dimpled cheeks and puppy-dog eyes imploring him not to stop as he pounded deep into her from behind.

"Addison," Joe nearly shouted as his legs locked. His back arched and he let out a roar, snarling and gnashing his serrated teeth as he shot his seed across the room. His legs grew weak and he collapsed. He slid down the wall onto the floor with a satisfied smile on his face. When he looked over at the door, still panting and trembling with the aftershocks of his violent climax, he saw Officer Addison's face peering in at him from the barred window in his cell door. Joe stared back at her and took himself in hand once again, rubbing his cock back to full erection as he watched her watching him. This time, he didn't imagine fucking her in her magnificent ass. His mind took him to dark places. He imagined ripping chunks from her gluteus maximus in a feeding frenzy. Jerking his head from side to side as he tore into her with his sharpened teeth. He stroked himself more vigorously and called out her name again.

"Addison."

In minutes, he found himself nearing orgasm once more. He growled low in his throat and bit his lip. The blood dripped into his mouth and he probed the wound with his tongue. The taste of pennies and meat added to the fantasy. He saw the officer's eyes widen. She covered her mouth and let out a tiny squeal as he ejaculated again, still staring into her eyes, still imagining gnawing her buttocks down to the coccyx and pelvic bone.

12

Officer Charles Belton sat in the control booth watching the new CO ogle Joseph Miles while he beat off in his cell.

"This bitch is crazy," he whispered, shaking his head. Despite his own disgust he felt his own manhood stiffening uncomfortably in his Fruit of the Looms. It only served to anger him more. He adjusted his erection so it was less noticeable and hissed in annoyance, as if he felt his own sexual organ had somehow betrayed him.

She has got to go, he thought. But ratting on a fellow officer wasn't his style. There was a code and there was enough illegal shit going on between inmates and officers that breaking that code might start a chain reaction that landed them all in prison or on the unemployment lines at the least. Belton himself had been complicit in a few cockfights, including one that had ended in a fatality. Not to mention Joseph's cannibalistic castration during the last cockfight.

Belton hit the zoom on the camera outside Joseph Miles's cell and magnified Officer Addison times ten. He could now clearly see her right hand moving vigorously in the pocket of her uniform pants. She was masturbating too. Belton grimaced. He didn't know women could even do that. He tried to imagine her reaching her clit through her pocket and acknowledged that it was possible before banishing the vision from his mind. Addison was cute, but she wasn't exactly "hot." He'd fuck her in a pinch, but she wouldn't be his first choice. Still, he'd been working a lot of double-shifts lately because of recent layoffs due to the recession. Those late-night shifts got awfully boring. A blowjob every now and then would definitely help pass the time. If he could dig up enough dirt on Cindy Addison, he might be able to extort some occasional oral love from the crazy bitch.

It was almost time to deliver the mail. The normal control booth officer would be back from his break in minutes. Belton set the camera to its normal position and magnification right after Cindy Addison appeared to have finished and was now once again walking the tier. Belton thumbed through the piles of mail on the mail cart. Almost half of it was for Joseph Miles, and that was even after most of them had been censored and destroyed. Of these letters, 40 percent of them were from women who were turned on by the big cannibal's crimes. Quite a few were marriage proposals. There were rants from religious folks offering to help him find the Lord. There were a few angry letters from people disgusted by what he'd done, and these were sent through virtually uncensored. Then there were letters of support and encouragement from teenagers who thought what he'd done was cool. The few of these letters they sent through to inmate number 177252 were so heavily censored they were almost unreadable. Belton wanted to throw them all in the trash.

What the fuck do these sick perverts see in that murdering piece of shit?

Belton was sick of everyone treating this freak like some kind of celebrity.

This perverted freak needs to be taken down a peg. I think it's time for another cockfight.

13

"I want you to tell me what you think of this." Professor Locke slipped the DVD into his laptop and after a few moments booting up, the screen filled with the image of Joseph Miles doing pushups. He was completely naked. Every muscle was clearly defined through skin as thin as parchment. His percentage of subcutaneous fat was in the single digits. Professor Locke had to admit the man was an impressive physical specimen.

Watching the convicted serial murderer tirelessly pump out pushup after pushup was almost terrifying. The professor glanced down at his own withered and wrinkled body, his protruding stomach, skinny arms, hair that had turned from gray to white, his weakening eyesight and thickening eyeglass lenses. He would have no hope if the big convict ever attacked him, but so far Joseph Miles had never acted aggressively toward him. If anything, he'd been remarkably respectful, almost deferential.

He couldn't imagine trying to fight off a beast like Joseph Miles. The idea of someone that powerful and relentless lunging for his throat made the professor shiver. Joseph Miles was a near perfect killing machine. The professor had watched countless hours of footage of the killer alone in his cell. Joseph spent most of the day either working out, masturbating, reading books and letters, or doing bizarre fighting movements in the air as if shadowboxing or fighting off an assault from some unseen attacker.

Professor Locke fast forwarded the DVD past the pushups and other calisthenics. He stopped at a scene of Joseph Miles striking out at the air in quick savage motions. "So what do you think? What's he doing?"

"It's definitely some type of fighting art, but it doesn't look like a formal *kata*. He seems to be making it up as he goes along. It's pretty good though. His instincts are amazing. Who is this guy?"

The professor had been watching the DVD for several days, trying to make sense of the violent pantomime that Joseph was doing in his cell. He watched Joseph punch, kick, elbow, and even bite at the air in a perplexing frenzy of movement. At first Professor Locke thought it was a martial arts kata of some sort. He didn't know much about fighting, so he'd taken the video to an expert martial artist for his opinion.

Alex Martin was a former cage fighter and a black belt in Jiu-jitsu, Wu Shu, and Taekwondo with more than two dozen Muay Thai fights and twice as many cage fights, but Professor Locke had never heard of him. But when he'd asked around for an expert on different fighting styles, Alex Martin's name was the one most mentioned. So he'd sought the man out. He was not at all what the professor was expecting.

This expert fighter and professional badass stood barely more than five feet, five inches tall and weighed less than a hundred and fifty pounds. His body was hard and lean, like a gymnast's. Not at all what came to mind when the professor thought of a fighter. He was expecting someone who looked more like Joseph Miles.

"His name is Joseph Miles. He's a convicted serial killer under my care at the state penitentiary."

Alex Martin let out a long whistle, still staring at the screen as Joseph did some sort of dive roll before coming to his feet in a low crouch and lashing out again with his fingers curled into claws right at the height where a man's crotch would have been.

"Too bad. I'd have loved to train a guy like that. I'd make him a champion in no time. Look at his speed and his reflexes. Wow. And how long was he doing pushups for? He must have done close to a thousand."

"He does pushups for an hour every day in the morning and another hour at night. Three thousand pushups a day."

"Holy shit. That's amazing. And how long does he do this shadowboxing for?"

The professor frowned, disturbed by the man's enthusiasm. "At least an hour. Sometimes longer."

"What else does he do?"

"Crunches, squats, lunges, jump-squats, calf raises, pull-ups, and then he stretches and meditates for about half an hour. He's got an entire routine. He spends about six to eight hours a day doing this in his cell."

"Six to eight hours?" Alex Martin sighed again, still staring at the computer showing Joseph Miles destroying some imaginary foe with terrifying ferocity. "One thing you should know though. He's using all killing blows."

The professor's eyes widened. "What? How can you tell?"

"That move he's doing right now? It's called a rear-naked choke, or a lion kill. It can render a man unconscious in seconds, but the way he's doing it, how long he's holding it, that's permanent brain injury or death. That leg lock he's pantomiming now? You can snap all the ligament's in a man's knee easily with that. Painful and debilitating, but not deadly, but he's finishing the move by pretending to tear a chunk out of the man's hamstring with his teeth. The femoral artery is right there. His opponent would bleed out in seconds. Earlier he did a motion that looked like was pretending to tear off a guy's balls, and before that he did a head and arm choke that ended with what looked like this guy pretending to rip out his opponent's throat with his teeth. I take back what I said about wanting to train this dude. I'm glad he's locked up. From what I can see, he's right where he belongs."

The professor nodded. "Thanks. You've been very helpful."

"My pleasure. Oh, and one other thing. All those exercises this guy is doing in his little cell? If I was training one of my fighters for the battle of his life, that's exactly what I would have him doing. I'd watch him real close if I were you."

Professor Locke thanked Alex again and then quickly left the gym. The image of Joseph Miles tearing the testicles from some imaginary opponent was stuck in the professor's mind. He didn't know how he'd failed to recognize the movement before. After hearing Alex's narration of Joseph's murderous training regiment, it had seemed obvious, but the professor didn't spend all day learning the best methods to destroy another human being. He had an instinctive distrust of those who did. He wondered how many degrees of separation there were between a man like Alex Martin, who'd devoted his life to the fighting arts, and a sociopathic killer like Joseph Miles. If Alex Martin had grown up with parents like Joseph Miles's homicidal father, would he have wound up the same way? His nature was that of a fighter, a sport that was sadistic by its very nature. The stated goal of the sport of mixed martial arts was to cause the greatest possible pain and injury to your opponent until he gave up or was rendered unconscious. All it would have taken was different nurturing to turn Alex Martin into a killer. The question was, "What would it take to turn Joseph Miles back into a normal human being?"

Perhaps if Joseph had found an outlet for his aggression as Alex Martin obviously had, he would have been beating the hell out of trained athletes in a cage or a ring in some pugilistic blood sport instead of murdering and mutilating innocent victims.

Professor Locke couldn't help but wonder. He'd heard rumor of prison boxing programs, like the one in Angola State Prison, that had resulted in a dramatic decrease in violence between inmates, but he'd never found any reliable statistics to support the theory that pummeling someone senseless in an organized sport was somehow cathartic. It sounded reasonable enough that it would be better than cutting the breasts off women and eating them, but there was no research to suggest the two compulsions were interchangeable.

The professor drove back to the prison, puzzling over how to "fix" Joseph Miles. The Prozac did not appear to be working anymore. He'd staked his entire reputation on the hope that he could cure him of his homicidal compulsions. So far he'd done little but take some of the edge off the killer's cannibalistic cravings. If the serotonin wasn't the issue, then he needed to find a new approach to the problem. He'd heard recent studies where psychologists treated manic depressives and people with obsessive compulsive disorders with ketamine in cases where serotonergic drugs like Prozac failed. There was significant evidence that glutamatergic dysregulation may contribute to the development and progression of these types of disorders. Whereas, since the introduction of Prozac in the seventies, serotonin deficiencies were seen as the main cause of OCD and clinical depression, new research has indicated that glutamate may be more closely linked to the part of the brain that causes everything from depression and anxiety to compulsive gambling. According to recent studies, ketamine, the glutamate receptor antagonist has demonstrated rapid effects when delivered as a single intravenous dose.

If ketamine works on housewives who can't stop smoking and shopping, there's no reason to think it won't work on a man who can't stop killing. Despite the difference in moral extremes, the basic underlying pathology is the same. Joseph Miles's cannibalistic compulsion could be viewed as little more than an eating disorder, not dissimilar to a man who habitually binges on donuts. The professor smiled. He liked that analogy. It had just the right tone of clinical aloofness. He imagined how that quote would read in a peer-reviewed journal. It would be shocking and controversial. He would be applauded by some and condemned by others for his unflinching scientific objectivity. That analogy might be the line that made him famous.

Shocking though it may be, the professor thought the characterization of Joseph's murderous pathology as an eating disorder was perhaps the most accurate. The MRI tests he'd been performing on Joseph confirmed the same elevated concentrations of glutamate and related compounds demonstrated in the caudate nucleus and orbitofrontal cortex of OCD patients compared to normal controls. The professor knew of the dramatic results reported in studies of eating disorders being treated with low intravenous doses of ketamine. Eating disorders are a compulsive behavior disease, a disorder characterized by frequent recall of body dysmorphic thoughts. Whatever was driving Joseph to cannibalize other human beings was likely spawned by violent memories from his past, most probably his assault at the hands of Damon Trent. Evidence suggests that memory is a neocortical neuronal network. Excitation of this network involves the hippocampus where new memories are stored before being transferred to the frontal lobe of the brain, with recall occurring by re-excitement of this same network. There was every indication that excitement of the hippocampus by glutamate-NMDA receptors can be blocked by ketamine.

The Professor ran the numbers in his head as he steered his car to the side of the road and pulled out a pad to figure out the exact dosage he would need. In the eating disorder trials, he recalled them using infusions of 20 mg per hour of ketamine for 10 hours with 20 mg twice daily of nalmefene (Revex) as opioid antagonists to prevent the patient from losing consciousness. He would have to look up the studies to confirm the dosage, but if that was correct, then that's where he would start with Joseph Miles.

For the first time in weeks, Professor Locke felt hopeful that he could cure his former student. But then what? Joseph would remain behind bars for what amounted to a disease that was beyond his control. It was cruel and inhuman. If his crimes were the result of a disease, and it could be proven that he has been cured, then it would be wrong to keep him imprisoned.

But what if it didn't work? What if Joseph's compulsion was too strong? What if he no longer wanted to be cured? The professor remembered a conversation he'd had with his now infamous student during class:

"Is it possible that it's an evolutionary mutation?"

The professor had paused along with the entire class. Even then, before the discovery of Joseph's first murder, everyone could tell there was something not quite right about the big psychology student.

"A what?" he'd asked. At the time, the professor thought Joseph had just been trying to get a rise out of him. The idea that the gigantic sophomore had been talking about himself had been nothing but a grim and cynical suspicion.

"An evolutionary mutation, part of natural selection. Man is the only creature on Earth without a natural predator, except other men. Perhaps, as our population explodes, Mother Nature has felt the need to select certain individuals to act as population control. Perhaps giving them drives and instincts other humans don't have, which genetically predisposes them to mass murder—to cull the herd, so to speak... Perhaps nature is just seeking a remedy for the plague. Isn't it possible that murderers are a natural antivirus?"

Then, as now, the thought had awakened all the professor's fears about the efficacy of his profession. *If there are mental disorders that can never be cured, then what purpose does psychiatry serve?* If this was true, then his chosen profession amounted to the selling of snake oil. He was no better than the televangelists who filled the airwaves every Sunday selling false hope and lies. And if Joseph's particular condition was incurable, then the professor's hopes for a Nobel Prize-winning breakthrough in the treatment of signature sex murderers would be dashed to the wind and there would be no safe recourse but to lock Joseph Miles away forever.

Professor Locke thought hard as he steered onto the freeway and into the flow of traffic, heading back to the prison at seventy-five miles an hour. If Joseph was correct, and serial murderers were an evolutionary mutation, there still had to be a way to channel those violent impulses into something less destructive to society. He again thought of Alex Martin and again wondered if the violent world of cage-fighting might be a way to productively channel those impulses. He recalled the tape of Joseph Miles practicing his "killing moves" and tried to imagine such wanton violence in an organized sport. He shuddered and dismissed the idea. Even if it was cathartic and actually did help curb the craving for violence, there was no way the American people would go for convicted serial killers battling it out in a cage. The moral majority would be outraged. The professor smiled. *But the ratings would be atmospheric. Talk about reality TV.* He'd heard the rumors of inmates being forced to fight one another. Joseph had even been involved in a near-fatal altercation resulting in grievous injury to another inmate that sounded suspiciously like one of the so-called "cockfights." Before he wasted time considering the alternatives if he failed, he needed to set up the ketamine experiment … and pray.

14

Six officers came for Joe in the middle of the night. Three he recognized and three he'd never seen before. There was a nervous excitement in the air. Fear. Anxiety. Joe could smell it wafting from all six like cheap perfume.

"Let's go, Miles. We need to search your cell. We're putting you in a strip cell while we search it."

Joe didn't protest, didn't declare his innocence of whatever contraband they thought he'd smuggled inside and hidden away. There was a strong likelihood that it was all a ruse anyway. It didn't take six officers to transport one prisoner.

They brought him to the large concrete room with the chin-up bar that was referred to as the exercise yard. It looked different at night. Even smaller than it did in the day. It looked even more diminutive now because it was already occupied. A large Latino man covered in tattoos from fingertips to forehead stood in the center of the room, glaring at them as Joe was led inside. The man was heavily muscled and had scars on his face, neck, chest, and arms from fights, knife and bullet wounds, and surgeries. The wounds were interspersed with tattoos of guns, low-riders, tombstones, crucifixes, of large-breasted women in high heels, fishnets, and mini-skirts or micro shorts right beside a portrait of the Virgin Mary with hands clasped in prayer, all telling the story of the man's life. It was the story of most of the inmates in here. Sex, drugs, crime, and the dream of redemption in some illusory afterlife where a lifetime of atrocities would be forgiven. He, like most of the really hardcore Latino gangbangers in supermax, had already given up on this life

96

and now placed all his hopes on heaven and was anxious to get there and bask in the light of Jesus and Mary.

Joe was willing to do his part to arrange an introduction.

The man's head was shaved and one of his eyes had a splash of red in the corner of it where the capillaries had ruptured. An old jagged scar ripped down from his forehead over the eyelid. He looked like a fighting dog—and that's exactly what he was. He began to stretch, watching the guards remove Joe's restraints, and then he stalked forward, staring at Joe like he was dessert.

"Settle down, Armondo. We don't want no trouble out of you just yet. We brought you a new playmate for the night," Belton said with a wide grin.

The big Latin thug Officer Belton had referred to as "Armondo" backed away with his hands raised. His eyes were pinned on Joe, looking him over from head to toe. Joe knew the look. He was looking for weaknesses, deciding where to strike first and where to strike last to end the fight.

The door to the exercise room had barely shut before Armondo advanced. "I'm putting my money on Miles," Joe heard one of the guards say. The officers were all still in the room, fanned out in a semicircle, forming a loose ring. Joe dropped down on all fours like a dog and bared his serrated teeth. Armondo paused. The look in his eyes wasn't one of fear but of surprise, momentary confusion, and then caution, rethinking his approach. The hesitation was all Joe needed. He sprang from his crouch with his jaws wide. The hunger was fully upon him and the monster was in a fury. Saliva dripped from his jagged canines. Armondo's eyes widened in surprise but he stood his ground.

Armondo stood in a boxer's stance and danced backward out of the way of Joe's attack. Joe landed beside him. His teeth snapped the air inches from Armondo's face. Behind him, Joe heard the guards whoop with excitement.

"Get that son of a bitch!" someone yelled, but Joe

couldn't tell which one of them the guard was cheering on.

A fist caught Joe in the eye and a flashbulb went off in his head. He staggered backward. He felt his eye swelling. He looked up at his opponent and a knee caught him in the chin and dropped him onto his back. His jaw throbbed. The big Mexican jumped on top of Joe, straddling his chest, and began raining down punches. Joe bit the man's thigh through his prison-issue cotton pants. His teeth sank deep in the muscle and Joe immediately tasted blood, an explosion of it, spurting into his mouth. Joe had to swallow hard to keep from drowning in it. He'd hit the femoral artery. He continued to bite down, chewing a large avulsion in Armondo's vastus muscle, ripping through the orange fabric of his pants and leaving a bleeding hole that gushed blood.

"Ahhhh! *Puto loco*! You fucking bit me!"

Obviously the guards hadn't properly prepared the man for who he was facing. Armondo punched Joe several more times, breaking his nose and further swelling his eye, and then he tried to scramble away but Joe pursued. He grabbed Armondo's ankle and pulled, dragging him back within reach of Joe's blood-drenched canines. Blood lust raged within him. Joe could barely think. He was all fury and appetite as he bit down on Armondo's calf. Joe received several kicks that sent lightning bolts of agony through his already shattered nose. He held up an arm to defend himself from the kicks as he ripped and tore at the big convict's soleus muscle until he'd torn it away from the tibia. Hobbled, Armondo continued to fight. He spun around and began punching Joe again. The man's pain tolerance was off the charts, no doubt boosted by the methamphetamines wafting from his sweat glands.

Joe tackled the man and scrambled up onto his chest. He leaned down and clamped his teeth onto Armondo's face, biting through skin and cartilage, removing the Mexican's nose with a large, stomach-churning crunch!

"Holy shit!"

"That's enough! Stop! Stop!"

"The fight's over! It's over!"

Joe could hear the COs yelling at him, but he could barely understand what they were saying. The monster was roaring in his ears. It swelled in his pants like a third limb. Joe heard Armondo scream as Joe chewed up the man's nose and swallowed it then leaned down and attacked his face again as the guards tried to pull him away and Armondo continued punching him and screaming. Joe bit off one of Armondo's eyelids and punctured his eyeball with one of his teeth. He'd bitten through Armondo's lips and part of his left cheek before the guards successfully pulled Joe away.

"My face! He ate my face!"

Joe had made a ruin of the big convict. Armondo's left eyelid was gone and the ruptured eyeball drooled down his teardrop-tattooed cheek like a dead jellyfish. Where Armondo's nose had been was now a ragged mucus and blood-filled hole. Each breath bubbled with red-tinged snot. A flap of the convict's right cheek hung loose where Joe's teeth had torn it away from his face, revealing Armondo's teeth and gums and the pink muscle of his jaw. His face was now fixed in a perpetual grin. It looked less like a living human face with flesh missing and more like a skull with flecks of skin still clinging to it.

Joe roared like a lion as three of the officers wrestled him out of the room, forgetting about his restraints in their eagerness to get him back into his cell. Joe's mouth looked like a slaughterhouse, with meat and blood staining his jagged teeth. The front of his pants was tented, a tremendous erection straining against the fabric. There was a dark stain forming on the orange fabric. There was no doubt what it was. Joe had ejaculated while tearing Armondo's face off. The expression on Officer Belton's face was one of abject horror. Joe smiled and brought his hand to his face, wiping

99

away the blood and viscera before bringing the gore-soaked fingers to his lips, licking the blood and gristle from each digit.

"I want more," he said. "The monster is still hungry."

One of the officers seized Joe's arm and jerked it behind his back while another officer slapped handcuffs on his wrists. Joe locked eyes with Belton, who turned away and dropped his head.

"That's the last time, Belton! How the hell are we supposed to explain this?" one of the officers said, jabbing a finger at the large black officer. Veins were popping out all over his face.

"Yeah, that's the last time."

15

Selene was just getting home from another modeling job at the university when she steered her Vespa over to the bank of mailboxes on the corner, three houses up from the home she rented with her roommates Linda and Paul. It was springtime, just after six o'clock, and the fog had not yet started its languorous march through the streets. The afternoon sun began its fiery decent and Selene's neighbors were either just getting home or stuck in traffic somewhere. The street was quiet and the air smelled fresh and verdant, like fresh-cut grass and flowers in bloom, like she was standing in the middle of a forest rather than a little cul-de-sac in Hayes Valley.

She removed her helmet and her long black hair spilled out and cascaded down over her shoulders. She shook her hair out and ran a finger through it, feeling foolish, like she was recreating a scene from some movie where a starlet with perfect hair and makeup, dressed to look like a tough biker-chick, removes her helmet for no particular reason and stands there straddling the bike and flipping her hair around. The fact that Selene was straddling a scooter just made it all the more ridiculous.

She fumbled her keys into the lock and unlocked her little mailbox. It was all she could do to keep from squealing. She immediately recognized the handwriting on the plain white envelope. Amongst the advertising fliers, coupons, unpaid bills, and supermarket circulars was a letter from Joseph Miles. She tore open the tiny envelope and read the entire letter right there by the mailbox.

Joseph never wrote long letters. That was the odd thing

about him. She had two friends who corresponded with prisoners and they both regularly received letters at least ten pages long. Joseph Miles seldom wrote more than a page. He said it was because anything he wanted to say would have been heavily edited by the guards or destroyed before it ever reached her. But she had never received a letter that had been edited. She knew they edited the letters she sent to him but wasn't so sure it worked in reverse. She had no doubt they read them and would have turned over any incriminating statements he might have made to the warden or even the district attorney's office, but that would have only been if he'd confessed to a crime or was in the process of trying to commit one. That's what Selene thought anyway. She wasn't sure. So, to her, Joseph's short but sweet letters were just another of his many personality quirks.

Her heart was racing. Her palms perspired and her panties grew damp. The letter was written with Joseph's normal flourish of praise and promises that left her wanting more.

She didn't know why Joseph Miles affected her so powerfully, but she had never wanted anyone as much as she wanted the convicted serial killer. Just thinking about his massive, muscular arms wrapped around her, his lips against her throat, the feel of his teeth biting into her flesh, tearing her apart while he fucked the shit out of her made her literally swoon. She and Joseph Miles had never so much as exchanged a kiss, yet she was completely obsessed with him. She gunned the Vespa's engine and hurried home to read the letter again, hoping her roommates would not be home so she could take a nice long, hot bath with scented candles, bubbles, bath salts, a glass of wine, Joseph's letter, and the eight-inch dildo she had affectionately nicknamed "Big Joe."

The letter had once again confirmed Joe's affection for her. But it wasn't just Joe's affections she was after. She wanted his passion as well, not just to feel it but to possess it. She wanted to feel what he felt. She wanted to know the ecstasy he knew when he murdered and mutilated those people. She clutched the letter to her chest and turned the little scooter around. It wasn't quite time to go home yet. She had a few ideas first.

San Francisco was a serial killer's paradise. There were so many underground sex clubs, S&M dungeons, brothels, bath houses, seedy bars and night clubs, and other pick-up joints that a predator could go undetected for years—at least until the bodies began to surface. It was in one such club, called The Backdoor, that Joseph had met Alicia and his homicidal impulses had first roared out of control. It was to that same club that Selene drove now.

She'd driven past it many times since she'd first learned of its existence. South of Market, just east of Sixth Street was an innocuous-looking building that housed the now notorious swingers club, The Backdoor. Joe had been the one who first told her about the club as he described his meeting with Alicia over a prison payphone on one of the rare occasions he was allowed to use the phone. She'd probed him for details and he had eagerly supplied them. Joe had appeared delighted by her curiosity and happy to relive what was obviously a fond memory for him.

"What does it look like?"

"It isn't that exciting from the outside. It's just a regular storefront with blacked-out windows and a little silver plaque by the front door that says 'The Backdoor.' You'd easily pass by it a dozen times if you didn't know where to look. But once you know where it is, it's impossible to overlook."

He'd been right. Ever since he'd told her where to find it, she'd stared longingly at it whenever she passed by, wishing she had been there that night long ago when Joe showed up with a raging hard-on and an appetite to match.

"And what's it like inside?" she'd asked.

"It's magical! A sex addict's paradise. When you first

walk in, there's a coat check girl who you can leave your clothes with. They prefer everyone to be naked but a lot of people keep their clothes on. Inside, there's a bar, a dance floor, and even a stage where bands sometimes play. There's a hot tub and a pool outside. Then there are the theme rooms."

"Theme rooms?"

"Each room is different. There's a room called the Orgy Room that has a bed that stretches from wall to wall and can easily hold ten couples at a time. There's a dungeon that has a crucifix with shackles on it, stocks, and even a rack. There's a room filled with dildos and other mechanical sex devices, and there are condom dispensers and sanitizing gels in every room. Most of the people there are in their thirties, forties, and fifties and look kind of like your high school English teacher, but there are always enough twenty-somethings to balance out the fat, hairy, wrinkled perverts. Enough to make the trip worthwhile. There's always someone there who can get you off." She could almost hear the smile in his voice when he said it. "I met my Alicia there. It was one of the best nights of my life. I'd love to take you there someday," Joe had said.

For all of her jealousy at the constant mention of Alicia, Selene had been intrigued and aroused by the idea of fucking the big cannibal in front of an audience. She'd likewise been intrigued by the idea of a house full of sex addicts.

Selene piloted her little red Vespa scooter into the gravel-covered parking lot, bumping along like she was riding a horse rather than something with an engine and tires. It was only six o'clock in the evening. The sun had just begun its slow decent and the shadows were growing longer moment by moment. Already the parking lot was filled with sports cars, SUVs, trucks, and old Fords and Chevys. At least three dozen vehicles and two taxis pulled up as she sat there in the parking lot with her engine idling. One contained a couple only slightly older than Selene dressed in black leather and lace, the woman wore a corset and hip-boots with six-inch heels and he wore a leather vest and chaps, shirtless and pants-less. They held hands and skipped into the club, giggling like school kids.

The next car that pulled up held three guys in their twenties, frat boys by the looks of them, who looked like they were already drunk, and a young, freckled redheaded woman of about the same age who looked like they'd paid for her. She was wearing a catholic school skirt that barely covered her red panties, white knee-high leggings, and big clunky patent leather heels that she was having difficulty walking in. Her white button-down blouse was tied in the front to reveal her flat, freckled stomach.

The frat boys threw money through the window of the taxi and then staggered inside, dragging the girl behind them. She looked reluctant and borderline terrified. Selene rethought her assessment of the girl. She was obviously not a pro. The frat boys had probably dressed her that way for the evening. She was probably one of their girlfriends or at least thought she was or would be after this evening. It was more likely that she was about to be passed around and then sent home alone in that same taxi, dripping in semen and reeking of Astroglide. If she had the chance, Selene thought, she'd warn the girl before she lost everything that was innocent about her.

Selene pulled the scooter to a halt in front of the club next to the Harleys, Kawasakis, and Suzuki crotch rockets. The first person she saw when she walked in was a large bouncer sitting on a stool by the coat-check girl. He had short gray hair, gray-green eyes, and a handlebar moustache. His heavily muscled arms were covered with tattoos. He was dressed modestly in a black T-shirt and blue jeans with black motorcycle boots. Selene guessed that one of the Harleys parked outside probably belonged to him.

"ID."

Selene pulled a slim wallet on a chain from her front pocket and fished out her California driver's license. The big biker stared at the license for what seemed like a full minute. Behind him on a wall covered with photographs of swingers partying it up at the club from the early seventies to today was a sign that said "Couples $50, Single men $65, Single women Free!"

"Go on in. You can leave your clothes with coat check."

Selene wore a sundress that was practically see-through, and that was as naked as she planned to get until the situation demanded it. She was still not completely comfortable with the weight she'd gained and was not quite ready to strip down in front of strangers. It was different when she was modeling and getting paid for it. Anyone who hired her knew what they were getting. Since she'd gained the thirty-five pounds of fat and muscle for Joseph, she had gotten twice as many runway jobs, her first print jobs, and had become the most popular art model in the area. Had she known there was such a market for plus-sized models she would have gained the weight long ago. She knew there were many women who would have objected to her use of the term plus-sized. Even with the added weight she was still only a size nine, well under the national average of a size twelve or fourteen but a far cry from the size one she had been.

She walked past an emaciated coat-check girl with pierced nipples, two sleeves of tattoos completely covering both arms, and stars tattooed on both shoulders like the Russian mob. She had long black hair like Selene's, but hers was obviously a dye job. She looked just as Joseph had described her, with the exception of the star tattoos. She must have added those since Joseph was here last. She had the beginnings of crow's feet at the corners of her eyes. Those too must have been added since Joseph's last visit. Selene suspected that hard drugs, alcohol, and bulimia had prematurely aged her.

The smell of air-freshener, pussy, sweat, lubricant, and semen hung heavy in the air. The unmistakable scent of Pine Sol lingered in the air as well and that was a relief. At least someone had made an effort to clean and disinfect the place. Selene wondered how often the floors and walls were scrubbed, sheets changed, sex toys disinfected. No matter how often it was, it couldn't have been often enough to keep up with the constant deluge of bodily fluids. A sign pointed upstairs to the "Couples only" rooms where no single men or women were allowed and announced that this was the only place where couples were free to dispense with condoms. Downstairs, condoms were mandatory and anyone found not using them would be asked to leave. Selene tried her best to follow the logic and failed.

The bar was fully stocked and looked like what you would see at any nightclub in the city, except the barstools were wrapped in disposable plastic covers and the patrons were mostly nude, though quite a few of the women wore lingerie and a few of the men were fully clothed. Somehow the men who were still wearing their street clothes struck Selene as the creepiest. She wondered if she looked just as creepy as they did walking around in a yellow sundress and pink Crocs. She walked up to the bar and all eyes, male and female, instantly landed on her. Smiles widened, eyes blazed with lust, and a few of the men who were completely naked rose to salute her. Selene smiled and slightly blushed. It was probably the most flattering welcome she'd ever received. Joseph had been right though. Most of the men were old and fat and so were most of the women, except the ones who had come alone and Selene suspected that most of them were prostitutes. She wondered if they thought she was a prostitute too and then realized that most working girls didn't wear yellow sundresses. Her decision to come to the club had been so sudden she hadn't had time to change into anything more seductive.

Selene ordered an apple martini from the bartender and leaned against the bar, sipping her drink as she scanned the room. There was a small dance floor and several couples had taken to it as the DJ changed the music from techno to an old school Madonna song to George Michael singing, "I Want Your Sex!" Everyone looked absurd as they shook, shimmied, and gyrated to the music, sex organs and mammary glands bouncing and flopping, asses and bellies rippling and jiggling. This was perhaps the least attractive group of people Selene had ever seen. Perhaps coming so early had been a mistake. Most of the people she knew around her age didn't even leave the house until after 10:00 p.m. to go clubbing and it was only—Selene checked her watch—6:23 p.m. No one came out this early except people who had to get home to cook dinner for the kids or the truly lonely and desperate.

The frat boys who'd come in with the girl who looked like she might have still been a virgin as recently as last week passed by the dance floor on their way out to the pool. Selene followed, still sipping her martini. The guys all looked like assholes, but at least they were near her age. Besides, she was feeling protective toward the young girl and wanted to make certain that anything that happened to her was consensual, though she wasn't sure if the girl was even old enough to know the difference. If the guy at the front had checked her ID, he was either blind, stupid, or had been handsomely bribed. Of course it was possible the girl looked younger than she was. Possible, but doubtful.

The pool was filled with couples, threesomes, and even foursomes, furiously copulating in various positions. A black woman in her forties with huge fake breasts and fake platinum blonde hair was bent over a deck chair being fucked in the ass by a young, muscular Latino guy with acne on his back and shoulders and a tattoo of the Virgin Mary in the center of his chest. He looked almost ten years her junior. Beside him an even younger Mexican guy with skinny tattoo-covered arms and a fat belly had a large Mexican woman with big, flabby, pendulous breasts in a similar position, bent over a chair, grunting and thrusting in her dimpled, cottage cheese covered ass. Every now and then the two guys would high-five each other. In the hot tub, a curvaceous Filipino woman in her twenties sat on the edge of the tub while an older white guy in his late thirties/early forties knelt between her thighs, lapping at her clitoris like he was trying to remove a stain. At the other end of the hot tub, two gray-haired men were sharing a large woman in pigtails who looked close to Selene's age though easily twice her weight. Despite her size, the woman's breasts were disproportionately small. Her belly easily stuck out further than her tits. She was grinning like she'd won the lottery as she was penetrated from behind by one of the older gentleman and had her mouth full of the other. The hot tub was oily with bodily fluid. The thought of doing anything in that cesspool made Selene's stomach threaten to revolt. Yet the couples splashing around in the water seemed to be having the time of their lives.

"Disgusting," Selene hissed. She spotted one of the frat boys staring at her from the other side of the pool. He was tall with an athletic build, blond hair, blue eyes, freckles, and a cock that appeared slightly larger than six inches. Not exactly big, but far more than she would have given him credit for. He just missed being cute by an inch and a weak chin that disappeared into his neck. But he was handsome enough that, with a little sweet talking and a bit of confidence/arrogance, he could entice a few pretty girls with low self-esteem into his bed. He was the one who'd been dragging the young girl in the Catholic school skirt into the club earlier. Selene looked for the girl and found her by the diving board, sandwiched between the freckled kid's two friends, being double-penetrated. One of the frat boys, a tall lanky guy with long hair, thrust his stubby penis in her vagina with her legs draped over his shoulders while his shorter, chubbier friend stretched her rectum with his own impressive organ. It was the blonde kid who she'd thought was the girl's boyfriend.

The expression on the young girl's face was not one of enjoyment but of grudging acceptance. Her eyes remained on the freckled kid the entire time. Selene felt a white-hot rage burning within her. She wanted to tear all three of those college assholes apart and rescue the girl. She reached into one of the large pockets in her sundress and found the small can of pepper spray attached to her keychain. It wasn't much as offensive weaponry goes, and it wasn't very accurate either. If she sprayed the two guys, she'd get the girl too. It would be easy to explain why she'd pepper sprayed two college assholes in a sex club. Just about any lie would have worked, starting with attempted rape. But pepper spraying the girl would have been harder to explain. Besides, she couldn't play heroine to every naïve young whore who crossed her path.

The boy with the nice body was making his move toward her, and Selene's hand tightened on the pepper spray even as she plastered a seductive smile on her face and demurely dropped her eyes. The boy was just a few feet away from her when an idea came to Selene, the real reason she'd come here.

"You're much too pretty to still be wearing clothes," the boy said. "My name is Mark and you're …"

"Quite horny but disgusted with this place. I can't imagine how many diseases are floating around that pool."

Mark looked at the pool like he was seeing it for the first time. "Yeah, you're right. Want to go someplace else? Like to my place?"

Selene smiled. "How far is it?"

"I live just off Seventeenth and Mission Avenue. We can take a taxi."

"I came on my scooter. Just give me your address. I'll meet you there."

Mark looked at her suspiciously and then turned back toward his friends.

Selene reached out and stroked his cock, which immediately got his attention. "I promise, I'll be there. I told you I was horny. Do you need to say goodbye to your friends?"

He turned back to the threesome. His girlfriend was no longer watching him and that seemed to bother him.

"Is she your girlfriend?" Selene asked while still stroking his cock.

"Nope. Just a friend. Let's go."

They walked back inside and Selene handed Mark a cocktail napkin to write down his address while she finished her martini.

"That's not far at all. I can't wait." Selene grabbed the boy's cock again and stroked it a few times for emphasis and then smiled and walked out the door, waving the napkin with his phone number on it.

"See you in fifteen minutes!" Mark called after her.

Selene didn't answer. She continued out into the parking lot while Mark collected his clothes from the coat-check girl. She grabbed her helmet and straddled her little scooter. After strapping on her helmet, she gunned the throttle and quickly pulled out of the parking lot as Mark walked out of the club and hailed a taxi. She raced down Sixth Street, slipping between slower moving cars. She wanted to put some distance between her and Mark's taxi. There was one more stop Selene had to make before she met him at his apartment.

Hopefully, he doesn't have any roommates, she thought, pulling into the supermarket parking lot. She parked quickly and dashed into the store headed for the kitchenware section.

16

It had been two days since Officer Cindy Addison came to supermax, and Joe had been working hard to win her heart. He sat in his cell, painting on loose-leaf paper he'd glued together at the edges to form a four-foot by two-foot rectangle. He used water he'd colored with Skittles and Sweet Tarts from the commissary for his palate and wads of toilet paper as brushes. Keeping his passions in check as he painted was difficult, but he knew he would scare her off if he let even the slightest glimmer of the mayhem and destruction he saw in his mind whenever he looked at her seep onto his canvas. Instead, he channeled his passion into more pedestrian images. Still, even what he considered "pedestrian" was shocking by normal standards.

He layered body parts upon body parts in a kaleidoscope of flesh and sexual organs. It looked like an orgy of two, the same faces and bodies in different sexual positions; Joe and Officer Addison in a "69." Joe and Officer Addison in missionary position, doggy-style, cowgirl, reverse cowgirl, legs thrown over his shoulders, Joe performing analingus, cunnulingus, cumming on her belly, on her ass, on her breasts, her cherubic smiling face. The images were so layered they were almost unrecognizable, just delicate intersecting lines of pink and tan, unless you knew what you were looking for, and Joe knew Officer Addison could see exactly what he was painting.

Officer Cindy Addison was standing outside Joe's cell watching him paint. She'd been watching him for fifteen minutes. He'd made certain to position the canvas so she could see it as she walked by and peered into his cell.

112

"What you painting, Joe?"

Joe looked up for a second, smiled, and then returned to his canvas and continued painting. "You. I'm painting a portrait of you ... and me. Us."

Whenever he painted her face, he smoothed out the wrinkles at the corners of her eyes, and he made her belly smaller and her breasts slightly bigger. Her ass, however, he drew exactly as he imagined it. Big, round, smooth like a beach ball. He reached for a handful of red Skittles and soaked them in a cup with water from the faucet. He opened another pack of Skittles and separated out more red ones and tossed them into the cup as well. Then he opened another pack and another. He threw in a few purple as well to get just the perfect hue. He stared at the water as it began to redden and darken. The color was perfect, totally authentic, but he couldn't use it. He looked back at his patchwork canvas of loose-leaf paper. If he touched any of the red paint to the canvas he wouldn't be able to stop himself. He would turn it into a slaughter; the canvas would look like an abattoir.

He imagined the painting he wanted to paint and then imagined the acts they represented, all the things he wanted to do to Officer Addison. Joe paused and began to masturbate again. "I'm sorry, Officer Addison. It's just been so long and every time I think about you ... I-I can't help myself."

Officer Addison blushed but didn't turn away. "It's okay, Joe. It's flattering, actually. I like that you find me so ... that you get excited when you think about me. And you can call me Cindy."

Joe leaned back on his bunk and locked eyes with her just as he had the first time she'd caught him masturbating in his cell. He stroked himself aggressively, lip curled up in a snarl, growling out her name. "Cindy. Cindy. Cindy. Cindy!"

He pinched his nipple between his thumb and index finger, twisting and squeezing it until it turned purple as he rubbed the head of his cock.

"You're beautiful, Joe. You really are."

"So are you, Cindy," Joe said before letting loose a primal roar and ejaculating a stream of hot semen onto his painting, mixing his seed with the flesh-colored mayhem.

17

The frat boy's apartment was as unkempt as she would have imagined. It was right out of a teen sex comedy with nude centerfolds, football and basketball stars Selene had never heard of, and comic book and "World of Warcraft" posters on the walls. Empty beer bottles, pizza, fried chicken, and Chinese food boxes adorned the counters and tables, and a 52" flat-screen HD television was mounted on the wall, a World War II video game on pause.

Mark was all over her from the moment she knocked on his door and stepped over the threshold into his apartment. He stammered out an apology for the condition of his home and then kissed her artlessly and went right for her breasts. Selene endured the awkward groping and pawing and even returned his sloppy, alcohol-laced kiss. His breath reeked of beer and pot and she could smell sweat and perfume on him. The perfume was undoubtedly from the girl he'd left behind at the sex club. Obviously they were much more than the friends he'd said they were.

Selene unzipped, unbuckled, and unbuttoned his pants and slid them down to his knees. His throbbing pink cock bobbled above her head as she helped him out of his shoes. There was nothing particularly exciting about this boy who was so much smaller, so much clumsier, so much less passionate, less dangerous, less ferocious than the man waiting for her behind bars, yet Selene was so aroused she thought there was no way she would fail to cum this time, no matter how terrible a lover this moron was.

She took the frat boy's cock into her mouth. He moaned and shuddered as her tongue swirled around the head of his manhood and she took it deeper, deeper, past her tonsils, burying her lips in his pubic hair as his penis filled her throat.

"Shit! Oh, fuck! Oh, yeah! That's it, you sexy bitch! Suck this cock! Suck it, you nasty whore!"

It wasn't just his ridiculous attempt at dirty talk that pissed her off. It was the fact that she could already feel him approaching orgasm. She had wanted to enjoy herself a little and this selfish prick was going to get off and leave her unsatisfied … as usual. Fucking men were all the same. He grabbed her by the back of the head and began fucking her mouth, rushing toward orgasm. That was the last straw. Selene jerked away from him, biting down hard and taking the tip of his cock with her as she pulled away.

"AHHHHHH! NOOOOOO! YOU BIT OFF MY DICK! You fucking BITCH!"

For a moment, the bleeding stump of his cock bobbed in the air, still erect, spraying blood and semen from his urethra, spattering Selene's face like some gore-soaked bukakke session. Then the frat boy collapsed screaming and twitching. Selene chewed the bleeding lump of meat, retching and gagging as she attempted to swallow it, choked, and then vomited it back up. Mark was still on the floor, shrieking like a cat on fire and clutching his bleeding cock when Selene's stomach rejected his half-eaten glans and she vomited it onto the floor beside him. She waited for that orgasmic rush Joseph had described to her. Her entire body was on fire. Her clitoris throbbed and tingled and she felt like she'd cum immediately if she touched it, but that was just the adrenaline, the excitement, it wasn't what Joe had described to her. The powerful climax he had described did not come. Selene took out the pepper spray as Mark groped for his cell phone. She sprayed him in the face and then took out the filet knife she'd purchased from the supermarket.

"AHHHHHHFUUUUUCK! MY EYES! MY FUCKING EYES!"

The knife was still in its packaging. She'd been in such a hurry to get to the frat boy's apartment before he gave up on her and went back to the club that she hadn't bothered to unwrap the knife. Now that she needed it, it was encased in plastic so thick that she couldn't even tear it with her teeth. She climbed up from the floor and ran into Mark's kitchen. She opened the drawers on both sides of his stove, looking for a knife to use to open her knife. It never occurred to her how ridiculous that was. She finally found a steak knife in a drawer on the left of the kitchen sink and sawed through the packaging. Mark was still on the floor screaming and calling her words no man had called her since her father died. If she didn't silence him soon, the neighbors would summon the cops.

Selene ran out of the kitchen and straddled Mark's chest. Blood was pumping from his wounded penis and he was squeezing it, trying to stop the flow.

"Help me! You have to help me! Call an ambulance. I'm bleeding to death! Why are you doing this to me? I didn't do anything to you. I didn't DO ANYTHING! You have to take me to the hospital. I'm DYIIIING!"

Selene smiled. She slashed his face with the knife and snarled. "I don't have to do shit but bleed once a month, pay taxes, and die. But not before you do, you piece of shit!"

She raised the knife above her head and began stabbing him. The first stab was shallow, sinking no more than three inches into Mark's pectoral muscle. Blood spurted from the wound, but it wasn't the lush arterial spray she had been expecting. Mark groped blindly for her wrists and Selene sliced at his fingers with the filet knife while punching at his face with her other hand. She stabbed him in the chest again and this time the blade sank deeper. Selene needed both hands to wrench it free and bring it down again.

"AHHHhhhrgh! GET OFF ME, you CRAZY BITCH!"

Just as she brought the knife down into Mark's chest, he

threw a punch that caught her in the eye and knocked her sideways onto the floor with blue lightning flashing in her head. She dropped the knife and Mark scrambled over the top of her, groping for it with his eyes still squeezed shut, pouring burning tears. Selene brought her knee up into his bleeding cock and climbed from underneath him while Mark cried out and fell onto his side, vomiting his lunch along with a lungful of blood. Even as he regurgitated over and over, he still tried to grope for the knife. Selene's heart thundered in her chest and she could barely catch her breath. She could see exactly where the knife was. She snatched it away just as Mark's fingers were about to touch it. He grabbed her arm to keep her from stabbing him again, trying to pry the knife from her hands. Selene reached down between his thighs and seized his ravaged penis, twisting it and raking it with her nails.

"AHHHhhh! FUUUuuuck! NOOOOO! Let it go! LET IT GOOOOoo!" He seized her hand with both hands and pulled. She didn't let go, and the tender, bleeding flesh between Mark's legs stretched until it looked like it was going to tear off. Selene stabbed the filet knife upward into Mark's throat. He toppled over, holding his punctured trachea as blood sprayed in that delicious arterial eruption Selene had been waiting for. Rather than try to pull the knife out again, Selene stood up and walked back into the kitchen. She knew where the knife drawer was.

When she walked back into the living room, Mark was barely conscious. His face and chest were caked with blood and vomit and he was wheezing in long shallow breaths. She held a steak knife and a dull carving knife, but she barely needed either now. She straddled him again and could feel the frat boy's diminishing heartbeat against her clitoris. For a moment, she thought she was about to experience that orgasmic rush she'd witnessed when Joseph swallowed her nipple. Her vagina was drenched. The thrill of killing had her quivering at the threshold of orgasm, but she couldn't quite seem to get there. Something was holding her back as it always did. In frustration, Selene took the steak knife and stabbed Mark in the chest a few more times until she'd buried it so deep in his pectoral muscle that the handle broke off and the blade remained embedded inside him. Mark finally stopped moving. She could no longer feel the pulse of his heart against her swollen clitoris.

"Wow. Oh, shit. That was fucking incredible," Selene whispered breathlessly. Her thighs were trembling. Her clitoris throbbed, engorged with blood. She reached down between her thighs and rubbed it, flicking her fingers across the swollen nub. So close. So close. Nothing. Selene screamed in rage. She stood up and began kicking Mark's body. She stomped his face until it was unrecognizable, little more than a bleeding, misshapen lump.

She collapsed, panting with exhaustion, across Mark's chest. She lay there on Mark's bleeding corpse for several long moments, trying to calm her breathing. She couldn't believe she'd just murdered a man. She felt enormously powerful, unstoppable, like a goddamn juggernaut, but she still had not reached orgasm. Joseph had been wrong, wrong, wrong! Maybe if she hadn't spit out Mark's cock? Maybe if she had been able to keep it down she would have felt it? Still, even though she hadn't been able to cum, this had been the closest to orgasm she'd ever been. It was close enough that she knew she'd have to try the experiment again.

She had just regained control of her breathing when she realized that Mark was still breathing as well, faint, hoarse breaths whistling out from the gash in his throat, up from his ruptured lungs. Selene lifted herself from Mark's chest and raised herself back to a sitting position. She studied the frat boy's face for some sign of consciousness before reaching out to grab the hilt of the filet knife still protruding from his throat. Slowly, she slid the blade from his trachea.

Blood spattered her face again as Mark's ventricles filled and his heart contracted a few final times, emptying his blood vessels onto the floor. Without bothering to feel for a pulse, she began to saw off his pectoral muscle. She slid the thin, sharp blade beneath the muscle and scraped it along his ribcage, exactly how Joe had once described removing a woman's breast. She lifted the muscle from his ribcage and carried it into the kitchen.

The taste of the frat boy's penis had caused her to gag. The chewy texture of it, like munching on raw chicken ... just thinking about it made her want to vomit all over again. She didn't even like her steak rare and could only eat sushi when it was rolled in seaweed with rice, cucumber, avocado, and cream cheese. Eating raw human flesh had been absolutely revolting and only the expectation of ecstasy had permitted her to keep chewing it. Perhaps it was the nauseating taste that was getting in the way of her enjoyment. She opened the white cabinet doors and removed a frying pan and a paper plate. She plopped the severed pectoral muscle on the plate and went hunting for something to season it with.

Years ago, Selene read an article about Jeffrey Dahmer cooking a man's bicep with garlic and onions. Selene opened Mark's refrigerator and found an onion in the vegetable crisper next to a moldy cucumber and a quarter stick of butter on the door shelf along with a couple prepackaged slices of American cheese. Besides a jar of mayonnaise that looked like it had seen better days, a package of bologna, and a two-liter cola, there was nothing else in the refrigerator. Obviously, Mark didn't cook much. Selene discovered a couple packets of garlic powder and dried oregano from a place called Pizza Buffet in the same drawer she'd found the steak knife now buried in Mark's chest. She turned to the stove and lit one of the burners.

The corpse bleeding on the floor in the next room was all but forgotten as Selene placed the pan on the flame, added the butter, and watched it sizzle. Blood had soaked through the paper plate and covered the counter. She lifted the plate and dumped the muscle into the pan with the butter. The blood and butter mixed to form a brown gravy. Selene wondered what it tasted like but wanted to wait until it had been seasoned properly before trying it. She emptied the packets of garlic and oregano into the pan and tossed the meat with a half-melted plastic spatula she found in the utensil drawer. She let it simmer as she quickly diced half the onion and added it to the pan. She wished she had a glass of wine. Everything went down easier with wine.

The smell of butter and onions filled the kitchen. The aroma was delicious, but the memory of her attempt to swallow the disembodied head of Mark's cock still troubled her. She flipped the meat over several times, basting it in the butter until it was brown on all sides with a slight crisp to the skin, and then she grabbed another paper plate and slid the meat out onto it. She walked over to Mark's rickety kitchen table and sat down on a chair with one loose leg, almost pitching herself over onto the floor. She stared at the meat, trying to figure out how to begin. There were a couple hairs sticking out of it that she reached out and plucked. She realized that it would have probably been a good idea to remove the nipple. Even after being sautéed with butter and onions, it still looked like a human chest. She stood up and walked back into the living room.

Mark looked like something from one of the more gratuitously violent Lucio Fulci or Dario Argento movies. His ribcage was completely exposed on the left side and the right side of his chest had been slashed and stabbed viciously and now resembled ground beef. The knife wound in his neck yawned wide and continued to leak a sluggish drip of blood onto the carpet.

Selene was surprised she didn't feel the slightest bit of remorse over the frat boy's death. All she felt was disappointment. The kill itself had been exhilarating, a tremendous high, but his flesh had been disgusting. She wanted the profound ecstasy that Joe felt when consuming human flesh, but that had been unreachable for her. She'd even failed to finish the job with her own hand just as she had every time she did anything sexual with a man, with the same results.

Selene couldn't even get off on her own and no man or woman had ever brought her to climax. Her sexual trysts always ended with her kicking some loser out of her apartment and trying desperately to satisfy herself with the help of one of her battery-powered friends or with her cursing and breaking things before collapsing to the bed in tears. She was tired of being sexually frustrated. That's why she'd been so intrigued by Joe and his unique style of passion.

She lifted the filet knife from where she'd dropped it on the floor beside Mark's body. It was coated in a thick sheen of blood. Selene brought it over to the sink and washed it off under the faucet. She shook it dry and then sat back down at the table and sliced off a piece of meat. The knife slid easily through the moist, tender flesh. It looked a lot like turkey or lean pork. She brought the meat to her lips and bit into it. The taste wasn't bad. She took another bite and then another and another, slicing off piece after piece, hungry for that orgasmic tidal wave that Joe described. She began ripping off chunks of the meat with her hands and cramming it into her mouth, tears streaming down her face.

18

A week went by without a letter from Selene, then a month, and then two. Joe wrote to her every day with no reply. He accused the guards of keeping his mail from him, but Cindy had assured him that no mail had been withheld. Selene had forgotten him.

Today, Cindy had finally managed to change her work schedule to the morning shift, midnight to eight a.m. They had been flirting for weeks and tonight they would finally consummate their mutual affections. She came for him just after midnight. Cindy unlocked the door and stepped inside. It was too dark to see anything, but he knew it was her. She was wearing the perfume he'd asked her to, the same kind Alicia had worn: White Shoulders. Her skin smelled fresh and clean. She'd washed for him. He stepped forward and inhaled the intoxicating scents.

"Cindy?"

She kissed his lips to quiet him. It was the first time he'd been kissed by anyone in several years. Alicia had been the last woman he'd embraced before being caged.

"Shhh. Don't say anything. I could lose my job if anyone catches us."

Joe didn't say another word. Cindy took his hand, and he allowed himself to be led from his cell, down the hall, to the stairwell. The stairwell smelled of both urine and disinfectant, as if it had been recently cleaned but the cleaner had missed a few spots or his work had literally been pissed on.

The prison library was in the basement. All the inmates were locked down for the night, so the basement was completely empty. They passed the library, the laundry, the kitchen, and the exercise yard. Joe stared longingly at the yard used by the inmates in general population. It had a basketball court, a wall for playing handball, and even a weight training area. He wished Selene had not abandoned him; even if he never escaped, just being allowed back amongst his fellow inmates would have made an immeasurable difference in the quality of his life.

They made it to the library without incident and Cindy used her keys to let them in. Bookcases lined the walls and filled every available space, arranged in even rows just slightly wider than Joseph's shoulders. There were several eight-foot banquet tables with chairs and even a couple of computers, though Internet usage was restricted. Two small windows located at the top of the wall above the bookcases let in light from the spotlights in the yard, illuminating the room with a blue-white glow like starlight. In the daytime, the place would have looked just like any library you'd see in the average inner-city high school. At night it looked eerie and haunted.

The glow from the guard tower's roving spotlights made shadows dance and rage across the room. The smell of Cindy's perfume, the touch of her hand in his, enflamed his senses and made the monster rage in Joseph's pants. He could smell her slow-burning soul, smoldering with the scent of blood and flame. His mind was a riot of lascivious images of sex and death. Joe tried his best to bring the monster under control before the door closed behind them and they were completely alone.

Cindy turned and locked the door. "Has anyone ever told you you look just like Superman? The same black hair and blue eyes. Even your amazing body. Except for your teeth. Why did you file them down like that?"

Joe squinted at her. "You haven't read my file? You didn't read about me in the news?"

"I know a little about you. They said you ate a woman. Is that true? Did you do it?"

124

"Yes."

Cindy took an involuntary step backward. "Why? I mean, why did you kill her?"

"I loved her and she asked me to."

"Do you want to kill me too?"

"I won't kill you, Cindy."

The searchlight outside passed by the library window, illuminating the room briefly. Joe could see Cindy's bottom lip trembling in fear. She'd apparently just realized the reality of her situation. She was alone in a room with a serial killer and nobody knew where she was.

"What if I wanted you to? What if I wanted you to eat me?"

"Do you?"

"N-no. No, I don't. I just want you to make love to me."

"Then come closer."

Officer Cindy Addison stepped into Joe's arms, pressed her soft, trembling body to his unyielding flesh … and the monster roared.

PART THREE

Drunken Long Pig

One medium-size adult 150 to 160 lbs
2 gallons vegetable oil
2 gallons sesame oil
3 tablespoons ginger root, shredded
2 gallons Chinese wine
2 1/2 tablespoons salt
1 cup sugar
2 cups fresh cilantro

Drown one medium-size adult (male or female depending on personal preference) in 1 gallon of Chinese wine until reasonably intoxicated. This works as a sedative and helps marinate the meat. Heat oil in large pot or steel tub big enough to accommodate one adult.

Add drunken adult and fry for 1 minute. Add remaining rice wine and stir-fry until tender and brown. Add ginger. Blend in salt and sugar. Serve immediately with cilantro for garnish.

19

Cindy would barely look at him. She hurried past his cell as she walked her rounds. Her uniform hid the scratches, bruises, and bite marks. Joe had been unable to completely control himself. He'd drawn blood in several places but he'd retained enough self-control to keep himself from tearing her apart. Her bruises would heal. At least the ones that could be seen.

As soon as she'd closed the door, all the tender words, all the loving caresses he'd intended had fled his consciousness. All that remained was the monster's ravenous hunger and lust. He took her down like a wolf taking down a fawn. His sharp canines dug into the back of her neck, piercing the skin.

"Ouch! Wait! That hurt!"

Blood filled his mouth and Joe eagerly gulped it down. The taste was maddening. He pushed her to the floor and dragged her pants down to her ankles.

"Easy, Joe! Easy! Slow down."

Joe nodded. He reached out and rubbed her massive buttocks. He squeezed and caressed it lovingly. Slowly, he removed her red, lace thong.

"You like it?"

"I love it. I adore it!"

Cindy smiled while wiping the blood from the back of her neck. "You hurt me."

"Let me kiss it and make it better."

He grabbed her by the hips and pulled Cindy's ass toward him. He kissed and sucked each pale globe. "It's so beautiful. You're exquisite."

He buried his face between her buttocks and slid his tongue inside her, flicking his tongue from her rectum to her vagina and back.

"Oh, Jesus! Oh God, Joe!"

He dug his hard fingers into her hips, bruising the skin and leaving the impression of his hands in the soft, doughy flesh as he pulled her closer, fucking her puckered anus with his tongue. His eyes rolled backward in his skull. He saw into his own mind. His inner consciousness, at all the things the monster wanted to do with Cindy Addison. He abruptly withdrew his tongue and flipped her over onto her back. Cindy spread her legs and purred, grinding her pelvis in the air.

"Fuck me, Joe," she moaned.

"Yes."

He pulled off his prison clothes and lay on top of her, entering her quickly, desperate to fuck the gruesome thoughts from his mind. He fought hard to suppress the voracious beast roaring within him, straining to get out, to feed. As much as he desperately wanted to indulge his feral instincts, to let the monster out to play, if he killed her now he'd be stuck in supermax forever. They would bury him in one of the strip cells until he went completely mad and tore out his own throat with his fingernails.

She was tighter than expected. His cock was so swollen with blood it felt like it had gained an inch on its already impressive length and girth. Cindy gasped as he eased the tip in and then screamed as he rammed the rest of his length deep into her loins.

"Oh, God. You're so huge!"

Once inside her he pounded her sopping wet vagina with maniacal fervor. The monster wanted blood, and if he couldn't tear it from her flesh he would fuck the blood from her sex, ripping her wide. But the monster was still not satisfied. He pounded harder and harder as it fed him images of her beautiful ass and all the fun he could have biting chunks from it. Delirious fantasies of cannibalizing her labia and clitoris, biting off each delicate fold one at a time flashed through his mind as he thrust deeper, harder, faster.

"Oh my, God. Joe. It hurts! It hurts so good! Fuck me harder, Joe. Harder!"

He withdrew from her and flipped her over, entering her from behind so he could watch the bounce and jiggle of that most perfect ass. Joe grabbed her by the hips again and pulled her forward to meet each thrust.

"Oh shit, Joe! Oh shit! I'm cumming! Oh God!" Her body trembled and shook. Her already tight pussy contracted as the orgasm wracked her body. The sensation was overwhelming and Joe could feel his own orgasm building. Joe licked his thumb to coat it in saliva and then eased it into Cindy's ass. He slid his cock out of her vagina and replaced his thumb with his engorged and throbbing sex organ, easing it in slowly, inch by inch.

"Oh no, Joe. I don't think I can. I think you're too big. I don't think it will fit."

But his cock slid in easily, despite its size. Her anus was slippery with the lubrication of her vaginal juices and Joe's saliva. Joe began to slowly thrust in and out of her anus. It was even tighter than her vagina, and now his view of her large wobbly ass was at the perfect angle. Moonlight alternated with the guard's spotlights, spilling through the window above the bookcase to illuminate her pale skin so her ass appeared to glow. Joe sped up his rhythm, thrusting harder and deeper as Cindy continued to moan. Her sounds switching from grunts and groans of pain back to cries of ecstasy and pleasure.

Joe knelt down and bit her neck again.

"Ouch! That hurts! Stop it, Joe. Don't bite. That hurts. Stop it, Joe! STOP!"

But the blood tasted so delicious. It wasn't the meat he

craved, but it was a suitable surrogate. He bit deeper into her neck as he fucked her harder and the monster's thoughts filled his mind. Suddenly, he erupted. He maintained his grip on her neck as he shuddered and thrashed and roared, spilling his seed deep inside her succulent ass. When he was spent, he withdrew from her and collapsed onto the rough carpet. His knees were bleeding from scraping against the floor, but even that was a welcome sensation, more proof of his existence.

He licked the rest of the blood from his lips as he lay back, staring at the light dancing across the walls and luxuriating in each tremor of pleasure. Cindy was already getting dressed. She was pressing a rag to the back of her neck that Joe realized was an undershirt. He couldn't tell if she was angry or not. He'd taken great care to avoid any major arteries, but his sharpened teeth had lacerated the flesh at the base of her skull to a bleeding ruin.

"Get dressed, Joe. I need to get you back in your cell and I need to get down to see the doctor and have her stitch me up."

"I'm sorry, Cindy. I didn't mean to hurt you."

She nodded, with her back to the window so her face was obscured in shadow and Joe could not read her expression.

"Hurry up and get dressed."

She barely spoke to him as she led him back to his cell and locked him in for the night.

"I really am sorry. I didn't mean to hurt you."

"Goodnight, Joe."

She walked off quickly down the tier, still holding the blood-soaked rag to the back of her neck. Joe wondered what she would tell the doctors when they asked what happened. He wondered if he had fucked up his best chance for escape.

She walked past his cell several times throughout the day. He could see the bandage on the back of her neck. It wasn't as large as he would have expected. He figured she must have had stitches. Joe wondered how many times she'd had to explain the bandage and what explanation she'd used. Running through rose bushes and being snagged by thorns? A car accident? A pit bull attack? Sex with a convicted serial killer during her watch? He was certain the latter explanation was unlikely. He was already in prison for life. There was little more they could do to punish him, but such an admission would have ruined her.

It dawned on Joe that he now had power over Officer Cindy Addison. Sex between inmates and COs was expressly forbidden, not just because of the potential for inmates to receive preferential treatment but because of the power the guards held over them. Inmates were not in any position to refuse. It was akin to statutory rape. If he told, her career was over and she might even wind up in jail. All he needed was proof of their affair. That meant he had to convince her to have sex with him again. He needed to start a new painting.

Joe took out his last remaining bag of Skittles and separated the different colors, placing a handful of each color in its own plastic cup and adding a small bit of water. He then took out a piece of typing paper and several wads of toilet paper. Painstakingly, he mixed the colors on the page, taking care this time, not letting the monster take control. It was a portrait of her, naked, a look of ecstasy on her face, her body idealized, smooth, not a wrinkle or ripple. She was bathed in moonlight, glowing. Even the fat on her hips and thighs was smooth and sensuous. Before long, Joe could sense her at his door. Curiosity had gotten the better of her and she was staring in at his painting.

"It's you, Cindy." Joe said.

There was no reply.

"You really are beautiful, you know? Exquisite."

Again, no reply.

Joe opened his pants and took out his cock. He began to masturbate.

"Save it. I'll be back later."

Joe smiled. He hadn't ruined everything between them after all.

It was already getting dark outside. It would be lights-out soon. Cindy was on swing shift today, probably working a double shift. If not, then her shift would end at midnight, just two hours after lights-out. That wouldn't leave them much time. But, if she was working a double-shift, they had all night. He hoped he was in luck. Even more, he hoped he could control his violent urges this time.

Time passed with little to mark its progression. Joe had a hard time distinguishing night from day. In supermax, there were no routines to mark the passage of time except breakfast, lunch, exercise time, and dinner. Joe could not remember how long it had been since Cindy brought him his dinner.

The TV in Joe's cell was on, another televangelist station blared an unending torrent of anti-intellectual bullshit designed to leech as much currency as possible from the legions of true-believers. Joe missed the lectures and discussions he'd participated in at school, arguing politics, religion, psychology, and sociology with his professors and fellow students. Even though they all thought he was weird and creepy, the discussions had been amazing. It was during one such discussion in Professor Locke's abnormal psychology class that he'd first developed his theory of homicidal impulses as a symptom of a communicable disease. But, there was no arguing with the television. The dogma spewing forth hour after hour from the 13" TV screen embedded in the wall and covered by a steel cage was completely one-sided. Joe growled and snarled and paced in his cell. After months of this type of aural assault, it was beginning to get to him.

A black preacher in a four thousand dollar suit was talking about how God didn't want anyone to be poor and how tithing generously would increase your economic fortunes. He was asking for everyone to donate 10 percent of their income to the church. When he spoke, he waved his hands in large grandiose gestures that displayed the platinum Rolex and diamond rings God had given him by way of his congregation's generous tithing. Obviously he selectively ignored the part in the Bible where Jesus said a rich man has as much chance of entering heaven as a camel has of passing through the eye of a needle. Joe wasn't sure how he managed to reinterpret that into believing God wanted everyone to be rich, but obviously his congregation had made the same cognitive leap. He wondered how many of his fellow inmates believed the same thing and how many were here because of their effort to claim their God-given right to luxurious wealth.

One thing was evident—the prison was dominated by Christians. That's why Joe thought it was odd that they pushed religion so hard in supermax as if it were some kind of panacea for crime when obviously it hadn't kept anyone from committing the offenses that had brought them here. It seemed odd that the prison officials expected it to work the second time, but the evangelical stations were some of the only stations they allowed in supermax. It was either religious programming or prison programming that consisted of announcements from the warden and "educational" programs on anger management and literacy, and some basic entertainment channels, primarily news, game shows, soap operas, and sitcoms. Since the guard in the control booth operated the TV, game shows, sitcoms, and even the news were rare treats. The programming on most days were never-ending streams of religious propaganda followed by patronizing videos on how to avoid conflict and other anger management tools.

The religion and race of the CO in the control booth could usually be determined by the TV programming. If

Officer Belton was in the control booth, Benny Hinn and Creflo Dollar would play nonstop. If the big, red-headed CO, Officer Bruce Finley, was in the control booth, Joe could count on Joel Osteen or Robert Schuller dominating the TV for six to eight hours. The only time he was permitted to watch regular programming was when Cindy was in the control booth. Today, it was obviously Officer Belton's shift.

Joe dropped down and began cranking out pushups, trying to drown out the preacher's fanatical diatribe with sweat and pain. The preacher was railing against everything from homosexuality to violent video games to the president of the United States. His answer to everything was prayer and money. The more the televised minister droned on the more Joe's enmity toward Officer Belton increased. He wished it was Belton rather than Cindy being set up for the kill. *Set up for the kill? Is that what I'm doing with Cindy? Setting her up?* He hoped it wouldn't come to that but didn't see a way around it.

"Lights out!"

It was ten o'clock. Lights out. The shouts of "Allah Ahkba!" from the jihadists, imprisoned for various acts of terrorism, competed with screams and angry shouts for the "screws" to turn the lights back on so the inmates could finish reading or to turn the TV back on or to let them use the telephone or for things like new toothbrushes or toothpaste or washcloths. This was the same din that filled the prison twenty-four-hours a day. It was just easier to tune out the madness with the television on. Now the darkness resounded with rage, fear, desperation, and despair. The vicious super-predator, Joseph Miles, clamped his hands over his ears as he began a series of lunges and squats that would last for nearly an hour, past the point of fatigue, until he'd taken his muscles to total failure.

One thousand squats and five hundred lunges later, Joe collapsed onto his cot in exhaustion. The dreams came almost immediately.

Joe was ten years old again. His father was angry. He could hear him upstairs in the bedroom. Each footfall sounded like a small explosion. The elder Miles was not a small man. Joe's father rarely turned on the lights so the house held a constant crypt-like gloom that darkened gradually into a solid fortress of night as the sun disappeared. He said it was to preserve energy, but Joe always suspected his father simply enjoyed the darkness, that he felt more at home in the shadows. Soon the grim pall of night enshrouded every corner of the room. The lone light in the entire house came from the exhaust hood above the gas cooktop and Joe concentrated on it. Staring at that one ray of light as the roars and shouts increased. His father's shouts of anger seemed to shake the house to its foundations. Little Joey knew his father would come downstairs with the belt and the pain would begin. If he was lucky, the belt was the only thing his father would use.

He heard the first thunderous footstep on the stairs and Joey began to tremble and wet his pajamas. He wasn't sure what he had done wrong. He wasn't certain his father knew either. He was certain it wouldn't matter either way. His father was drunk and angry and Joe was there. His mom had left again and gone to live with her mother. She would be back. She always came back but, in the meantime, Joe was left alone with his father's explosive temper.

His father reached the bottom of the steps and Joe screamed as the big man came for him, only it wasn't his father anymore, it was Damon Trent, the fat, teenaged, child-murderer who'd kidnapped him when he was young.

He wasn't in his own home anymore. He was back in Damon Trent's basement, in the rusty, blood-filled tub. The basement windows were painted black and nailed shut. He was duct-taped and bleeding and Damon was coming to hurt him again.

"No. Don't hurt me. No. Nooo!"

Joe awoke in darkness—screaming. He looked around and for a moment expected to see Damon Trent coming to cut him and drink his blood. When he remembered that Damon Trent was already dead, that he had butchered the murderous pederast, vivisected him in his bed, Joe was filled with sudden and overwhelming joy and relief. Then he remembered where he was, locked in a cage, and was overcome with a sudden soul-crushing malaise. He had to escape. He was dying in here.

20

It had been dark for several hours when Cindy finally came for him. Joe was in the midst of another nightmare when his cell door unlocked and Cindy stepped in. He leapt to his feet when the door opened and took a defensive stance, expecting an inmate to come through the door for another cockfight. He was relieved to hear Cindy's voice.

"I turned off the camera in your cell. No one can see us."

She rushed into Joe's arms then pulled away and reached for her neck.

"You won't bite me again will you?"

Joe smiled, but in the dark, the expression went unseen.

"I'm sorry if I hurt you. It had just been so long since I was with a woman. I couldn't control myself. I'm okay now. I won't hurt you again." He stroked her cheek and heard her gasp. Cindy trembled beneath his fingertips.

"I wasn't going to come. I was afraid."

Joe nodded. "I know. I didn't mean to scare you. I won't hurt you again. I promise."

There was a flurry of motion and the sound of cloth rubbing against cloth. She moved closer to him, pulled his hard body against her soft flesh. She had removed her clothes and the feel of her smooth, warm flesh put steel in his manhood. The monster roared awake, but Joe quickly suppressed it. He would not lose control again.

She kissed him, deeply, passionately. Her tongue probed his mouth and he met it with his own. He nipped at her lips and then sucked them lightly. He kissed her cheeks, her forehead, the bridge of her nose, her chin, her jawline. He kissed his way down her quivering neck and heard her breath quicken in fear as he nipped at her throat. His hands caressed her narrow shoulders. He circled her throat with his fingers and then squeezed gently before pulling her forward into another kiss.

"Your body is incredible," she whispered.

"So is yours," Joe replied as he reached around to cup her large buttocks in both hands. He knelt down and sucked one of her nipples into his mouth. Her breasts were small but the nipples were large and erect. Joe flicked his tongue over them and sucked harder, drawing her entire breast into his mouth, just barely controlling the instinct to tear it off her chest. He kissed, sucked, nibbled, and bit his way down her chest to her stomach and from her stomach down between her thighs.

Joe still held Cindy's voluptuous ass in both hands as he knelt between her thighs and wriggled his tongue inside of her, luxuriating in the acrid, tangy, sweet taste of her sex. Her thighs shuddered as he sucked and lapped at her clitoris. She grabbed the back of his head, put one leg up onto his cot, and pulled his tongue deeper inside of her, grinding against his face. Joe eagerly lapped at her sex and the steady flow of juices as she quivered on the precipice of orgasm. He swirled his tongue around the engorged nub of her clitoris, bringing her to a convulsive climax. As she came, Joe stabbed his tongue deep inside of her. He licked the walls of her sex, swallowing the deluge of juices as orgasm after orgasm shook her to her core.

"Oh, fuck! Oh, God! OH GOD!"

She plopped down onto his bunk, her legs still trembling, struggling to catch her breath. Joe stood, dropping his pants to his ankles as he rose from between her legs. Cindy took Joe's massive endowment into her mouth and sucked on the very tip of his cock. Her tongue circled the rim of his gland, sending delirious bolts of pleasure down the shaft. Joe grabbed Cindy by her hair and eased his length further into her mouth until the head of his cock brushed her tonsils and she gagged slightly and pulled away, withdrawing his cock from her mouth abruptly and gasping for air.

"I can't take it that deep. You're too big."

She dragged her tongue down the length of his shaft and then cupped his testicles in her hand and sucked each one. Joe let out a low, rumbling growl while Cindy stroked his cock and licked his testicles. He could feel himself nearing orgasm.

"Suck it, Cindy. Suck it again. I'm so close."

Cindy took Joe's cock in her mouth again and grabbed him by his buttocks, slowly easing him deeper and deeper until she'd swallowed every inch and his full length throbbed deep in her esophagus. This time, she did not gag, even when Joe threaded his fingers into her hair and began rocking his hips forward and back, gripping her skull tight and fucking her throat. A growl reverberated low in his chest then came roaring out as he ejaculated thick gouts of warm semen, filling her mouth, spilling out over her lips, and dribbling down her chin. She licked her lips and lapped the semen still spouting from Joe's cock as he twitched and spasmed with what felt like an endless orgasm. In his mind, the monster roared too.

When Joe looked down at Cindy, who was smiling up at him with lips glazed with his seed, he saw her through the monster's eyes, her features distorted by its voracious hunger. What he saw was meat, bones, blood, and food. He saw sex and sustenance combined into one glorious, voluptuous, scrumptious delicacy.

Drool hung from Joe's mouth in long ropes as he stared down at Officer Cindy Addison and she looked up at him with an expression near reverence. His face betrayed the war within him, and he watched Cindy's face change from ecstasy to terror, seeing the murderous appetite contort his features.

She stood and wiped his semen from her lips with her fingertips and then sucked each digit clean.

"Okay, I think it's time for you to get back to your cell before you lose control again. A little at a time. I think that's best. The more you learn to control your urges, the more of me you can have," Cindy said.

Joe seized her by the throat and kissed her, tasting his own sex on her lips. His hands trembled. Joe could feel her pulse beneath his fingers and he wanted to crush it. He felt her swallow deep and he squeezed a bit harder. He could have easily snapped her neck like a twig.

He let her go and backed away. "It's okay. I can wait."

21

It was Cindy's day off. Joe spent the morning doing push-ups and crunches until his arms and abs burned with lactic acid and began to cramp. He couldn't get Cindy out of his mind.

Professor Locke sent the guards to fetch Joe for more tests. The professor wanted to try a new medication on him. Joe shuffled along the tier in chains escorted by Officer Belton and Officer Ramirez, a short, skinny Mexican guy who'd been there longer than Belton. They walked without speaking except for the usual commands:

"Stand here."

"Turn here."

"Keep going straight."

"Stop at the end of the hall."

There was a surliness to Belton's demeanor today that was even worse than his usual air of unpleasantness. He seemed almost hostile, and Joe was thankful for the presence of Officer Ramirez. If Belton had been alone with him, Joe was certain the man would have taken the opportunity to take his aggression out on Joe while he was chained and helpless. The only thing preventing him from doing so now was Officer Ramirez and his own fear of the massive cannibal killer. Belton had seen what Joe did to the big Mexican, Armondo, and he'd no doubt heard about his castration of the big transvestite they'd thrown in the cell with him. Joe was sure every guard in the prison had watched the tapes and none of them were exactly eager to experience the same.

"Wait here."

Joe stood silently as they unlocked the door to the prison medical facility where the professor had set up his lab. They walked past beds filled with sick and injured prisoners, some who'd been shanked, beaten, raped, or all of the above, and some who were dying of AIDS, cancer, and other illnesses. The place reeked of pain and despair, death and hopelessness. Joe could feel his own prey drive respond to the weakness surrounding him. His primal instinct to cull the herd awakened the monster within, sensing so many easy kills. Joe began to salivate as he walked past, staring at row after row of meat. Those he passed stare back at him. Some held expressions of fear, obviously recognizing who he was. Others appeared to recognize what he was and crossed themselves or mumbled prayers as he shambled past their beds. A few challenged him with words of defiance.

"Fuck you lookin' at, muthafucka?"

Joe grinned and licked his lips in response. He saw the goose bumps rise on their skin and smelled the fear wafting from them despite their continued show of bravado.

"I'll whoop your fuckin' ass, white boy," one of the inmates challenged. He was a huge, bald, heavily-muscled black guy with bandages on his arms and waist. He'd obviously been in a fight. Joe stared at him long and hard, remembering his face. He had a feeling he'd be seeing him again.

They took him to a separate room from the rest of the inmates and strapped him to a gurney, leaving the shackles on as well. The professor came in not long afterward.

"Good afternoon, Joe. How was your morning?"

"It was fine, Professor. How is the cure coming, sir? Will I be ready to leave soon? I can't stand it here."

Professor Locke gave him that look you give a child when he asks why he can't eat ice cream for dinner every night. "I'm working on that cure and I have a few promising new ideas, but I want you to understand, Joe, that even if I cure you, there's no guarantee the courts will release you. They still consider you to be a danger to society."

"But if I'm not dangerous any more they'd have to release me. If you can prove to them that it was the disease that made me this way, that it wasn't my fault, they would have to let me go if I was cured, right?"

Professor Locke bowed his head and then looked up into Joe's eyes, and shook his head, and shrugged. "I don't know, Joe. Let's just work on getting you cured first and then we'll see."

Joe nodded, clearly dejected.

"I promise I'll do everything in my power, once you're cured, to get you out of here. I'm going to stick an IV in your arm now, Joseph. It contains a sedative called ketamine. You may have heard it referred to on the streets as 'Special K'."

Joe nodded. He wasn't exactly from the streets. But he'd heard about Special K from students on campus. "That's an animal tranquilizer, isn't it?" Joe asked, sneering in disgust. "I'm not an animal, Professor."

"Yes, I know Joseph, but ketamine has shown remarkable promise in the treatment of addictions and obsessive-compulsive disorders. We've been attacking the problem as an issue with your serotonin production because of the low serotonin levels seen in patients with chronic addictions, but recent studies suggest that it could be an issue with your glutamate receptors. People with addictive personalities, like those with OCD, experience intrusive, anxiety-provoking thoughts and obsessions. They feel compelled to perform repetitive behaviors or to indulge and over-indulge in behaviors that are potentially destructive, such as gambling, smoking, drug abuse, and over-eating. The only medications that have proven effective so far are serotonin reuptake inhibitors like Prozac, but even with SRI treatment, most patients still experience significant symptoms and cravings."

"Is that why the Prozac hasn't been working for me?"

Professor Locke smiled and nodded. "I think so, Joseph."

"But I don't have OCD. I'm a murderer, Professor. I kill

147

and eat people. What does this have to do with me?"

The professor gave Joe that same indulgent smile he gave him whenever he asked a question. "I know you don't have OCD, Joseph. Not exactly. But your addiction is very similar. That's why you repeat these homicidal behaviors. That's why all serial killers do. They are compelled to do so. It is an irresistible urge, an addiction, and the same anxiety-driven depressions ensue when those compulsions are ignored. Am I right? The same euphoric high results from indulging these compulsions and the same guilt and self-loathing sets in once the high dissipates. You know it's wrong, but you can't stop yourself. Isn't that right, Joseph?"

Joe nodded, remembering how he felt after killing the librarian and seeing Alicia's horrified expression. Remembering how he felt seeing Alicia in the hospital after cannibalizing her breasts, how he felt seeing her sister's face the other day. The professor was absolutely correct. Whenever he allowed the monster to take control and sate its hunger for flesh, he felt terrible afterward, but if he were being totally honest, he'd have to admit that he was feeling less guilty every day.

"Professors at Yale University have been conducting experiments that suggest a different neurotransmitter, glutamate, may be responsible for many of the symptoms of addiction. In the Yale study, medications that modulate the neurotransmitter glutamate through the N-methyl-D-aspartate receptor, a major type of glutamate receptor in the brain, were shown to ameliorate these symptoms. And ketamine is a potent antagonist of the N-methyl-D-aspartate receptor. Small intravenous infusions of ketamine were used, which produced a mild euphoria that lasted less than two hours but then, three hours after infusion, the depression many OCD sufferers say they experience when not indulging their compulsions was gone. This anti-depressant effect lasted for up to three to or four days. During that time, the subjects were free of compulsions. Do you hear that, Joseph? If it worked for them, maybe it will work for you too. It's at least worth a try."

Joe looked down at himself. He was still handcuffed to the gurney and there were leather restraints across his chest, cinching him to the mattress. His legs were still in shackles. Officer Belton and Officer Ramirez stood behind the professor, leaning against the wall, ready to summon the SORT team to beat Joe to a pulp if he made the slightest gesture of hostility. It didn't look like he had much choice in the matter.

"I won't force you, Joseph. If you don't want me to try, I can call off the experiment and have these gentlemen take you back to your cell. You can spend the rest of your life here in peace. I won't bother you again. Ever."

He looked back down at his restraints and then at the two guards. Officer Belton was still glowering at him.

"If I do it, and it works, then I'll never experience that high again, will I? I'll never feel the same ecstasy I felt before."

Professor Locke shook his head. "No, Joseph. I won't mislead you. You will never feel anything like what you feel when you consume human flesh. That 'high' as you put it, will be gone for good. But you won't crave it the way you do now either. Addicts have difficulty producing the endorphin dopamine without indulging their addictions. The experiences that produce endorphins in normal people, such as dancing, riding a bike, eating ice cream, getting a hug, will no longer produce dopamine in those with addictions and that's why you have these depressions when you don't act out. Nothing else does it for you. My hope is that your brain will form new nuero-pathways so you will be able to produce endorphins through normal healthy experiences. You'll be able to appreciate the little things normal people enjoy, experiences you are oblivious to now."

Joe felt his heart sink. As much as he hated the ravenous beast inside of him, Joe could not deny how much he enjoyed the orgasmic ebullience he felt when the monster claimed another victim, when his tongue was wet with blood and his belly filled with meat, the soul of his prey circulating through his veins.

"Yes, but it won't be the same transcendental ecstasy will it?"

"No, Joseph. It won't. The choice is yours. You can try it and maybe find some release from this thing inside you that you used to call your curse, or you can keep this curse forever."

Joe nodded. He remembered the look on the faces of Alicia's mother and her little sister, Lana. They hated him for what he did, Lana especially. She looked so much like Alicia it made his heart hurt and she was appalled by him. To her, he was a reprehensible abomination. The psychotic deviant who'd ended her loved one's existence.

"You're a sick, perverted bastard and you deserve to be locked up forever! No one could ever love you, Joseph Miles. You're a fucking MONSTER! No one could ever love you!"

The memory of Lana's words stung. Joe had never wanted to be the man Lana accused him of being, but he was. He was a monster, a sick perverted monster and no one would ever love him unless he was cured of this curse. Every day the guards brought him stacks of mail from people wanting to save his soul or to see him burn in hell for what he was, what he'd done. Then there were the letters from women like Selene and men like his cousin, Dirk; people who got off on the thrill of knowing a famous serial killer. His choice was either life with the perverts and sycophants or life with regular people, real people, like Lana.

"I made my choice when I first came to you and asked for your help. If you say it will work, Professor, I trust you. Do what you have to do."

Professor Locke smiled warmly. "That's good, Joseph. Very good."

He called for one of the prison nurses, a short, skinny black man with big glasses and a head full of short dreadlocks. The male nurse's hands shook as he swabbed the crook of Joe's arm with alcohol, patted the prominent vein pulsing there, tied his enormous bicep with a short length of medical tubing, and eased the IV into place. While the nervous nurse stabbed an IV needle into Joe's arm, Professor Locke busied himself preparing the ketamine drip.

A heart-rate monitor and EEG wires were placed on Joe's head and chest. Professor Locke withdrew to a swivel chair across the room where he monitored Joe's vitals and waited for the ketamine to take effect. A sense of calm descended over the massive human predator.

"I feel kind of woozy."

"That's normal," Professor Locke replied. "It will pass."

The monster was not merely silent. It seemed to have slipped into a coma. Even when Joe ran the previous evening's activities through his mind, the monster remained in hibernation. After a couple of hours, Joe was escorted across the hall to the small room where the PET scanner was kept.

"How do you feel now, Joseph?"

"Peaceful."

"Do you still feel lightheaded?"

Joe shook his head. "I'm okay."

"Good. Good. I'm going to put you in the scanner for a few tests. I'll be showing you pictures again. You just breathe and relax, okay? This won't take long."

The professor asked again that Joe's shackles be removed and again Officer Belton called the SORT team to be present first. Six men in riot gear filed into the room and took positions around the PET scanner before Belton unlocked the cuffs on Joe's wrists and ankles. As he unlocked the handcuffs he leaned in and whispered to Joseph.

"Please try something. I saw what you did to Addison's neck. You should be put down like a rabid dog and I'd love to be the one to do it."

Joe smiled back at Belton. There was no confusion between them. Despite the power Belton's position gave him and the relative powerlessness of Joe's circumstances, there was no doubt who the alpha wolf was. If all things were equal, Joe would tear Belton apart with ease and they both knew it.

"Okay, just relax and look at the slides."

Professor Locke put what looked like virtual reality goggles on Joe's face, headphones in his ears, and slid him into the machine. He started up the scanner and it began to whir and click. Music filled the headphones, Beethoven, orgasmic music. It drowned out the sound of the scanner. Then the pictures began.

This time, there was little preamble. Joe was shown a few pictures of apples and kittens and trees, presumably to establish a baseline, and then came pictures of plus-sized models and porn stars with enormous breasts, hips, thighs, and asses. Joe stared rapturously. He was aroused, but the monster was silent. He wanted to fuck them, to ejaculate all over their large breasts and buttocks, not eat them. Then came the photos of Alicia, and Joe felt a sudden and overwhelming sorrow. He finally saw the beautiful woman's death as Lana saw it, as a tragedy and nothing more. They showed him the same photos he'd been shown before of Alicia in an evening gown, in a low-cut blouse, and finally of her as she'd looked in the hospital before and after surgery, with her breasts eaten away.

"Turn it off. Turn it off! I don't want to see anymore! TURN IT OFF!"

The final image flashed before him. It was of a pile of splintered bones that had been picked clean of flesh, gnawed, the marrow sucked out. It was all that remained of Alicia.

Joe ripped off the goggles and pulled out his headphones, but he couldn't extract himself from the scanner. He was too big and the PET scan was too small. He was trapped. He began to hyperventilate. "Get me out of here!"

"I'm coming, Joseph. You have to calm down. You're making these gentlemen nervous."

The whirring and clicking stopped and the platform on which he lay began to slide out of the machine. Once free of the scanner, Joe sat up and was slammed back down just as quickly as the SORT team rushed in and pinned him to the gurney. He was cuffed at the wrists and ankles and quickly dragged to his feet.

"I need to go back to my cell. Take me back to my cell!"

"Joseph, wait! Calm down. I need to show you something. Please."

Joe was being held by three guards. One had his left arm wrenched behind his back and the other had his right and there was another guard behind him with a baton lodged under his chin, pulling back on it so that Joe had to lean backwards at a painful, spine-wrenching angle to avoid being choked to death. He took several deep breaths, closed his eyes, and when he opened them he was calm again. He was surprised how easy it was to regain his composure.

"Gentlemen, please. You can let him go now. He isn't going to hurt anyone."

"This is bullshit! You said he was medicated!" Officer Belton yelled, jabbing a finger at the professor. His eyes were brilliant with rage. He appeared on the edge of physical violence. He was scared. Joe could see it as conspicuously as if he'd been wearing a sign. He could smell it in the man's perspiration, a gamey odor full of adrenalin like that of a frightened doe. The man was terrified, even with more than half a dozen specially trained officers in the room, and that pissed him off.

Professor Locke turned to Officer Belton and looked down his nose at the angry corrections officer. It was clear that Belton wanted to strike him and would have if he didn't know he'd lose his job because of it.

"He is medicated, Officer Belton. He isn't resisting, is he? Perhaps you'd be interested in seeing these results as well?"

"What results? What the hell are you talking about?"

"Come. Take a look."

Professor Locke gestured toward the small booth where the monitors for the PET scanner were kept. Belton followed him along with Joe and two of the SORT officers. The professor pointed to a red, blue, and yellow image of what was clearly a brain on the monitor screen.

"This is your brain while I was showing you those images just now. It is the brain of an addict. Your brain shows the same changes one would expect to see in the brain of a heavy cocaine or methamphetamine user. Here's what your brain looked like while I was showing you those photos. That yellow spot right there in the amygdala indicates increased brain activity. The amygdala is the part of the brain that's critical for memory and emotions. It's often called the rage center of the brain because that's where our flight or fight emotions are stored. It's also where our sexual desires originate from. For an addict, when something stimulates a craving, the amygdala becomes active. A cocaine addict, for instance, will show increased activity in the amygdala at the mere mention of the word or upon hearing sounds or seeing images that remind the addict of cocaine. For you, Joseph, this increased brain activity happens when you see women, particularly voluptuous women."

"So, I guess the drug didn't work. There're flashes of yellow in the amygdala when you were showing me the pictures."

"Yeah, you ain't fixed shit, Doc," Officer Belton added.

The professor smiled giddily. "But wait. I have something else to show you."

The professor went to a keyboard and began furiously typing in commands. Another image of a brain leapt onto a nearby screen.

"I want you to look at this image. This was your brain a few months ago viewing those same images."

The image on the screen now showed an explosion of yellow in the area of the brain the professor identified as the amygdala. It looked like Joe's brain was on fire. Comparing the two images, that small spot of yellow on the first screen was like the flare of a match compared to an inferno.

"The drug works, Joseph. It works."

22

"Cannibal Killer Suspect Convicted!"

"Six Victims Identified in Cannibal Case"

The headlines were sensational, but the details of the murders were even more lurid. She read about the librarian whose cannibalized remains were found at Joseph's old apartment, cremated in an arson fire; the body they'd found roasted on a spit, most of the flesh torn from its charred bones; the child-killer who'd been butchered and nearly filleted at the state hospital; the orderly with his throat torn out; Joseph's father who was found beheaded and burned with Bible pages stuffed in his mouth; and finally Alicia, eaten down to her bones. Cindy didn't know what she was doing. She had allowed herself to fall for another inmate, perhaps the most dangerous prisoner in the entire prison system.

Cindy knew that men never changed. All the promises, all the therapy, even incarceration didn't change a thing. A bad man was always going to be bad. Still, there was something about Joseph Miles that contradicted everything she read. She remembered watching him cry when one of his victim's family members came to visit. It hadn't been an act. He'd been genuinely remorseful. And the things he'd said to her, the way they'd made love the last time. He'd promised her that he wouldn't hurt her and he hadn't. He could have killed her if he wanted to. She'd been a fool to sneak into his cell like that. It had been just as foolish of her to sneak him out of his cell the night before. She could have easily been another victim, but he hadn't killed her. He'd bit her neck and it had hurt, but he'd stopped when she told him to stop and he hadn't done anything close to what he'd done to the people in these stories. He'd ripped out that orderly's throat with his teeth, but he'd let Cindy go. Maybe his treatments were working. Maybe he was changing.

23

Joe had a visitor. He was allowed to shower and shave before being led down to the visitor's room to receive his guest. The entire time, Joe hoped that it was Lana who had come to visit him again. He was surprised to find a tall, gray-haired man in a dark blue suit and light- blue pinstriped shirt waiting for him in the visitor's booth behind the thick Plexiglas wall. The man had a lean athletic build, clearly the result of hours in the gym. His face was lean and hard and had few wrinkles. His eyes were battleship gray, hidden behind thin spectacles with lightweight titanium frames. He smiled and picked up the phone when Joe entered. Joe sat down and picked up the phone as well.

"Hello, Mr. Miles. My name is Jon De Salvo. I was hired by a friend of yours to represent you. I believe you are acquainted with Ms. Selene Cassaro?"

"Is she here?"

Joe stood and looked behind the lawyer into the hall. Mr. De Salvo gestured with a slight wave for Joe to sit back in his seat.

"Ms. Cassaro is not here today. She is still barred from visiting you."

Joe slumped in his chair.

"I do have good news, however. I am very close to getting you moved back into general population."

"Really? How?"

"It's been five years since you committed the crimes you were sentenced for. You spent most of that time in the state mental hospital before being transferred here several months ago. They were able to transfer you to prison because they

158

declared that you were now mentally competent and able to understand the difference between right and wrong and why you were being incarcerated. They declared you legally sane, in other words. Now, you are being kept in what amounts to solitary confinement because you are considered violently insane and a threat to your fellow inmates. They can't have it both ways. Either you're insane and should be returned to the state mental hospital or you're sane and should be released back into general population. Since you have been incarcerated here, there have been no documented instances of violence toward either the guards or your fellow inmates."

Joe was shocked. "What about the convicts they made me fight? What about the one I castrated?"

Mr. De Salvo smiled.

"As I said, Mr. Miles, there have been no *documented* instances of violence toward your fellow inmates. If the guards were engaged in anything as illegal as what you described, setting up inmates to fight one another, I don't think they would be careless enough to keep reports on these events. Would you? On paper, you have been a model prisoner. Any testimony to the contrary would have to include blowing the whistle on the practice of cockfighting. I doubt the corrections department would risk such a scandal to keep one inmate in supermax. I have several noted psychiatrists prepared to testify that your crimes were the result of your mental illness and that you are now sane and therefore not a threat to yourself or others."

"Will they let me go then? If I'm not a threat anymore, then why am I still locked up?"

Mr. De Salvo shook his head. His expression was one of genuine remorse, but Joe knew better. The man was a pro and his facial expressions were as calculated as his choice of suits, his haircut, and his words.

"No, Mr. Miles. They will not let you go. You have been sentenced to life in prison. That hasn't changed. You still killed those people, sane or not. This is the best I can do for you."

Joe balled his hands into fists, squeezing until his fingernails broke the skin of his palms and blood seeped out from between his fingers. He was leaving one cage for another, but at least he wouldn't be locked in his cell twenty-three hours a day.

"I have one more thing to tell you, Mr. Miles. Ms. Cassaro wanted me to deliver a message. She said it didn't work. She tried to experience what you experience, the way you experience it, and it didn't work. She didn't feel anything. She wants to know what she did wrong."

Joe frowned. "What I experience? The way I experience it? I don't know what she's talking about."

Mr. De Salvo leaned forward, tilted his thin, titanium-frame glasses down to the tip of his nose, and peered at Joseph over them, locking eyes with him. There were few men who could so easily stare unflinchingly into the eyes of a killer. Mr. De Salvo had probably locked eyes with many such men throughout his years as a criminal defense attorney. Joseph wondered exactly who Selene's parents were that they had required the services of such a man and could so easily afford them.

"I think you know what she means, Mr. Miles. There's only one behavior of yours she would emulate that would require such clandestine discussion."

The lawyer continued staring at him until his meaning sank in, then he eased his glasses back up onto his nose with his index finger, and leaned back in his chair.

Joe was stunned. *What has this crazy bitch done?* "You mean she— she killed someone? She ate someone?"

"These phones may not be completely private, Mr. Miles, and I'm only her lawyer. I am just the messenger in this case, delivering a message she is unable to deliver herself. I would prefer not to try to interpret the message. I am simply delivering it as directed."

Joe thought about Selene killing someone and eating them. He wondered who her victim was. Some portly business man she'd picked up at a bar? A prostitute she picked up off the street? *Why would she do that? What was she looking for? What did she mean "it didn't work"?*

"Is she— is she in trouble?"

"She's fine. She's in no legal trouble, if that's what you mean. Now, I was hoping you might have a reply to her query."

Joe thought about it a moment more. She said it didn't work. She hadn't felt anything. She was talking about the ecstasy of the flesh. She was talking about orgasm.

"She didn't feel anything because she's not infected. She doesn't have the curse."

The lawyer smiled but his eyes showed obvious confusion and just the slightest hint of annoyance and perhaps disgust. It was there for only an instant before the calm, reassuring expression returned to his face.

"I'm afraid I don't follow you, Mr. Miles."

"I had this theory— I *have* this theory— that what I am is the result of a communicable disease, a genetic retro virus like AIDS, transmitted through body fluids like blood and saliva. It's like the vampires and werewolves in the movies. The only way to get it is to be bitten by me or someone like me and she hasn't been bitten. She's not infected."

Mr. De Salvo nodded.

"Thank you, Mr. Miles. You've been extremely helpful. Oh, and while I'm working to get you released from supermax, I'll also be working to get Ms. Cassaro's visitation ban lifted. Perhaps you two will see each other soon. Good day, Mr. Miles." Mr. De Salvo hung up the phone, stood, and left the room.

Joe sat there a moment trying to collect his thoughts. Selene had murdered someone. It didn't make sense. She wanted the curse? She wanted to be like him? *Why would anyone want to be a monster?*

Officer Ramirez came to collect him. Belton's shift must have ended. When he stepped outside the visitor's room, Cindy Addison was waiting to help Ramirez escort him to his cell.

"Good to see you, Officer Addison."

"Good to see you too, Joseph."

24

"But isn't ketamine addictive?"

Joe nodded. He'd have to discuss that with the professor. Trading one addiction for another was not the type of recovery he was looking for.

"It's better than killing people, though. Besides, people get addicted to Prozac. I would have to take it for the rest of my life anyway, so addiction would be a moot point."

Cindy smiled, but she didn't look convinced. Half the people in supermax were there as a result of drug addictions.

"That's great, Joe."

Officer Ramirez was silent as he helped Officer Addison escort the big serial killer back to his cell. Joe's familiarity with Officer Addison was obviously bothering him.

Joe tried to bring the man out of his shell. He extended an olive branch. "What did you think, Officer Ramirez? The professor says he can cure me."

Officer Ramirez looked up at Joe and scowled. He snorted derisively and shook his head. "I grew up in LA, in the gangs. There were lots of killers in my old neighborhood. Some killed because they had to for protection. Some killed for money. But some were like you. They killed because they enjoyed it. Those types of murderers don't change. They get killed or they wind up in here. There ain't no kind of miracle drug to cure you of what you are. You're right where you belong."

Ramirez let out a slight chuckle and nudged Joe forward, ending the conversation. Joe could tell Officer Ramirez was still haunted by many of the things he'd witnessed and perhaps even participated in on the streets of Los Angeles.

There was no one in this place who had not been scarred by violence in some way. Joe thought it best to let the matter drop. He wasn't certain himself if he really could change.

Finally, they arrived at Joe's cell and Cindy called to the control room for the guard to open the door. Joe deliberately brushed against Cindy as he stepped into his cell, rubbing his bicep across her breasts. Her nipples became instantly erect.

Joe smiled coyly as he turned to face Cindy. "Thank you, Officer Addison. And you, Officer Ramirez."

Ramirez scowled. "Yeah, don't mention it."

Cindy was blushing. She stammered a nervous reply. "I-I-I'm really h-happy you found something to help you."

"Thank you. For the first time, I feel completely in control of myself, like I can finally control all the passion inside."

Cindy looked into the big cannibal's eyes and her blush deepened. Joe could see her struggling to keep the smile from her face. "I'll be back later with your lunch."

Joe stood quietly as his cell door closed. "Can you bring me something from the library?"

"What do you want? I'll see if they have it."

"I want a book about the human brain … and one about vampires."

Cindy nodded. "I'll see what I can do."

25

"What did he say?" Selene asked.

They sat in what was once her father's study. Large cherry-wood bookshelves lined the walls from floor to ceiling. Two red leather recliners sat side by side in the center of the room, separated by a small table upon which sat a single reading lamp. The attorney who'd represented the Cassaro family for the past two decades occupied one recliner and Selene fidgeted nervously in the other.

Jon De Salvo chuckled and shook his head. "What he said was—it was just crazy."

The flash of rage that sparked in Selene's eyes was sudden and terrifying. "I didn't ask you to judge, I asked you what he said!"

Mr. De Salvo smirked and then nodded in deference to his hot-tempered client. "Sorry if I offended you, Ms. Cassaro. I only meant that his theory was highly unorthodox and, I dare say, implausible."

"Well, what the hell did he say?"

"He said it didn't work because you haven't been infected. He said he has a communicable disease, some sort of genetic virus that turned him into a killer. According to him, this virus is what makes him the way he is. It's what makes the experience of killing so sexually invigorating."

Selene leaned forward, eyes locked on the lawyer, studying his mouth, waiting eagerly for each word to emerge.

"His vampire theory, right? It didn't work because I haven't been turned, right?"

"Yes. He said you had to be bitten to get the curse."

"And I'm pretty sure he didn't use the words 'sexually

165

invigorating'."

Mr. De Salvo smirked again."I was paraphrasing."

Selene sat back in her recliner. Her fingers drummed on the armrest.

"You have to get me in to see him—and not with two inches of glass between us. You have to get him out of supermax and into general population so we can meet face to face and touch. You have to arrange conjugal visits."

Mr. De Salvo raised an eyebrow.

"Conjugal visits?"

"Yes, conjugal visits."

"I'm pretty sure you have to be married for that. Just getting him out of supermax is going to be hard enough."

"I know you've arranged conjugal visits for my father's friends, bringing their girlfriends in for private visits, even arranging for them to have prostitutes. Some of them were in supermax too, as I recall. Uncle Tony was in supermax when you brought his mistress to see him. You'll do this for me, Jon. Do it!"

The high-paid criminal attorney with the meticulously quaffed silver mane, smiled and bowed.

"I can do this for you, of course, but it won't be cheap."

"It never is," Selene replied, reaching for her checkbook.

26

Weeks passed with the monotony and inevitability of the alarm clock going off each morning. Only, Joe Miles was not waking for a day of work as an office drone or blue-collar worker. Each morning came and went staring at the same cinderblock walls and metal door. His breakfast of overcooked eggs, cereal, milk, and bacon was shoved through a slot in the door, and he returned the empty tray through the same slot.

Officer Cindy Addison's late-night visits had become more frequent. They'd made love almost every night in every conceivable way, and, with his twice-weekly ketamine injections, he'd been free of the urge to tear her apart. The monster languished within him, defeated but still alive. Then, Cindy had stopped coming. She had disappeared.

At first, Joe assumed her shift had simply changed, but he didn't see her on day shift either. She had vanished. Joe asked Officer Belton and Officer Ramirez what had happened to the new guard, trying to sound as casual as possible, but it was obvious they were aware of his romantic relationship with her and were delighting in withholding the details of her removal.

"She's gone," Officer Belton finally said after days of repeated questioning.

"Gone where? Did she get fired?"

"Just gone," Belton answered and continued on his rounds. That was all he ever got out of him. Then, one day, it was Joe's turn to leave. The announcement came over the cellblock PA system.

"Inmate number 177252! Miles! Gather your belongings. You're being transferred!"

Transferred? Transferred where? Had Selene finally come through? Joe wondered. A serial killer being transferred to general population was uncommon these days, though certainly not unheard of. Joe wondered, not for the first time, just how much money and influence the Cassaro family had. That lawyer she'd hired for him was certainly not your average ambulance chaser.

Joe gathered his toothbrush, toothpaste, soap, shoeboxes of letters, his paintings and books, and whatever else he could carry and stood by the door, waiting for it to open. Officer Belton came to get him along with a big, goofy, redneck nearly Joe's size, but soft and flabby. He had dark freckles on his cheeks and reddish blond hair buzzed into a military high-top. Three of his teeth were missing in the front of his mouth and Joe wondered if it was from fights or poor hygiene. The guard was noticeably uncomfortable standing so close to Joe without a gun in his hand.

"This is your lucky day. You're going to general population with all the rest of the killers, rapists, and gangbangers. There's no one to protect your ass there. Good luck!" Belton said with a chuckle.

Joe turned toward him, smiling with those teeth shaved to points so he looked like a six-foot-six, blue-eyed piranha.

"I don't think I'll be the one who needs protection. But thank you for caring."

The big redneck's mouth fell open and he groped for his baton. Belton merely shoved Joe forward. He was used to the big cannibal's intimidation tactics by now and went out of his way to deny that they still worked.

If supermax had been noisy, the cacophony that rose from the cells in general population was like stepping inside Yankee Stadium, or, more accurately, like stepping inside The Mandalay Bay Event Center during an Ultimate Fighting Championship match. Taunts, threats, catcalls, random curses, hoots, whistles—a tidal wave of sound buffeted Joe's eardrums. He looked up at the rows and rows of cells filled with convicts and felt a sudden jolt of adrenaline. His body was preparing to fight, to defend itself or, perhaps, to hunt.

The cell block was divided into tiers with a combined forty-eight single cells. It resembled a pet store piled high with cages of unloved animals. There were sixteen cells on each tier with inmates packed in two or three to a cell. A far cry from the oppressive solitude of supermax. The cells opened into a dayroom area with a television at one end and stainless steel tables in the middle. The showers were at the other end of the dayroom and, unlike supermax, the inmates were encouraged to shower every morning.

Each cell had a bed, a sink, a toilet, and a wall-mounted metal shelf or desk. Joe knew Belton was watching his face, hoping to see some sign of fear. Joe closed his eyes, inhaled deeply, smelling sweat and sex and blood and meat. He smiled that same carnivorous grin.

"I'm home."

"Yeah, well get your ass upstairs. Your cell is on the second tier. Cell number thirty-four," Belton said. "This is where we house all the 5150s, the nut jobs. You should fit right in here."

"If you're lucky, maybe these animals will throw you a welcome home party," the big redneck officer added.

Still smiling, Joe locked eyes with the big redneck.

"I look forward to it."

Joe stepped into his cell, where for the first time since he'd been locked up five years ago, he had a roommate. The man was a large Mexican, six-foot-two and nearly three hundred pounds, covered in gang tattoos.

"Joe, meet your new roommate, Fausto Cardona. Fausto, meet Joseph Miles. You two play nice now, ya here?" the big redneck said.

Belton waved and scowled simultaneously as he walked down the tier and back to supermax.

Joe began unpacking his things.

"You can put your stuff over there, homes. I hang my pictures on that wall. You can hang yours on this one. I take the bottom bunk 'cause I'm too big for the top one. I know you's supposed to be some crazy killer, but you don't fuck with me and I won't fuck with you. Cool?"

Fausto held out his hand. Joe smiled and saw the big Mexican flinch. Joe took his hand and shook it.

"Deal."

27

"I guess it's only fair I tell you what I'm in here for since I already know what you're here for, right? You got a right to know what kind of *vato* you roomin' with, right? Most people in the pen don't like to talk about why they here and it's not cool to ask. You just mind your own business. That's the best way. You know, right? I killed a couple vatos that were trying to steal my coke. I had like half a kilo I was selling and when I caught them trying to take it, I blasted those fools with my shotgun and tried to feed them to my pit bulls to get rid of the evidence, you know? But my dogs, they didn't eat enough, you know, right? The neighbors saw arms and legs and heads and shit all over my yard and called the cops. Stupid, huh, right? I can't believe I did that shit. I tried to plead insanity and lost, but they put me in here with the loonies anyway."

Joe nodded, remembering his two Rottweilers, Hades and Beelzebub, from when he was a kid and how he'd fed his best friend Mikey to them after they accidentally attacked and killed him. Joe remembered how they'd torn Mikey apart and how aroused he'd become watching the carnage. He'd masturbated for the first time watching Hades and Beelzebub devour his best friend. He could feel himself getting an erection, just thinking about it and instinctively reached down and stroked himself.

"Jesus, homey! What the fuck is you doin'! You can't be doin' that shit in here while I'm awake and shit!"

Joe snapped out of his reminiscence.

"S-sorry. I didn't mean to…"

"That shit turn you on? Talking about dudes bein' torn

apart and shit? That's what you did to the muthafuckas you killed, right? Tore 'em apart and ate 'em, huh? That shit is crazy, huh, right? Just don't try none of that shit with me. I swear I'll cut you up."

"We shook on it, remember? We're cool," Joe smiled.

"You know, until you smile, you look just like that dude who used to play Superman. Not Christopher Reeve but the dude from like the fifties. Seriously, though, right? You look like mutherfuckin' Clark Kent and shit! That's a trip, homey. Why'd you file your teeth like that though, homey? So you can rip fool's throats out and shit, right? You can't be doin' that shit in here though. The screws would know it was you. Ain't nobody else got teeth like that. You need to get yourself a shank. Stab a fool if he fucks with you, huh? Nobody's gonna fuck with you anyway cause you're a crazy mutherfucker and you're big as shit. Everybody says I'm crazy too, right? So as long as you don't start no shit, we're cool, right?"

"Right."

Joe climbed up onto the top bunk and opened a book. *The Anatomy of The Human Brain.* As he studied about the amygdala and the hippocampus and how they related to impulse control, memory, and emotions, Joe couldn't stop thinking about eating a brain. There was so much protein and vitamins in the human brain, not to mention that it was the seat of consciousness, the home of the human soul. Eating one was like drinking from the very fountain of creation. The only brain he'd ever eaten was Alicia's and it had been delicious, transcendental. Joe could not wait to do it again. He wondered if the ketamine was still working. Maybe it was time for another dose. He didn't want to break his word to his new roommate the way he had with Alicia.

He had a few unopened letters he hadn't had time to read before the transfer. Joe sat in his bunk and opened the first one. It was from his cousin, Dirk.

Hey, Cuz!

    I'm comin' to see you! I finally saved up enough to buy a new car, so I'm driving up this weekend to visit. I can't wait! I spoke to your friend Selene again. Dude, she's kind of crazy. She's sort of hot though. A little thick for my tastes, but I know that's how you like 'em. I found a few pictures of her online modeling lingerie and bikinis. I printed them out for you. Thought you might like to have them. Anyway, she said her lawyer was arranging for you to be moved to general population. You think that's a good move? There's some dangerous people in that prison. I mean, I know you're dangerous too, but they've got gangbangers and shit in there. Be careful, Cuz. I'll see you this weekend. I still need to tell you what she has planned. Dude, it's fuckin' brilliant!

    See you soon!
    Dirk

Joe pulled out the pictures of Selene. There was a picture of her in a black lace body suit, lying on her belly on white satin sheets, staring up at the camera with an expression that clearly said "Come fuck me." Selene had definitely gained a few pounds, though not as much as she'd claimed. She was curvaceous now, though not nearly as voluptuous as Alicia or Lana. Joe could not stop thinking about Lana. Maybe Dirk could help him find out how to get in touch with her. He had to see her again.

    Another photo showed Selene modeling a bikini. Joe's breath caught in his throat and the monster roused from its slumber. In this one, she looked particularly delectable. Selene had her back to the camera, looking over her shoulder at the photographer. The pose displayed the marvelous swell of her buttocks. It was an amazing sight. When she said she had been doing squats and lunges to build more mass in her gluteus maximus, she had underrepresented her success in the endeavor. Her glutes were now two massive globes of muscle perched high on her back like that of a sprinter. A layer of fat engulfed the muscle, adding to its size and softening its appearance. It was heavenly. Joe felt his mouth water at the sight of her.

"My God."

The tilt of her head, the subtle smile touching the corners of her lips, the way her eyes found his through the photo across a distance of weeks and miles, all added to the allure of what was the most sensuous thing Joe had ever seen. Selene's skin was wet, hair dripping with seawater that ran over the succulent mounds of her buttocks in long rivulets that traced their way down her voluptuous thighs.

There was a vast body of water behind her and a beach with black sand. Joe had been to that beach before. It was across the bridge from San Francisco in Marin County. Black Sand Beach, a nude beach. He wondered if perhaps there had been other photos of her without the bikini and the guards had helped themselves to them.

The sunlight dappling through the droplets of water on her skin made her flesh glisten and shine. It was like seeing a glimpse of the fiery essence within her, the one he'd tasted in the tiny morsel of flesh she'd given him. Selene's thighs, like her round buttocks, were thick with muscle and just the right amount of adipose tissue.

The last photo was of Selene lying on a beach towel with her head tilted back so her long neck was exposed to the sun and her breasts stuck out prominently. Here was Joe's only moment of disappointment. Her breasts were indeed larger than the last time he'd seen her, but still dwarfed by the memory of Alicia's impressive bosom. Selene's lone nipple poked hard against the thin, satiny fabric of her black bikini top and Joe hungered to make the two breasts symmetrical by consuming the one that got away.

Joe taped the photographs to the wall above his bunk and stared at them.

"That your woman, homes?"

Joe nodded.

"She's fine, right? I bet you miss that."

Joe nodded. There were no words.

28

"How are you feeling, Joseph?" Professor Locke inquired. He aimed a tiny penlight at Joe's pupils and peered deep into his eyes. "Any side effects?"

"None, so far."

"And how about the urges? Have they returned?"

Joe thought about the last time he'd made love to Cindy Addison. There had been no violence. The monster had not tried to take control. He had kissed every inch of her, sucked her nipples, licked her thighs, the cleft of her buttocks, the silken folds of her labia, tasted her womanhood, and never once felt the urge to do her harm. Their love making had been almost tender, sweet, normal. He had reached orgasm in the missionary position, staring into Cindy's eyes. The moonlight streaming in through the library windows had illuminated her face as she whispered the words, "I love you" and he hugged her in lieu of a reply. The very next day she'd disappeared.

"No, the urges haven't come back. But, I'm afraid."

Professor Locke looked at him with an expression of concern, eyebrows knit, peering over the top of his glasses.

"What are you afraid of, son?"

"I'm afraid I'll get addicted to it, the ketamine."

Professor Locke nodded, pushing his glasses back up on the bridge of his nose.

"There are worse things to be addicted to. But I'll look into some alternatives."

Joe nodded.

"Thanks, Professor."

He laid back on the gurney and a nurse stepped forward

to insert the IV in his arm. Joe felt instantly relaxed. All his worries and fears, lusts and carnal obsessions, were momentarily lost in a narcotic haze.

29

Joe had been nervous about going out to the yard with the other inmates. There were several other convicts just as big as him and a few who were even larger. Everyone seemed to show him respect, giving him a wide berth. It was a relief even though he found it confusing. Joe asked his cellmate about his seeming status.

"You're a serial killer. Serial killers are high on the food chain here. Besides, you bit off Luscious Jones's dick, man! That dude had been fucking people up for years, raping guys, stabbing guys who didn't let that big *maricón* fuck them. A lot of homeys were afraid of him, but not since you whooped his ass. Now, you're the man!" Fausto said.

Joe didn't know how to take it. He was flattered, but he was more interested in how he could use this sudden celebrity to his advantage. Fear, he'd long ago discovered, could be a valuable asset.

In prison, the social order devolved to its most primitive state. The strongest and most vicious ruled and the meek did their best to stay out of the way. Joe sat on the bleachers, staring up at the guard towers and over at the two rows of fences topped with barbed wire. Between the two rows of barbed wire fencing, guards patrolled with dogs. Escape seemed impossible. If he couldn't hop a fence or tunnel out of the prison, that left only two alternatives: fight his way out, which would end with him either being bludgeoned to death by the SORT team or shot down by the guards in the lookout towers once he made it outside, or he could somehow stowaway in a package that was leaving the prison. Joe began cataloging the various deliveries that came to and left from the prison.

The most frequent deliveries were food. Trucks filled with meat, vegetables, and canned goods rumbled through the door of the gates to be unloaded by convicts at the loading bay. Almost as frequently, trucks came delivering denim and cotton for the flags and blue jeans manufactured inside the prison by inmates and taking the finished products away to be shipped to distributors all over the country, then there were the coffins that were taken out to be buried in the prison cemetery and finally, there was the sewage. Sewage tunnels ran beneath the massive correctional compound, transporting tons of waste to a treatment plant a hundred miles away. Joe had many options. He smiled up at the sun. It was good to see the sky again. He had been in supermax for so long he had almost forgotten what the heavens looked like.

Joe was watching a dark cloud shaped like Buddha drift slowly across the blue firmament when a large shadow abruptly blotted out the sky. The large, athletically built black man with the shaved head and gangland-style tattoos covering his arms, chest, and stomach with rap lyrics, biblical verses, crucifixes, tombstones, firearms, and tribal designs stood above Joe with his fists clenched and a malevolent grin scarring his face. It was the inmate who'd threatened him when he was walking through the prison hospital on his way to see Professor Locke.

"You supposed to be some kind of bad mutherfucker, huh?"

Joe shrugged. He began sizing the man up, looking for weak points, places where he could do the greatest amount of damage in the shortest amount of time without leaving any evidence behind that could send him back to supermax.

He looked at the man's slender legs. One kick to the convict's patella would shatter his kneecap and render him helpless.

"Leave him, Devon. He ain't lookin' for no trouble. He just tryin' to do his time like the rest of us," Fausto said.

179

"Did I ask your fat ass, Fausto? You want some too?"

Fausto stood up. Layers of adipose tissue rippled and jiggled as he rose.

"You want some of me, Devon, you know you can get some. But you know I ain't alone," Fausto answered, raising his forearm and pointing to a tattoo of the Mexican flag with a crucifix in the center bordered by an uzi sub-machine gun on one side and a machete on the other. Beneath it in thick gothic lettering were the words: Latin Mafia Lords.

"I ain't tryin' to beef with the Latin Lords. This is just between me and the white boy that bit Luscious's dick off and almost tore out his throat."

Joe looked up at the tower to see if any of the guards were watching them. They weren't. Most of the guards were busy monitoring an aggressive basketball game that seemed to be on the verge of turning violent. Joe looked over at the door that led back to the cells, counting the steps it would take to make it back inside. He estimated it would take four seconds to break the big black man's leg and make it back to the cellblock.

A fight erupted on the basketball court between a Mexican guy and a small black guy and soon the game became a race riot. Joe took the opportunity. He gestured to Fausto to head for the exit, and the big Mexican, his instincts honed from years in the penitentiary, understood and began to move. Joe stomped his foot hard against the big convict's knee, driving it backwards against the grain and snapping tendons as the ball joint of his tibia tore free from its moorings and bulged against his skin, threatening to tear its way out. The man howled in pain and collapsed in the dirt, holding his injured joint. Joe dismissed the man and turned to make a quick dash for the exit, trying to make it back inside before the guards noticed anything, but his opponent wasn't done fighting yet.

A strong hand gripped his ankle with crushing force. Joe tripped and went down hard. In seconds, the big convict had scrambled on top of Joe and was raining down powerful blows. The first punch split his lip and the next swelled his eye. Two more blows caught him on the forehead and jaw, before the last punch hit his temple and everything went black. When Joe regained consciousness, he felt something jab into his chest and then his stomach. The large, muscular inmate was still on top of him and Joe saw the man raise his hands over his head, holding what looked like a sharpened toothbrush wrapped in duct tape and tipped with something sharp and metal. It was a shank, a makeshift knife. The sharpened metal tip was wet, dripping red down the convict's arm. It was then that Joe realized he'd been stabbed. He'd been badly stabbed.

Blood spurted from some artery in his torso and Joe felt weak, woozy. From what he knew of such injuries, Joe estimated he had minutes to live, less if he let the big convict stab him again. He grabbed the man's wrist with both hands and halted the blade's downward arc. He wrapped his legs around the man's waist and pulled him into his guard like a Jiu-Jitsu fighter. He shifted his grip so he was holding the big convict's wrist just below the back of his hand. He then reached over his attacker's shoulder and grabbed his own wrist. With one hard jerk he separated the man's shoulder and the shank fell onto the floor. Joe felt the sudden powerful urge to feed. It would be easy to rip out the convict's throat now, to taste the big man's raging spirit in his blood and meat. But that would take this from an act of self-defense to a brutal murder and proof that he was unfit for general population.

While contemplating the pros and cons of cannibalism, Joe took another punch, far lighter than the first ones, still powerful enough to turn out the lights. Joe collapsed in the dirt. He could hear the sound of scuffling and what sounded like a whistle before the darkness rushed in. This time, he awoke in the prison infirmary. He recognized it immediately from his many trips down here with Professor Locke to use the PET scanner. It was a large gymnasium-sized room filled with single beds. It seemed as if every bed was occupied. There were separate rooms for surgery and rooms filled with medical equipment. Each room had a lock and one even had chains on the door. Joe assumed that was the room where the meds were kept. The walls were painted a sallow tan that was almost yellow and fluorescent lights hung from the ceiling, making the room uncomfortably bright. The place reeked of bleach and ammonia.

Fausto stood above him, his huge pie-shaped face smiling down at him, breathing a cloud of halitosis.

"I can't believe you're alive, homes. You got stabbed like six times by that big *negrito*. You fucked Devon up bad though, right? Broke his leg and separated his shoulder and shit. You know, right?"

Joe looked around confused.

"What are you doing here? They let you come up here just to visit me?"

The big Mexican laughed. Billowy rolls of adipose tissue rippled and jiggled as he chuckled.

"No, hermano. We ain't that tight! I work here. I'm like a nurse and shit, right? I was a medic in the army, in Iraq and shit. You know, right?"

"How long was I out?"

"Six days. They rushed you into surgery to stitch up your guts. You lucked the fuck out, right? Devon didn't get any major organs or anything, right? He hit an artery though. You almost bled out. You know, right?"

Joe looked down at the bandages crisscrossing his torso.

"How long before these stitches heal?"

"Probably another week or two as long as you don't do anything stupid to open them up again, you know, right?"

"Yeah, I know."

Joe's plans for escape would have to be delayed. He

looked around the infirmary and spotted Officer Cindy Addison as she walked in, smiling. Her eyes looked watery and she quickly wiped them away with her sleeve. Fausto looked from the CO back to Joe and then smiled, winked, and backed away.

"I'll talk to you later, hermano."

"Thanks for everything, Fausto."

"Hey, I told you, it's my job, homes. You know, right?"

Joe nodded and then turned his attention back to Cindy Addison. His mind was already working all the angles.

"I thought you'd been fired. I haven't seen you for days."

Cindy shook her head and wiped her eyes again with her sleeve, and then tugged on her uniform to straighten it.

"Not fired, transferred to another cellblock. I think Belton said something to the warden about us. He tried to get me to fuck him. Said he knew I was fucking you and that he even had it on video. I told him to fuck himself. Next day I was called into the warden's office and transferred."

Joe nodded.

"I'm sorry. I didn't mean to get you in trouble."

Cindy shrugged.

"I ain't the only one around here … well … you know. And it ain't just the female guards."

"I've heard the rumors. It's good to see you, Cindy."

Cindy looked down at Joe's wounds and sucked in a deep breath then almost choked on it as a sob escaped.

"I'm okay," Joe said. "I'll be good as new in a couple weeks."

Cindy nodded and then wiped her eyes again.

"I'm so sorry, Joe. This shouldn't have happened. I'll put the word out to the COs in your cellblock to keep an eye on you, okay?"

Joe motioned for her to lean in closer. Cindy looked around to make sure no one was watching them and Joe did the same. The inmates were watching TV or begging nurses for painkillers. The other nurses and doctors were busying themselves with other patients.

"Do you love me, Cindy?"

Cindy giggled nervously then wiped her eyes again as fresh tears welled up in them. She nodded her head vigorously.

"I know I shouldn't, but I do. I do, Joseph."

She covered her mouth as another sob escaped and the realization of what she'd just confessed hit her.

"I love you too, Cindy. I want to be with you forever. I want to make you happy."

"Well, what are we going to do?"

Joe gestured for her to lean in closer. Cindy checked her surroundings again before obliging.

"You have to get me out of here, Cindy. You have to get me out before they kill me. They're going to kill me, Cindy."

30

The trip to the state penitentiary was a long one. The Mercedes E-Class devoured the road in quick gulps, bringing her ever closer to the man she loved, the only man capable of giving her the ecstasy she desired.

Since her parents' death, Selene had slowly begun to re-accustom herself to the luxurious accouterments of wealth. Her modeling career had been put on the back-burner now that the investigation into her father's "mysterious" death had been concluded and his millions had finally transferred to her. She ran her hands over her voluptuous curves, squeezing her hips and breasts, imagining they were Joe's hands, caressing her, appreciating her as no other man could. She closed her eyes and squeezed her nipple. She could see Joe's mouth close over her breast, his savage teeth biting through the supple flesh to remove the tender nub. It would be a worthwhile sacrifice to have his gift.

Selene remembered her own experiment with cannibalism with a shudder. She'd been a fool. Hadn't he told her his unique proclivities were the result of a curse? Didn't he explain to her in his letters how he had been assaulted by Damon Trent as a child, how his father had murdered more than thirty young boys and girls, and how this disease had been passed along to him through his bloodstream? That's why he murdered both of them, trying to put an end to his curse. Now he thinks the curse originated with his grandfather and he wants to get out of prison so he can hunt the man down and murder him. His idiot cousin, Dirk, had filled in that last tidbit. But Selene didn't want the curse to end; not until she could get herself infected.

All the money in the world couldn't purchase the ecstasy she craved. Only Joseph could give her that, but her money could get her closer to him. Selene's lawyer had spread liberal donations and campaign contributions around in her name to secure her a few conjugal visits with her "Cannibal Cassanova," and she was going to make the most of them. She was determined to experience the pleasures of the flesh, the all-consuming ecstasy burning inside Joseph Miles, even if she had to tear the curse from his bleeding corpse.

31

When Professor Locke came to visit him, Joe was poking at his stitches, trying to determine the extent of his wounds. He had refused a dose of dilaudid. He didn't want anything clouding his mind or dulling his pain. Pain provided necessary information about the health of his body. What he felt now was tolerable, and after three hours without pain killers, the nurses had assured him all the narcotics were out of his system and the pain wouldn't get much worse than this.

"Good morning, Joseph. How are you feeling?"

It was the professor's standard greeting. Usually it meant: "How are the treatments affecting you? Still feeling like killing and eating people?" But today there was a hint of genuine concern in his voice.

"I've had better days, Professor."

The professor took a quick glance at his bandages.

"I heard you were in a pretty vicious altercation."

Joe shrugged.

"I guess so."

"You broke the guy's leg, tore some muscles in his shoulder, and he stabbed you a few times."

Joe nodded.

"But you didn't bite him."

"No, sir. I didn't bite him."

The professor stroked the whiskers on his chin, and then looked over his glasses at Joe.

"That's progress, Joe. I'm sure you could have ripped him apart had you wanted to."

"Oh, I wanted to. I just didn't. I didn't want to get sent back to supermax."

"Still, that's progress. I don't think you'd have been able to exhibit that sort of control even a few weeks ago. Do you think the ketamine is helping?"

"I don't have the same urges. Not as often or as intense as before."

The professor nodded and then scribbled something in a small notebook he carried.

"May I ask you a question, Joseph?"

"Of course. Anything, professor."

The professor continued staring at Joe for a while before speaking. His eyes were like microscopes, studying Joe on some subatomic level where all his pretensions and affectations became transparent.

"I watched you in your cell, before you were transferred out of supermax ..."

Joe's eyes narrowed and his brow furrowed.

"Yes? And?"

"And you were doing some sort of shadowboxing routine..."

Wincing, Joe sat up in bed. Clearly interested now in what the professor was about to ask him.

"Is this what you were training for? This type of thing?"

"In a manner of speaking, you could say that."

The professor nodded, but his face did not look entirely convinced.

"I met a man the other day, a mixed martial artist. I told him about you."

"Me?"

"Yes, you, Joseph. He said you'd probably make an excellent fighter. What do you think about that, Joseph?"

Joe shrugged.

"I don't know, sir."

"Well, I think that might be a good career for you if you ever get out of this place. It would be a way to channel your natural aggression."

Joe shrugged.

"Maybe. I don't think they'd let me take ketamine before fights though."

"Maybe you won't need it. There's a sea sickness drug that affects the glutamate receptors the same way as ketamine. It's non-addictive and I don't think any state athletic commission would have a problem with it. In the meantime, I found a new drug I'd like to try with you called Riluzole. It is specifically designed to modulate the glutamate receptors just like ketamine."

Joe cocked his head and smirked at Professor Locke, searching the aging scholar's eyes for whatever was motivating this talk.

"Professor, do you want me to fight?"

Professor Locke took a long, deep breath.

"Joseph, I am just considering all the possibilities."

Joe raised an eyebrow.

"Do you think fighting would help me control my urges?"

"I think it would help you channel those violent impulses. Now that we know you can protect yourself without losing control. It may be something to look into."

Joe stared at him for a long moment before he responded. He thought about his fight with the big transvestite and his destruction of Armondo.

"I don't really enjoy fighting, Professor. I don't want to be violent anymore. I want to be cured."

Professor Locke nodded and patted Joe on the shoulder.

"I understand, son. I am merely trying to present you with options."

The professor handed Joe some pills and a cup of water.

"Is this the Riluzole?"

"Yes. The ketamine might cause a bad reaction with the other pain killers you're on. This should be safe."

Joe palmed the pills as he pretended to take them and drink the water. He opened his mouth and lifted his tongue so the doctor could see that the pills were gone. Professor Locke nodded and turned to leave then turned back around and looked at Joe over the top of his glasses.

"Joseph?"

"Yes, Professor?"

"If you don't enjoy fighting, why do you spend so much time in your cell practicing fighting moves?"

Joe suppressed a grin, but not before the professor caught it. They stared at each other, reading one another's thoughts as clearly as if they had been written in the air between them.

"Those are just exercises, Professor."

They both knew he was lying. Professor Locke opened his mouth to reply but thought better of it and turned to leave again.

"Take care of yourself, Joseph."

Professor Locke patted Joe on the leg and smiled warmly before walking down the hall and exiting the infirmary.

Joe stared at the closing door for several long minutes before he slipped the pills into a book he was reading, Mary Shelley's *Frankenstein*. He then closed his eyes and tried to go back to sleep. The sights and smells of the hospital ward were awakening all of Joe's predatory instincts. The smell of blood was overpowering. The sick, injured, and elderly lined both walls. Even injured, Joe knew he could have taken down any one of them and fed until his stomach burst. It had been more than a week now since his last ketamine injection. Not since before his injury. Its effects had worn off and his prey drive was at full throttle for the first time since his incarceration. Every instinct within him was calling out for him to feed the monster, but it wasn't time yet.

His eyes were closed and he was breathing in slow, measured breaths when he heard and then smelled the man standing above his bed. He smelled like Skittles and cigarettes. Joe opened his eyes and looked at the wild-eyed man smiling down at him. He was dressed in a blue trustee's uniform and carrying a mop. He had brown eyes and hair and was wearing thin, rectangular glasses. Joe recognized the man. He'd seen him around mopping the floor, changing bedpans, and bringing mail to the patients. He always had some sort of horror novel sticking out of his back pocket. Today it was something about zombies by an author named Nate Southard that Joe had never heard of. The trustee was just under six feet and soft in all the right places. Joe felt his stomach growl and the monster slowly unfurl in his pants, awakening, mean and ravenous.

"You're Joseph Miles, right? I read all about you. Damn, you really do look like Clark Kent! Well, like a twisted, evil version of Clark Kent, like Superman after a dose of red Kryptonite. But I bet you look just like him when you're all cleaned up."

Joe continued to stare at the trustee, watching his carotid artery pulsate along the side of his neck. He could feel his self-control slipping. He needed to feed. It was the only way to heal his injuries fast enough. The doctors would take weeks, but Joe knew that a fresh kill, devouring the living energy of a vibrant soul, would make him stronger.

"There was a girl here to see you a couple days ago."

Joe paused.

"A girl? Lana?"

The trustee shook his head.

"She said her name was Selene. That's what the guards told me. They tell me everything. People trust me around here."

"Did she say what she wanted?"

The trustee grinned and blushed a little.

"They said she was here for a conjugal visit. It was unusual. That's why they told me. She had permission from the warden and everything. They don't usually allow conjugal visits in this prison. Not even for married inmates. That's what was so unusual. The trailer they used to use for conjugals is just used for storage now. She isn't even married to you. I'd have known if she was. I've read all about your case. How you ate that librarian alive and then roasted that guy alive on a spit. That was so sick! I couldn't believe it when I read about it."

The trustee leaned down and whispered in Joe's ear. Joe had an almost irresistible urge to bite a chunk out of the man's face as he leaned in close.

"I tried it. After I read about what you did. I tried it. I'm in here for attempted rape, but they don't know about the others."

The man stood back up, puffing out his chest, waiting for Joe's approval.

"Is she coming back?'

"Who? The girls I …"

"Selene. Did she say she was coming back?"

"Yes. She said she was going to stay in town and she wasn't leaving until they let her have her conjugal visit. She wants you bad, man."

He leaned down and whispered in Joe's ear again.

"I can get you out of here."

Joe looked at the man in surprise. The trustee was smiling and nodding.

"I help take out the inmates that don't make it. You know, the ones that die. I put them in a pine box and stick them on the truck and the state takes them away and cremates 'em. I can put you on that truck."

Joe's eyes narrowed.

"Why? Why would you do that for me?"

The trustee's smile widened.

"Because you're my hero. I read all about your case and then when I found out you were coming here I couldn't wait to meet you. But they put you away in supermax where no one could see you." His voice dropped even lower. "Then I heard you mutilated that piece of shit Luscious."

Joe couldn't place the name at first and his confusion must have shown on his face because the trustee quickly refreshed his memory.

"That big, black fucker with the braids that you were in a cockfight with. He used to try to hurt me. He said he was going to fuck me in the ass. That's just how he said it. That crude bastard. If he's going to try and rape me, you'd think he could at least be a little nicer about it. Try a little romance or something. I was scared to death of that big sonuvabitch. I heard rumors about what he did to people. Hell, I even saw some of them come through here with their anuses prolapsed from that big, black bastard's cock ripping up their insides. And he wanted to do that to me? No, thank you. My asshole is strictly exit only. I made a shank just in case he tried anything, but I didn't really think I'd have a chance even with a shank. But you fixed that. He ain't gonna be hurtin' nobody no more. Not without a dick."

Joe nodded.

"Then, that Mexican guy you ripped apart? He was going to shank me because I wouldn't give him my cornbread. He asked me for it in the cafeteria and I was hungry and they don't usually have cornbread. It might be a year before they have it again. So I said no and he tried to stab me. I climbed up on the table and was running around the cafeteria trying to get away from him. Then the guards grabbed him and threw him in a strip cell. Next I heard, he was in a fight with you and got his face ripped off. You're like my guardian angel. It's like you were helping me out and you didn't even know it. Like we were destined for each other. I'm not a homo or anything. Don't worry. I just like reading scary shit and you're the scariest of the scary and you're real. I can't even believe I'm talking to you! It's like having a conversation with Jeffery Dahmer or Ed Gein. What a trip!"

Joe was patient and just let the man talk before interrupting with a single word.

193

"When?"

"Whenever you want. You can go tonight if you want. I've got a couple stiffs to take out in the morning. As long as that truck leaves the yard before they notice you're gone and lock the place down, then you're home free. You got anyone who can pick you up on the outside? Eventually they're going to notice you're gone. You want to be off that truck and on your way before they stop it and search it."

"I may know somebody," Joe said. "What's your name by the way?"

"Nathan. Nathan Felizzi."

"Okay, Nathan. Let's do it tonight."

Nathan smiled and seemed on the verge of jumping for joy. Then he paused and looked over Joe's injuries.

"Are you sure you can make it?"

Joe considered it a moment. He wanted to get out of here so bad the idea of waiting even until the sunset was killing him. He needed to feed. He needed to find his grandfather and destroy the curse forever. He needed to be free in every sense of the word. But realistically, he'd probably die if he tried to escape now. At the very least, he'd be caught or wouldn't have the strength to kill his grandfather when he finally found him. He needed to wait until he was stronger, but not too long. The hospital was the perfect place to escape from. If he missed this opportunity, he didn't know when he'd get another.

"A week. Give me a week."

"Awesome!"

Joe stared at the man, thinking how much he resembled his old friend, Frank. Older, pudgier, but otherwise the spitting image. He wondered if he'd taste the same.

"Will you be coming with me, Nathan?"

"Really?"

"Yes. Really."

"I don't know. I think the screws would notice if we both

194

left. I practically run this place. I wish you *could* take me with you though. I'd love to go on the run with you. Talk about a story to tell the grandkids."

Joe was already imagining the many ways Nathan could come in handy on a long road trip. Joe watched Nathan as he continued talking about his love of horror novels and how he felt so lucky to have met the infamous serial killer, Joseph Miles, and how they were linked by destiny. He was starting to believe him. What else but destiny could have brought them together right when Joe's appetite was at its peak? He imagined Nathan flopping around like a fish while Joe plopped sushi-sized morsels of flesh from his vivisected body, rooting around in the trustee's guts with chopsticks.

"Okay, Joe," Nathan whispered, shielding his face with one hand to block his face from any lip-reading inmates. "I'll be back in the morning to talk more."

Joe nodded and smiled. It was all coming together. He had a couple more people he needed to talk to. Even with another week to rehabilitate, there was no way he could get out of the prison with just him and Nathan. Not without some inside help. He needed to talk to Cindy. He would also need help on the outside and that meant getting in touch with Selene and Dirk.

"Nurse? Nurse? I need to make a phone call."

PART
FOUR

Yin Yang (Dead and Alive)

1 dozen egg yolks
7 1/2 cups ice water
9 3/4 cups flour, sifted
One small long pig (alive)

In a large bowl, place the egg yolks. Add iced water gradually, stirring (preferably with hashi(chopsticks)) and blending well. Add flour all at once. Stir BRIEFLY, well enough to coat but leave the lumps and bumps! To fry long pig, heat a large frying pan with 6-inches of oil (or more if necessary) and heat on high. Coat selected body parts in batter and fry until golden brown. Recommend restraints be used during this process as there will be much screaming and thrashing about during the cooking process. While coating the long pig's entire body up to the neck in batter and frying whole is preferred, this is often difficult. Frying them piece by piece is acceptable and still produces the desired freshness and crispiness. Long pig should still be alive and breathing, preferably still crying and moaning when served.

32

Waiting alone in the hotel room was maddening.

How dare they keep me from my Joseph, Selene thought. *I'll sue the fuck out of these bastards!*

The more Selene thought about it, the angrier she became. It had been days since she'd arrived and no one would let her anywhere near her cannibal lover. She couldn't even call him on the phone because there were no telephones in the prison hospital and the warden told her Joseph was still too weak to walk to a phone.

How could they let this happen?

She could not imagine Joseph ever being weak. He was like a force of nature. The warden said he'd been stabbed multiple times, but that he'd broken his attacker's leg and shoulder. It was good to know he hadn't just laid there like a punk and allowed himself to be victimized. That would have completely shattered her image of him. She didn't know how anyone could have hurt her powerful super-predator. Part of her didn't want to see Joseph laid up in a hospital, humbled, but she needed his curse in order to finally be free of her own. If she had to scoot his bed pan over and crawl into bed with him in order to get what she needed, she would.

Back in high school, they called her a "cold fish," "ice princess," "prude." At first, the guys had all been afraid of her because of her father's rumored Mafia connections. Then, it was her puritanical clothing and her conservative ideas, the product of a strict religious upbringing, that had branded her "unfuckable." Even after Selene had shaken her Catholic guilt and deeply-ingrained aversion to sex, her inability to achieve an orgasm had solidified the painful labels. So, she'd begun faking it to fit in.

She feigned an interest in sex she didn't really feel, and mimicked and then exaggerated the passion she saw in others. Sex was a dramatic performance done to convince her partners that she actually felt something, that she felt anything. She endured a long procession of inadequate lovers, lying beneath them as they grunted and thrust inside of her or lapped at her clit like they were in a race to the finish, trying to win a prize at a carnival in a maddening effort to bring her to orgasm until, frustrated and annoyed, seething in a silent fury, Selene would scream and moan and fake a quiver in her legs so they'd stop fumbling around with her private parts. When they were done, she quickly ushered them out the door, out of her sight.

By the time she was a junior in college, Selene had completely transformed herself. She wore suggestive clothing, tank-tops, baby T-shirts, short shorts and mini-skirts, walking and talking in a manner that would have made any man within eyesight think she was for sale. She looked and acted like a nymphomaniac, all to profess a sexuality she didn't possess.

In her quest to avoid total asexuality, Selene began to experiment. She tried both women and men; sometimes simultaneously. The women were better, but in the end, she was still left teetering on the edge of orgasm, never finding someone who could tip her over that awesome precipice. She tried bondage, S&M, humiliation, both as a submissive and a dom. Again, she found the thrill exhilarating, like a rollercoaster that left her breathless, entertained, but far from satisfied. She participated in orgies, gangbangs, tried tantric sex, golden showers, skat, blood play, bestiality, nearly every conceivable act of debauchery known to man short of pederasty. Nothing worked, but every experience altered her, changed her, warped her.

Selene's father had paid for her to go to Catholic school and wanted her to become a nun. Seeing his little girl strutting around with half her ass hanging out of her miniskirt had almost driven him insane. He was on the verge of disowning her and striking her from his will when, just a month ago, he was shot by an unknown assailant coming out of a whorehouse owned by one of his clients. His death was ruled an attempted robbery and Selene's inheritance was secured. The only thing in the way of her and daddy's millions was her pill-popping, bulimic, cosmetic-surgery-addicted stepmom with the drum-tight skin, basketball-sized, saline-filled mammaries, and sausage-shaped, collagen-injected lips. It hadn't taken Selene long to feed her enough Xanax and vodka to kill her. Everyone assumed she'd overdosed trying to handle the grief of her husband's death. No one suspected Selene.

When the police tried to question Selene, she'd cried so long and hard they'd given up and had never returned. Orgasms weren't the only thing Selene had learned to fake well. They buried her stepmother a week ago. Now, Selene had all her daddy's wealth and still couldn't get a decent fuck to save her life.

The innocent, prudish Catholic girl she'd once been was a distant memory now. The idea of joining a monastery and becoming a nun, as her father had wished, was laughable considering all she'd experienced. Once, she'd actually taken it seriously. Sex hadn't meant much to her anyway. Why not marry herself to the "Almighty" and live a life of celibacy? Now, it was almost inconceivable. She still believed in God and could technically still become a nun even after all her sexual trysts, but that would mean first giving a total confession. She'd have to tell some child-molesting priest about her homosexual experiences, the group sex, the bondage and whips and scalpels and cattle prods and dildos the size of a man's arm, even her experience with a Doberman pinscher. None of that bothered her much. At least she wasn't sodomizing little boys and girls, though she'd considered it more than once. Even what she'd done to her stepmother could be considered a mercy killing and she'd feel comfortable arguing the point. What worried her was what she'd done to that frat boy. That wasn't something she could ever see herself copping to in a confessional. On the bright side, no one called Selene an ice princess anymore. Now, she was a slut, a pervert, and apparently a sadist, and had still never had an orgasm.

To date, her little experiment with cannibalism had been by far her most profound sexual experience. It had been her closest near-climax experience. The violence, the blood, even the taste of Mark's pectoral muscle sautéed in butter and garlic, had been amazing. Biting his cock off while Mark was still alive had been the most exhilarating part, but the taste and texture of the raw meat had been unbearable. Eating the frat boy's cooked flesh had tasted much better, but hadn't given her the same thrill. There had to be a way to combine the two experiences. She had to try anyway, either that or wait another month for Joseph to get well enough for visitors. She remembered a dish she'd tried once on a trip to Beijing, China, for the 2008 Olympics. It had been a delicacy called "Yin Yang Fish." Then, she'd thought it was the cruelest thing she'd ever seen. Now, it sounded like a wonderful idea.

Tired of sitting around the hotel room watching bad horror movies and reality TV shows about obnoxious teenagers and housewives from New Jersey, Selene decided to check out the hotel bar. First, she went online to find a local store that sold electric deep fryers. Just in case she got lucky.

33

Joe walked around the hospital, dragging his IV behind him as he traveled from his bed to the bathroom to the hallway and back three or four times. The doctors and nurses had made him walk the day after surgery. They said it helped prevent blood clots or something. He'd made a ritual of it ever since, gradually increasing his distance until he estimated he could now walk a mile. It wasn't much, but it was progress and it might be just enough to get him out of here.

The phone call to Dirk was promising. His cousin volunteered to come into town this evening and find Selene. Together they would prepare everything for his escape. As many times as Joe had told his cousin that the prison phones were monitored, the kid had still almost given away the plan several times during the conversation.

"I need you to get a hold of Selene. I think she's already in town. She's been trying to get in to see me. Just tell her to hang tight. I'll see her soon."

"Don't worry, Cuz. I'll handle it."

"Tell her there's a truck that leaves the prison almost every morning, taking dead inmates to the crematorium. She might want to find out the truck's route, where it stops, what roads it takes, where the crematorium is. You understand? And she might want to rent an SUV. Something big like a Navigator or an Expedition."

"For what?"

"Just tell her."

"Why not something fast like a Charger or a Mustang or even a Porsche or a Lamborghini? She can afford it with all that money she's got."

"Dirk. Just tell her what I told you, please."

"Okay, sure. I just don't see why you wouldn't want something faster. I mean, if we get chased."

"Dirk. All you're doing is coming to visit me in prison. Why would you get chased? Now keep quiet and listen. I told you these lines are monitored."

"Yeah, okay, Cuz."

"Tell her she needs to get some hair clippers and sunglasses too."

"Ohhhh! Okay. I got it. That's smart. That way she can—"

"Shut up, Dirk. What did I tell you? Make sure she understands that I'm still injured."

"Oh, that's why you don't want her to get a Porsche, huh? You can't be hidin' in a trunk or anything when you're all stitched up, huh?"

"Hang up the phone, Dirk."

"What?"

"Goodbye, Dirk. Remember what I told you to tell Selene."

"Okay, but—"

Joe slammed the phone down and looked around to see if anyone was watching him. No one seemed to be paying any attention to him, but he knew that didn't mean they weren't listening to his call from a control booth somewhere or taping it to listen to later. That idiot cousin of his had almost fucked everything up. Now, all that remained was for him to convince Cindy to help get him out of the hospital and down into the morgue. That would be the hardest part. Joe decided to do a couple more laps around the hospital. He was feeling good today.

34

The hotel bar was full of empty barstools and bored waitresses. The bartender was an older woman, mid- to late-thirties, with platinum blonde hair and big pendulous breasts. The woman stared at Selene hard as she walked in. It immediately occurred to Selene that this bartender was exactly the type of woman Joseph Miles would have been attracted to. Looking at her large breasts and hips made her miss the big cannibal all the more. Even though she'd never been physical with him, he'd shared a piece of her, and after all the letters and phone calls, she felt like she knew his soul.

At first she thought the woman was another jealous bitch mean-mugging her to compensate for some insecurity or inner self-hatred projected outward as animosity toward anyone prettier than her. A "hater," in other words. Selene was used to that sort of reaction from women. Then the bartender smiled and looked Selene over from head to toe, and Selene realized what the long stare had been for—the woman was checking her out. She was a lesbian and she was attracted to Selene and not making any attempt to hide it. Selene returned the bartender's smile and took a seat at the bar.

"What can I get you?" the woman asked.

Selene grinned and licked her lips.

"Something wet, exotic, and intoxicating."

The bartender smiled back coyly and once again dragged her eyes over Selene's body, slower this time, more deliberately, and without the slightest pretense of modesty.

"Sex on the beach or a slow comfortable screw?" The bartender asked, sucking on a maraschino cherry and twirling her tongue around it like it was an engorged clitoris.

"I'm really in the mood for a screaming orgasm."

The bartender pursed her lips, made a whistling noise, and then smiled.

"So am I, sister. So am I."

The woman began making the drink. Her eyes never wavered from Selene's except to sweep salaciously over her breasts.

"Maybe," Selene began. "Maybe we can both have one. What time do you get off?"

"I'm here until the place closes. Midnight tonight."

Selene checked her watch. It was just after seven p.m. She would have to wait five hours if she wanted the woman and Selene really wanted her.

"What's your name, gorgeous?" Selene asked.

The woman smiled and nodded approvingly. She was obviously not used to being so brazenly pursued by another woman. It was evident from her mannerisms that she was usually the pursuer, but she was enjoying the role reversal.

"My name's Wendy."

Selene held out her hand and the large woman took it and held it rather than shake it and release it.

"Nice to meet you, Wendy. My name's Selene."

"Are you staying here at the hotel?"

Selene held up her door key.

"Room 212. You're welcome any time."

Wendy smiled then and suddenly looked over Selene's shoulder and frowned.

"Is he with you?"

Selene turned and frowned when she saw a large man standing behind her in a faded, black *"I Spit On Your Grave"* promotional T-shirt, wearing baggy, black cargo jeans and black, retro Adidas shell-tops. He had long, greasy, black hair that was all one length and he wore black fingernail polish and eyeliner like an Alice Cooper or Ozzy Osborne wannabe. He smiled with a mouthful of yellowing teeth. He looked like he hadn't bathed in days and hadn't brushed or flossed in months. Selene looked him over, scowling in disgust.

"Selene?"

"Yes? And who are you?"

"I'm Dirk, Joe's cousin. We talked a few times? We need to talk."

Selene turned back to Wendy the bartender and rolled her eyes.

"I'll be back," she said, then Selene stood up and walked toward the exit.

"Follow me," Selene said, swinging her Prada handbag over her shoulder and storming past the greasy Heavy Metal/ Goth kid. She could hear him struggling to keep up with her as she strode in long purposeful steps toward the elevator.

"Wait! Hold on. You're walking too fast!"

Once inside the elevator, Selene whirled on him, jabbing a finger in Dirk's chest and pinning him in place with her angry dark eyes.

"What the fuck are you doing here, Dirk?"

"Joe wanted me to find you."

Selene's features softened.

"You spoke to him? When?"

"Yesterday."

"And he asked for me?"

She knew she sounded like a schoolgirl with a crush on the high school quarterback. She was practically gushing, but she couldn't help herself.

"Yeah, he wanted me to let you know that he's escaping next week and he needs you to get an SUV. Something big like an Escalade or a Navigator or one of those huge Yukon, Denalis or something. He said to remind you he's still going to be pretty sore. I guess he got cut up bad. I told him you should get something fast like a Mustang or a Porsche so we can outrun the police, but he said no. I don't get it."

"That's because you're an idiot, Dirk. The last thing we want is to be running from the police. You can't outrun an entire police force. He needs something he can stretch out in and relax on a long trip. Something with a big rear storage. I'd better make sure it has tinted windows."

"Yeah! He said that too!"

Selene looked the big scraggly kid over. Except for his size, well over six feet, it was hard to imagine he was related to Joseph. He was so skinny he was practically bony, but still managed to sport a beer belly. He reeked of clove cigarettes, candy, and body odor. She couldn't help but wonder what he would look like cleaned up though. Perhaps with that ridiculous hair pulled back out of his face, a shave, and a bath, he might actually look presentable —and he was from the same bloodline as Joseph.

"How is he getting out?"

"He didn't say. Oh, he said you should check the routes on the truck that takes the bodies from the prison morgue to the crematorium. You know, where it stops, what streets it turns on, that sort of thing."

Selene nodded.

"What did he want you to do when he escapes?"

"He didn't say that either. He just wanted me to get you that message."

Selene smiled and gave Dirk another head to toe appraisal.

"You smell terrible, Dirk. When we get upstairs, you're taking a shower and you're shaving."

"But I don't want to shave."

"What you want doesn't matter right now. Now, does it?"

Dirk locked eyes with Selene for a moment and then looked away, dropping his eyes to the floor.

"No. I guess not. I just don't see how me shaving is going to help get Joe out of prison."

"You don't need to understand. You just need to do what I say. Me and Joe are the only ones who need to understand."

The elevator stopped and Selene strode down the hall with Dirk still struggling to keep up despite the fact that his legs were easily twice as long as hers.

"Have you ever heard of drunken shrimp?"

Dirk looked confused for a moment.

"Uh, no. What is it?"

"It's one of my favorite Cantonese dishes. Have you ever had saki?"

"You mean like sushi? I don't like raw fish."

"Saki. Not Sushi. Japanese rice wine. The Chinese make a similar drink. It's very potent. You'll like it. I'll get us some from somewhere while you get showered." She looked him over again, and Dirk squirmed uncomfortably under her gaze.

"What do you keep looking at me like that for?"

"Do you have any body hair? Like on your chest or stomach or your back or anything?"

"A little, I guess. Why?"

"Shave that off too and your pubic hair."

"Shave my pubes? What the fuck for?"

"It's part of the plan, Dirk. You'll understand it all soon. Just use my razor when you get in the shower and come out looking like you did when you left the womb."

"You're not going to dress me up like a woman or anything are you?"

Selene snickered.

"Why? Does that get you off, Dirk?"

Dirk scowled in exaggerated outrage.

"No! I like girls."

Selene smiled and wagged her finger at him.

"Not all transvestites are homosexuals, Dirk. I used to date a guy who liked to wear women's clothes. He was hung like a horse and fucked like a demon. You should be more open-minded."

"Are you really going to get wine?"

"Chinese rice wine, yes."

"Like saki?" Dirk asked, repeating her previous description of the drink with obvious delight.

"Sort of."

"Sweet! Can you get me some tequila too and some Coronas?"

Selene paused and thought about it as they stopped in front of room 212 and she used her credit card-shaped room key to unlock the door.

"Tequila, yes. Corona, no. I hate the taste of beer."

"Well, you don't have to drink it. I'll pay for it."

"I think the rice wine and tequila will be enough, Dirk. You just get in the shower. One more thing, did Joe say exactly what day he wanted to escape?"

"No. He said he'd call me."

"Do you have your phone with you?"

"Yeah. It's right in my pocket."

"Let me have it."

Dirk pulled it out and placed it in her hand, this time without questioning her until she turned to walk away.

"Why do you need my cell phone?"

"In case he calls while you're in the shower. Use plenty of soap. I'll be back soon."

Selene waved and shut the door.

35

The infirmary was a dark maze of shadows when Cindy came to visit Joe. The fluorescent lights that normally lit the place with a stark, white incandescence were out and the cavernous room now resembled a morgue with row after row of bodies laid out under sheets. The smell of vomit, blood, feces, and disinfectant roared in Joe's nostrils. Moans, snores, and heavy, labored breathing echoed off the sterile walls in a sonorous chorus broken by the sound of Officer Cindy Addison's leather boots clip-clopping along the vinyl floor.

Joe knew those footsteps. He'd listened to them walk past his cell night after night while he was locked up in supermax, hoping they would stop at his door. Now, they traveled to the side of Joe's bed.

"Hello, lover," Joe said.

"Hey, Joe."

"Help me up," Joe said, holding out his arms.

Cindy leaned down and slipped an arm around Joe's shoulders and started to lift him up when he pulled her down into the bed with him. She giggled as he tried to spoon with her, pressing his erection against her back.

"We can't. Someone will see us," Cindy whispered.

"Okay, then help me up for real."

Joe swung his legs off the side of the bed and Cindy rushed over to help lift him to his feet.

"Let's go for a walk."

"Are you sure you're up to it?" Cindy asked.

"I can make it."

"Where do you want to go?"

"Anywhere but here. How far is the morgue?"

"The morgue?" Cindy paused and Joe could feel her tense up. Joe's old awkwardness had reared its ugly head. He had been trying so hard not to appear creepy. He wanted—*needed*—Cindy to trust him and he hoped he hadn't just ruined it all. He shuffled nervously from foot to foot and stared down at the floor, drooping his shoulders to appear smaller. He knew that even the most ferocious beast could appear adorable in the right light and he was doing his best impression of a cuddly bear.

"I, um, I heard some of the other inmates talking. They said that's where a lot of people go for…for some alone time."

Cindy smiled and visibly relaxed, letting out a quick breath as if she'd been holding it.

"You can barely walk, Joe. I don't think you're ready for any alone time quite yet. I don't want you popping any stitches."

Joe nodded.

"You're probably right, but I thought it would be nice to just go somewhere quiet and talk without worrying about people listening in on us."

Dimples burst on to Cindy's face as her smile widened, making her look absolutely adorable, like an aging cherub. Joe wondered how he'd failed to notice them before. He leaned down and kissed and then lightly bit her dimpled cheek. He then brushed his palms and fingertips along her jawline, staring at her like she was the most beautiful woman he'd ever seen, and at that moment she almost was. She was certainly the most beautiful thing he'd seen in months besides Lana who wanted him dead. Joe pushed the image of Lana's luscious body and sad, angry, beautiful eyes from his mind and leaned down to kiss Cindy's other cheek. Cindy closed her eyes and let out a satisfied moan.

"Okay, Joe. It isn't far actually. The infirmary's right on top of it."

Cindy led the massive serial killer out of the infirmary and into the dimly lit hallway. Joe lumbered along behind her, watching her unlock one door after another with her electronic key, taking mental note of the directions in case things went wrong and he had to come this way without her. The pain in his chest and stomach was just a dull ache. Maybe he could perform after all.

36

Why the fuck does this crazy bitch want me to shave my sack? Dirk wondered, standing in the shower, lathering up his testicles with shaving cream. His face, chest, and arms were already smooth and hairless. There was only one area left to address.

"I can't believe I'm doing this shit," Dirk said out loud to no one. He took several deep panting breaths, steeling his nerves for the task ahead. He tried to tell himself he was doing it for his big cousin, but he honestly couldn't see how making his genitals look prepubescent was going to help Joe escape. He was hoping Selene was just trying to get him to clean up and groom himself a bit before she fucked him. Yeah, she was a bit heavier now than she was in the pictures. She'd no doubt put on the extra weight for Joe. He liked those chunky chicks, but she was still incredibly sexy.

Something about Selene made Dirk uncomfortable though. There was something sort of off about her. Something unstable. Talking to her gave him the same nervous, uneasy feeling he got when he talked to his cousin Joe. There was this primal aura of threat and menace radiating from her. There was crazy in her eyes. And, as much as it frightened him, it also made him want to fuck the shit out of her.

Dirk took the pink disposable razor and scraped it gently over his wrinkled testes. Removing the hair along with an occasional sliver of skin.

"Ouch! Fuck!"

Dirk threw the razor down at his feet and checked his nuts for grievous injury.

"I'm gonna fucking castrate myself! Fuck this shit!"

Dirk said, but, contrary to his words, he obediently retrieved the razor and finished the job. He had just stepped from the shower when he heard the door to the suite open. Moments later , Selene stepped into the bathroom and Dirk's modest erection swelled.

This is it, he thought. *I'm gonna get laid!*

"So, let's see how everything turned out."

"What?" Dirk said, covering his genitals with both hands while water sprayed his back and shoulders.

"Let's see how you look." She reached into the shower and turned off the water, and Dirk shrank away from her. His hair was wet and plastered to his face. With his bony arms and legs, hunched shoulders, his hands cupped between his legs, and his pale skin, Dirk looked like a prisoner of war or a terrorist captive. He felt uncomfortably vulnerable. Selene reached out and brushed the hair away from Dirk's clean-shaven face.

"That looks much, much better. Very good. No chest hair. Good. Let's see your arm pits. Good. Okay, now let's see the rest of you."

"Seriously?"

"Now, Dirk, don't tell me a big boy like you is shy around the ladies?"

Selene winked at him and suddenly Dirk felt even more powerless. He wanted to crawl through the cracks in the shower tiles and hide where her piercing stare could not reach him. Instead, he allowed her to pull his hands away from his private parts. Selene's smile widened and she nodded, appraising him with obvious approval.

"Very good, Dirk. Very nice."

Selene grabbed the hem of her shirt and lifted it over her head, tossing it to the floor. Dirk's eyes immediately dropped to her breasts. He was transfixed as she reached around in back of her and unhooked her bra. Her breasts bobbled free while her bra slid down her arms and fell to the floor. One of her nipples looked as if it had turned inward. It was merely a dimpled scar on her left tit, but the other one jutted out like a .22 bullet. Dirk could hardly breathe. His cock was so hard he could feel the skin on his shaft stretching. It felt like it was about to rip.

"Fill the Jacuzzi. Let's relax." Selene dropped her pants then, hooked her thumbs in the waistband of her underwear, and slid them slowly over her heart-shaped hips and ass, down her smooth, thick thighs and muscular calves. Dirk felt faint.

"Oh my God, you're beautiful."

Dirk had forgotten his modesty and was standing there with his erection bobbing in the air like a divining rod as he stared at Selene's naked body in slack-jawed amazement.

"Damn, I don't think I'll ever look at another skinny chick again."

Selene smiled and blushed. It was the first genuine expression of emotion Dirk had seen her display since he first laid eyes on her.

"Thank you, Dirk. Now fill the tub while I get our drinks."

Dirk walked over to the large tub, which sat on a raised platform halfway between the bathroom and the bedroom in the center of the suite. As instructed, he turned on the faucet and began filling the tub. Selene walked back over to him carrying two large jugs with Asian characters written all over them. She held the two bottles underneath her own impressive jugs. Dirk drank in her naked form. Her hips were wide, tapering into a narrow waist and down to thick but muscular thighs parted by a thin rectangle of perfectly groomed pubic hair. Her labia appeared engorged. She was clearly aroused, which Dirk found confusing. Earlier she'd seemed apathetic toward him, even annoyed and disgusted by his very existence. He'd like to think the shave and shower had turned her around, but something still felt off. There were alarm bells going off. The prospect of pussy, however, was seriously muting his self-preservation instincts.

Selene turned her back to him and Dirk appraised her ample buttocks, an enticing combination of muscle and fat though a bit more fat than Dirk usually liked. Something about this woman defied all his normal preferences. Perhaps it was just that it had been so long since he'd been laid or because she was forbidden fruit, his cousin's girl. There were just too many thoughts going through his head. He just wanted to get drunk and shut his mind off for a few hours, lose his inhibitions in alcohol and let the night unfold.

"Saki?"

"Chinese rice wine," Selene replied holding out the big, blue jug to him. "Try a swig."

Dirk took the bottle and looked around for a glass.

"Just drink. You're not a germaphobe are you?"

"Hell no!"

Dirk turned the bottle up and took a large gulp. His eyes widened and he swallowed hard.

"Whew! That's some strong shit!"

Selene opened the other bottle and took a gulp of the wine herself. She cocked one hand on her hip and stuck her breasts out further. Dirk's eyes raced her curves from her feet to the superior grin on her luscious lips. Dirk took another long swig.

"You like? It's one of my favorite wines."

"It's not bad." Dirk took another drink. "I never pictured you as the type of girl who drinks wine straight from the bottle."

"I'm probably going to do a lot of things tonight you couldn't picture me doing."

Selene walked over to the edge of the Jacuzzi tub and took another long swig from the bottle of rice wine. She leaned down and kissed Dirk, pouring the wine from her mouth into his. Dirk reached out for her breasts, rubbing his hands over her one stiff nipple and feeling the buoyant weight of each breast. She pulled his mouth to her breast and poured wine down her chest where it gushed down her cleavage and into his mouth. Dirk gulped again and again, swallowing large quantities of alcohol faster than he wanted to but unable to pull away. This was the sexiest shit he'd ever done with a woman without her actually touching his dick and he didn't want it to end. He wanted to see what Selene was going to do next.

Dirk was already feeling woozy and lightheaded when Selene grabbed him by the hair and jerked his head back. She took the bottle from his hand and poured it into his open mouth. Dirk sputtered and coughed. It felt like he was drowning, like he was being waterboarded with rice wine. Selene laughed.

"Too much?"

"Fuck! I almost gagged. Slow down."

Selene continued to giggle.

"How about a little more? Stick out your tongue."

She sat on the edge of the tub now and pushed Dirk down between her thighs. He slid his tongue inside of her and felt her vagina contract, sucking it in deeper as she poured wine down between her breasts, over her stomach, through her patch of pubic hair, and down his throat. Dirk lapped at her swollen clitoris while the intoxicating cocktail of her sweet vaginal juices mixed with wine flowed into his mouth. He gulped it down like the last drink of a dying man.

The tub was full now and Selene reached over and pressed a button that started the bubbles, then she shut off the faucet. The combination of the warm bath, the water jets massaging him from all sides, and the alcohol was making Dirk sleepy. More than sleepy, suddenly Dirk felt like he could barely stand. He tried to climb out of the tub and stumbled backward, splashing down in the tub and smacking his head on the edge of it, which made the fuzziness in his head even worse.

"I feeeeel fuuuunnnyyy."

"You're okay. It's just the wine. Relax and enjoy the bath."

The room blurred and began to wobble like he was in a slow-moving earthquake. His skin felt too hot and then like he was freezing. The last thing he remembered was Selene pulling the plug on the Jacuzzi and letting all the water out just before everything went black.

When Dirk reawakened he was still in the tub. His limbs felt heavy and everything was still blurred like he was looking at it from underwater. He tried to lift his arm and it didn't move. He tried to roll over, to stand, but his body did not move. He felt completely paralyzed. He tried to call out for help, but all that came out was an inarticulate jumble of slurred syllables.

Selene was still in the room, still naked, still completely fucking gorgeous. She had two more bottles of rice wine in her hands and she was slowly pouring them over his body. Dirk couldn't even feel the sensation of the wine pouring onto his skin.

She drugged me. This bitch fucking drugged me!

He remembered her turning her back to him while she was opening the bottle. While he was busy staring at her ass, she must have slipped something into the bottle.

Rohypnol. Roophies. It had to be. A fucking date rape drug. He'd used it himself a couple times in college. Not to rape anybody. He'd popped one at a club once to get high and then he'd given one to Jessica, his roommate's big-breasted, empty-headed girlfriend. He slipped it into her drink one night when his roommate wasn't home and then undressed her and jacked off on her tits, but he hadn't raped her. He wasn't that degenerate. Now, someone had used it on him and Dirk had the feeling that, whatever Selene had planned, it was much worse than what he'd done to Jessica.

Selene poured another bottle of rice wine into the tub.

She must have put the stopper back in because the wine had filled the bottom of the tub. Selene walked out of the room. He could hear her moving from room to room fiddling with something. When she walked back in, she had three smoke detectors in her hands. She set them down on the bathroom counter and walked over to Dirk with a book of matches. That's when everything finally began to click. Selene looked in his eyes and smiled.

"You've figured it out I see. Remember when I told you about my favorite Chinese dish, drunken shrimp? Do you know how they make it? Traditionally, live shrimp are doused with a strong rice wine. The shrimp ingest large quantities of the wine, hence the name. Then they are set on fire and flambéed. The result is a crispy texture with the taste of wine in every bite. The thing is, I realized after my last experiment that I don't like carrion. I can only get off on eating something that's alive. The trick is to flash cook you without killing you. I want you alive right up until the final bite." Selene threw the match and flames leapt up immediately. It was all he could see. Burning tendrils of blue flame crawled all over his body.

The searing agony was worse than anything he could have imagined. He tried to scream, but the Rohypnol had paralyzed his vocal chords. Dirk's mind, however, let loose a shrill cry. His very thoughts shrieked and begged and sobbed uncontrollably as his world became pain, a landscape of white-hot anguish that obliterated all other thoughts or sensations. His flesh sizzled, turned brown, and then began to blacken. He could feel the subcutaneous fat boiling beneath his skin, frying his muscles and fusing tendons. His fingers and toes shriveled and burned away to nubs. He could smell his own hair burning like the scent of boiling tar. Then he realized why Selene had wanted him to shave. Between his legs, Dirk's penis now resembled a barbecued sausage link that had fallen from the grill onto the charcoals. He finally found his voice.

"Aaaaaargh! AAAaaaaaahhhhh!"

Dirk inhaled smoke and flame, singing his tonsils and scalding his esophagus. The flames grew higher until they looked like they would consume the entire room. Selene turned the water in the tub back on, dousing the conflagration before it got out of control. The cool water made Dirk's fried nerve-endings sing out in stomach-churning anguish. Selene sat beside the tub, smiling down at him with eyes that sparkled with madness and glee. It was the most terrifying sight Dirk had ever beheld … until he saw the knife.

The flames had felt like the last moments of Dirk's life but the first cut, the blade sawing through his fried muscles down to the bone, felt like the end of the universe. The smell of marinated meat filled the room. Even to Dirk, it smelled delicious.

Selene cut away one of Dirk's biceps, staring into his eyes the entire time. As she brought the scorched meat to her lips, Dirk could see her other hand down between her legs, furiously masturbating. She looked like she was crying even as she aimed the knife down at him again and punched it into his chest.

37

Dirk was dead long before Selene carved out his heart. His eyes had gone blank soon after she severed the first artery. There was a square-shaped section of flesh missing from Dirk's chest where she'd removed his left pectoral muscle and much of the surrounding flesh to expose his ribcage. Dirk's heart had still been beating when she'd first opened him up. She could see his purple and gray lungs expanding and contracting in a shallow rhythm as she cut away the large square of charred meat. Selene took the large carving knife she'd purchased for her first "meal" and began sawing through Dirk's ribcage. She wanted to eat his heart while it was still beating. The ribs were thick and cutting through it was taking a long time. Finally, after nearly ten minutes of sawing, she cut through to the heart. She pulled back the pericardium, the thin membrane covering the heart, and quickly severed the pulmonary and coronary arteries. She sliced the inferior and superior vena cavas, feeling her excitement peak once again. Her pussy was throbbing as she lifted the heart from the thoracic cavity. Dirk's lungs had stopped their rise and fall and his eyes had fixed in place. He was dead, but his heart continued to twitch and spasm in her hands.

The heart itself had been untouched by the flames. Selene held it in her hands as she lay back on the bathroom floor and massaged her throbbing clitoris, watching Dirk's disembodied heart pulsate in her hands. Selene took one small bite then and then another and another. The flesh was tough and rubbery, but not completely repulsive. She grabbed a half-empty bottle of rice wine and doused the heart in it before finishing her meal, still furiously fingering herself as she devoured first the left atrium and then the left ventricle, the aortic valve and much of the aorta itself before tossing the rest back into the tub when she began to gag. She had eaten too much food. Her stomach felt bloated, but she had still not achieved the orgasm she craved. Selene was still furiously fingering her swollen clit when she climbed to her knees and looked into the tub for something else to eat.

She picked through the rest of Dirk's charred remains. His heart had been okay. It would have been much better cooked but the fact that it was still pulsing with life when she'd taken her first bite had been an incredible high. But Dirk's bicep had tasted wonderful, even though she'd overcooked it. Looking in Dirk's eyes while he watched her consume him had been almost orgasmic. Almost. The hideousness of Dirk's appearance post-immolation, his skin fried and crinkled, ears, nose, lips, and eyelids burnt away, had been so repulsive it had turned her off, spoiling her enjoyment of the moment. It had ruined the mood. Cutting out his heart and eating it had gotten her extremely horny again, but not with quite the same intensity she'd experienced eating Dirk while he was still alive. If she was going to cum, it would have been when she'd taken that first delicious bite and saw Dirk watching her with something like awe in his disbelieving eyes. Then she'd made the error of looking too closely at his face and the moment passed.

Trying to get back into the mood, Selene cut off Dirk's roasted penis and testicles and sat down on the bathroom floor again, poking at them with her fingers like a kid scooting vegetables around on his plate, trying to work up the nerve to eat them. Finally, she lifted his small flame-broiled sack to her lips and bit into his testicles. The taste, once again, was marvelous. She could taste the rice wine throughout the meat. What she couldn't taste was Dirk's soul. Not the way Joe had described it. This was just meat, dead lifeless meat. Whatever spirit had animated it had fled, or else her own taste buds were too dull to detect it. Another failure.

It was time to stop fucking around. She needed Joe and she needed him now. Killing these losers was just a tease.

38

Cindy was on her knees with Joe's enormous cock filling her throat. He was so sexy she couldn't believe it and he said he loved her. She had heard men say those words to her before, especially men behind bars, but she' had never heard them the way Joe said it. The intensity in his eyes and voice was almost scary. It was the same when they made love. Even as he fucked her throat with his beautiful eight-inch cock, he stared down at her with a raw primal passion in his eyes that was terrifying in its honesty and profundity. There was no pretense with Joseph. His lust was raw and naked and so was his affection. He would pound his cock in her ass like he was raping a street hooker one moment and then cuddle up against her, purring like a kitten the next. As much as she hated to admit it, she loved him.

Try as she might to fool herself, however, Cindy was not a fool. She knew a man who looked like Joseph would not have looked twice at a woman who looked like her, let alone profess his love for her, had he not been incarcerated and had his choice of women. In the penitentiary, she was one of few choices a highly sexual creature like Joseph Miles had. It was either fuck a middle-aged fat chick like her or risk HIV infection sodomizing some prison bitch. Cindy didn't care how this gorgeous man with the body that looked like it had been hewn from stone, the piercing blue eyes, and the porn-star cock had become hers. She was enjoying it while it lasted. They were exploiting each other. And she was okay with that.

She felt the serial killer's engorged cock expand in her throat, the head widen and swell. Joseph's legs locked and

227

his body tensed and quivered, and then he roared, a savage, snarling roar like the battle cry of a full-grown tiger. The sound made Cindy's legs weak and almost made her cum herself. Her pussy was dripping wet. She wanted Joseph to fuck her so bad she felt like screaming. She began fingering her engorged clit as Joe's throbbing hard cock spasmed in her throat and warm semen filled her mouth. She pulled his cock from between her lips and licked the massive head as he continued to cum, ejaculating thick gouts of semen onto her nose, cheeks, and outstretched tongue. His seed plastered her face and neck, drooling from her chin down her neck and splattering her tiny breasts. He lifted her to her feet and kissed her deeply, sucking his own cum from her tongue. Cindy dropped to her knees again and sucked his cock once more licking the remaining cum from the head, grabbing his hard muscular ass and pulling him deeper into her mouth, guiding his incredible organ past her tonsils and forcing him to fuck her throat again. The many weeks she'd spent fucking the huge cannibal, sucking his tremendous manhood, had completely rid her of her gag reflex.

She had almost reached orgasm on her own when Joe lifted her to her feet and laid her atop one of the few unoccupied autopsy tables. Cindy tried not to look around at the bodies filling the room in various stages of dissection, while the big cannibal knelt between her legs and began licking and sucking her clitoris. She felt his tongue circle and swirl around the swollen nub, sucking and nipping at it before stabbing his tongue deep inside her sex and fucking her with the long, serpentine appendage.

His mouth felt marvelous. She had already been so close to orgasm that it didn't take long before she felt the familiar tremors and tingles radiating through her sex. Joseph sucked her clit again, flicking it with his tongue while Cindy's legs shook. The first spasms of what promised to be a tremendous climax ripped through her muscles when Joe slithered his tongue deep in her anus and began fucking her asshole with his mouth. He slid one, two, three fingers in her sex, slowly fisting her as he flicked his thumb across her pulsating clitoris. Cindy screamed when the orgasm erupted. Her legs stiffened and trembled. Cords and veins bulged in her neck. Her eyes rolled heavenward. Her stomach sucked inward and her back arched violently, feeling like it was about to break.

The tenor of her scream changed when she looked sideways and saw the faceless, tattooed corpse on the next gurney. The man's face had been eaten away. His nose, lips, one of his eyelids, and part of his left cheek were gone and there was little doubt who might have done such a thing. Cindy stared in horror at the dead man's ruined face while Joe continued licking her asshole and fucking her wet pussy with his hand. The horror of the scene somehow added to the intensity of the next orgasm and the next and the next. By the time she came for the fifth and final time, she knew she was in love. Helping him escape was no longer an option. It was now a duty.

39

"I am buying you a plane ticket. I've made a bit of a mess and I need you to come clean it up for me."

"Who is this?"

"This is Selene Cassaro. Frank Cassaro's daughter. I need your help."

There was a long pause.

"Give me your number. I'll call you back."

Selene gave the man her cell phone number. He repeated it back to her then and immediately hung up the phone. Selene paced her hotel room. She'd opened the windows and the doors to the balcony to air the aroma of cooked flesh from the room—still the smell wafted from every surface. It permeated her skin. She'd already taken two showers, but she could still smell Dirk on her fingers, taste him on her lips. She was just about to take another shower when her cell phone rang.

"Hello?"

"This is Vincente. Who is this again?"

"Selene Cassaro. Frank Cassaro's daughter. I need you to make something disappear for me."

"Uh huh. And this thing you need to disappear, is it cold or warm?"

"It's cold, very cold."

"And was there an audience?"

"No. It was all very private."

"Will this little mess of yours be missed?"

"I don't think so. I'm not sure."

There was another long pause.

"You find out for sure and then send me a first-class ticket tooo …?"

"Seattle, Washington."

"Okay, Seattle, Washington, and have ten thousand in twenties and fifties waiting for me."

"Okay. I'm going to rent you a car too, an SUV with tinted windows. What name should I put this under?"

"Vincent Damien."

"Really?"

"Hey, I almost said D'Onofrio."

The phone went silent. Selene cradled her smartphone in her hand for a moment then scrolled through her contacts for the number to the State Penitentiary. She dialed the warden's office and waited.

"Warden Jeffrey's office. How may I direct your call?" said a bubbly voice full of practiced enthusiasm.

"I need to speak to the warden."

"And who may I say is calling?"

"Mrs. Joseph Miles."

40

A large black man with a shaved head limped by Joseph's bed on crutches glaring murderously down at him. Joe recognized the man's feral scent before he placed his face. It was Devon, the guy who'd stabbed him in the prison yard. Joe had left another victim alive. Luckily, he hadn't bitten Devon, and Armondo was dead, but the big transvestite was still alive somewhere as far as Joe knew. If the curse was real there would soon be at least one more serial killer in the world. But there was nothing Joe could do about that now. He couldn't risk another fight when he was so close to getting out of here.

Devon smiled at Joe and the big cannibal killer's blood ran cold. It was a big, leering, carnivorous grin filled with beautiful white teeth that had been shaved to sharp points. Had Joe somehow infected him during their fight?

The blood.

Joe had bled. A lot. Devon stabbed him and Joe's blood must have gotten all over him. If Joe had any remaining doubts about whether what he had was communicable, that display instantly dispelled them. Joe smiled back, and for a moment, he and Devon locked eyes, challenging one another. The message was clear. There was only room for one super-predator in this prison. There could only be one alpha male and Devon was not yet ready to concede the crown. If Joe didn't escape soon, one of them would have to die.

Joe maintained eye contact while Devon limped by, nodding his head to affirm everything Joe had been thinking. Moments later, the big transvestite Joe had fought weeks ago came through. Joe sat up in bed and placed one foot on the floor, ready to attack should Luscious make a move. Luscious saw the motion and took a few steps back. He smiled proudly, displaying the same sharpened teeth. Joe stood up and Luscious scampered away. He would not be a problem. Not for Joe anyway. Not unless he and Devon teamed up, which was certainly a possibility. Devon's attack had been partially in retaliation for what Joe had done to Luscious.

At least, Joe thought, the man wouldn't be able to rape anyone else. But that wasn't assured either. Even the loss of a penis wasn't a sure-fire cure for rape. Most likely, the big rapist would simply switch his method of attack and start assaulting the weaker inmates and the new fish that came to the prison with his teeth instead of with the cock Joe had eaten.

It had now been three weeks since the surgery and Joe felt stronger now. He walked around the hospital in endless loops and had even begun doing crunches, pushups, pull-ups, and dips again in the rehabilitation room. There were some light weights in there as well and Joe had begun using them, doing endless repetitions and supersets with twenty and thirty pounds. The nurses warned him that he was doing too much too soon, but Joe knew his own body. He knew what his breaking point was and he was far from reaching it. He just needed to get his strength back quickly so he could get out of here.

Selene had come to visit him the other day. It was his first conjugal visit and he could smell the blood on her immediately.

"You' have been a busy girl, Selene."

"I love you, Joe. I miss you so much."

She looked amazing. After being locked up for so long with no one to fuck but Cindy, he could barely keep his hands off of her.

"How long do we have?"

233

"Half an hour," Selene replied breathlessly. She was already pulling off her clothes, and the sight of her body instantly awakened the monster. Joe had taken one of the pills the professor brought him a few days ago to keep him from attacking the other patients. Being in that hospital surrounded by the sick and infirm had been wreaking havoc with his predatory instincts. His drive to cull the herd of the weak was almost irresistible.

Selene's breasts were definitely fuller, not as big as Alicia's or even Lana's, but much bigger than Cindy's. That thought reinforced in Joe's mind how complicated his love life had become. He needed Cindy to help get him out of this prison of violence and despair before he killed someone else and got sent back to supermax. He needed Selene to get him to San Francisco once he was out. But he wanted Lana. He wanted her like nothing he'd felt since he'd eaten the last morsels of flesh from Alicia's bones, but she hated him. And deep down, in the part of his soul that still felt sympathy and remorse, the part that knew right from wrong, the moral core of Joseph Miles, he knew that going to see Lana was a bad idea. He'd already brought enough misery into that family's lives.

"What's wrong?" Selene asked.

"Nothing. Why?"

"You're not getting undressed. Don't you want me?"

In reply, Joe grabbed her by the arms and slung her over his shoulders. He walked her across the small trailer the warden had set up for conjugal visits and threw her down on the bed. He watched her squirm out of her panties while he pulled his orange prison shirt over his head and dropped his pants and underwear. The monster bobbed free and he heard Selene gasp when she saw it.

"My God. I thought you'd be well-endowed but I had no idea!"

Joe didn't wait, didn't waste time with foreplay. He fell on top of her and impaled her on his engorged cock with one thrust that took the wind from Selene's lungs.

"Oh God, Joseph! Oh fuck! You're so huge!"

It felt wonderful inside of her. Joe leaned down and sucked her breasts. The nipple she'd cut off was now just a dimpled scar and Joe sucked and licked that as well. The urge to bite off the other nipple, to tear her mammary glands from her chest and devour them completely, was just a dull ache. Joe thrust deeper, harder, driving as far into Selene as he could, trying to pierce her soul. The scent of blood was all over her and it was maddening. She had killed. There was no doubt about it, and the kill had been not long ago. Days? No more than a week ago.

"Bite me, Joseph!" Selene shouted grabbing Joe by the back of the head while cupping her hand beneath her breast to offer up her remaining nipple. The monster roared in response and Joe bared his sharpened teeth. Saliva drooled over his lips onto her chest.

"Go ahead. I want you to. I want you to taste me. I want to watch you cum while you eat my flesh."

"I can't."

Selene nodded vigorously.

"Yes. Yes, you can!"

"There are guards outside, Selene. If I bite you … if you leave here bleeding and they find out I bit off your nipple, they'll put me back in supermax and I'll never get out of here."

Selene immediately went cold. All the passion that had been there moments before was extinguished. Joe felt the change and withdrew his cock from her.

"Then I'm getting you out of here tonight."

"What's the urgency?"

Selene placed her hands on either side of Joe's face and turned his head to look at her.

"Because I want you, Joseph. I don't want you holding back with me. I want all of you."

"But what if I go too far and accidentally kill you?"

Selene smiled and kissed Joe lightly on the lips.

"I trust you. You won't hurt me."

Joe leaned in and inhaled the rich scent of her pheromones. He could still smell the moistness between her thighs, the sweat, and the thick, overpowering scent of blood and cooked meat.

"Who have you been eating, Selene?"

A panicked expression crossed Selene's face. The question had clearly rattled her.

"Uh, um. No one. I mean. It was just some guy I met. He didn't mean anything to me. I promise."

Joe smiled.

"I'm not jealous, Selene. I'm just looking out for you. How was it?"

Selene's bottom lip quivered and her eyes filled with tears.

"It was awful. It was nothing like what you described. I couldn't … I couldn't cum. I was so close, but something just wasn't working."

Joe nodded.

"Your lawyer told me. And I told him it wouldn't work for you because you don't have the curse."

Selene was putting her bra back on when she paused and jerked it down, pushing her breasts up out of the bra. She stood up on the mattress and grabbed Joe by the back of the head again, pushing his face into her cleavage.

"Then bite me! Give me your curse."

Joe pulled away from her, scowling.

"You don't want this, Selene. Trust me."

"I do. We can be a team. We can fuck and kill together. I'll even find us someone we can kill when you get out. There's this bartender. She's just your type. Her breasts are as big as my head and she's got thick hips and thighs. She looks like the librarian from the University. We can fry her up and eat

236

her. You can fuck me while we tear her apart just like you did with Alicia when you ate Frank in the park, remember?"

Her voice sounded desperate. Joe remembered that moment in the park on the trip to Seattle. He'd impaled Frank with a piece of rebar and roasted him alive over a fire, and then he and Alicia made love while he ripped off pieces of Frank's sizzling corpse and ate him piece by piece. He and Alicia had reached orgasm together as they shared Frank's roasted cock. The idea of repeating that with Selene did have its appeal.

"What did you do with the body?"

"Whose body?"

"Whoever you ate. What did you do with it?"

"My dad has friends who take care of this sort of thing. I called one of them and he came and cleaned things up for me. He also rented us a car under one of his aliases. He's very discreet. There won't be a problem."

Joe's eyes narrowed suspiciously. It was obvious Selene wanted Joe's curse more than she wanted him. If he had any doubts about that, today had dispelled those. But did she want it enough to kill him for it? He imagined being held down by some big, burly mafia type while Selene drained his blood and drank it like Damon Trent had drank his blood more than a decade ago.

"Is this friend of your dad still in town?"

"No. I sent him back as soon as he rented the car."

"Okay. Tell me everything that happened."

"Have you ever heard of drunken shrimp?"

Joe shook his head.

"It's absolutely delicious. We'll have to try it together sometime."

41

Joe was led back to his room by a skinny CO with buck teeth, red hair, and a stutter. He looked like Howdy Doody. The guy was clearly nervous and Joe couldn't help feeling bad for him.

"I know what you're thinking. Don't worry, my friend. You're not my type."

Howdy Doody laughed nervously.

"That-that girl … um … is she really your wife?"

Joe cocked an eyebrow.

"Why?"

"She's just … well … um … she's beautiful."

Joe shrugged.

"She's okay."

"Well, here you are. Thanks for … well, uh … you know. Thanks for being so co-operative."

Joe smiled, proudly displaying a mouth full of ivory razors.

"My pleasure."

Joe walked alone into the hospital. Nathan was waiting for him with a handful of envelopes.

"Hey, Joe! I brought your mail."

"Thanks, Nathan," Joe said, taking the envelopes from him. "Oh, and Nathan, I heard you had another body to deliver to the morgue tomorrow morning."

Nathan smiled. "I believe I do. Tomorrow morning?"

"Tomorrow morning. It will be down there waiting for you."

"Uh, um, Joseph?" Nathan whispered, looking nervously around the room as if he thought the walls were bugged.

"Yeah?"

"Should I still get two coffins ready?"

Joe slung an arm around Nathan's shoulders like they were old pals. He pulled him close and whispered in his ear. He could smell the man's pastry-scented soul. The monster stirred and Joe pulled away before it could fully awaken and ruin someone's day.

"Two coffins. I need you, Nathan. Don't let me down."

Nathan nodded vigorously.

"Badass! You can absolutely count on me. This means everything to me. You have no idea."

"Okay. Now get out of here before somebody gets suspicious."

A small tremulous smile crept slowly onto Nathan's face and his eyes moistened. He looked at Joseph almost lovingly. There was an underlying sadness to the expression that confused Joe for a moment. Then he realized what it was. Nathan knew he was going to die. He knew and he didn't care. He was like the many long pigs who would come to the message board long ago, offering themselves to the "chefs" to be consumed, only Nathan didn't want to be consumed by just anyone. He was only interested in one chef, the famous serial killer, the monster of the moment, Joseph Miles.

Joe studied Nathan's expression closely, wondering how the man would taste. His death would have to be something spectacular, something that would live up to the man's fantasies. As if he was reading Joe's mind, Nathan offered a suggestion.

"Have you ever baked someone alive … like in an oven? You know, like Hansel and Gretel?"

"I've never put anyone in an oven if that's what you mean, Nathan. I don't think there's an oven big enough to put a full-sized human in it."

"There are at restaurants and bakeries. There's one here at the penitentiary."

Joe studied Nathan's face.

"Baking someone alive would be a very painful way to go, Nathan. That would be extremely excruciating."

Nathan dropped his head and looked down at the floor. His mouth worked soundlessly, grasping for words that avoided him, then he looked back up at Joseph with a sad expression, holding out his arms, pleading with Joe to understand him. Joe tilted his head like a dog hearing a strange sound, regarding Nathan like some alien species. Eventually, Nathan found the words.

"When I was a kid, my mother used to tell me that story, about Hansel and Gretel, and the gingerbread house, and the witch. I would try to imagine what the witch felt like when they pushed her into the oven and she was cooked alive. It terrified me. I would look at that book with dread whenever she reached for it. I wanted to tell her not to read that story, to pick something else, but I kinda wanted to hear it too. I liked that feeling of being terrified. I liked the goosebumps that would spring up on my skin when she described the witch. I liked the way my mom would hold me and laugh when I would turn away and bury my face in her chest. I liked the way the images stayed with me all night long. I still like that feeling. That's why I like reading about serial killers. The fear. The goosebumps. That's why I liked reading about you, Joseph."

Joe nodded and patted Nathan on the back.

"I understand, Nathan. I understand."

Nathan nodded back and walked off with his eyes still glistening with tears that did not spill. Joe told himself they were tears of joy, but he couldn't be certain. There was a deep well of pain within Nathan that seemed to be bubbling to the surface. Joe hoped the man would stay stable long enough to see this through. Getting the coffins on the truck was the most important part of the entire plan.

The hospital was bustling today. There had been a fight

in the exercise yard and five inmates were wounded. One of them had been nearly gutted. He came in on a gurney, screaming and holding his intestines in with his hands. The smell of his insides jolted the monster awake. Joe turned his attention from the carnage with great effort and instead looked down at the stack of envelopes in his lap. The first thing he noticed was one from Lana. It was long and rambling, handwritten in a shaky cursive script that seemed almost formal.

Dear Mr. Joseph Miles,
    I have been trying hard to find the right words to express my feelings after seeing
    you. I have hated you for so long and now I don't know what the fuck to feel. Confused. Angry. Repulsed. Sad. Grateful. Yes, I was grateful. I wanted closure and seeing you, speaking with you, gave me that. I can't pretend to understand what went on between you and my sister, but it was clear to me that you had genuine feelings for her. It was obvious that you loved her. I don't know if she loved you or not. You clearly believe she did. That was obvious too.
    I have been reading a lot about serial killers lately, trying to understand, and something about you doesn't quite fit. They say serial killers are usually narcissistic, anti-social, incapable of feeling empathy or remorse. I didn't get that impression from you. I saw you cry. I saw the love in your eyes for my sister. You're not the monster I imagined you to

be. You're still a fucking monster. I'm sure about that too. You murdered my only sister. You're a sick, twisted, fucked up individual. You're just more complex than the evil villain I thought you'd be, the villain I thought I needed you to be. You're pretty fucked up though. You're a horrible bastard, but I don't hate you anymore. I've wasted too much damn time on hate. I just pity you now. You're a very sad person, Joseph Miles. I think you eat yourself up as much as you have eaten your victims. That's a fitting punishment I guess. When my mother said I should forgive you, I thought she was crazy. I didn't think there was any way I could ever forgive the man who took Alicia's life so brutally, so horribly. I wanted to find a way to hurt you, not forgive you. I wanted to make you feel what Alicia felt, what we feel. Now, I think my mom was right. I need to let all this anger go. All I know is that my sister's life hadn't been happy for a very long time. She bounced from one abusive relationship to another, messed around with drugs, drank too much. She was ruining her life. It was no surprise that she wound up dead. So don't torture yourself anymore over her. If you think she died happy, I have to believe you, for my own sanity. I think you need to believe it too. I forgive you.

    Sincerely,
    Lana

Joe's hands trembled. He tried to hold back the tears and failed. They came in a downpour of anguish that threatened to wash him away in its tide. The other inmates were watching him. Joe didn't care. They recognized his pain. They had all felt it before, even the crazy ones. It was the torment of realization. That moment of self-recognition when evil realizes itself. For the past few months, Joe had only been concerned with escaping. He had seldom thought seriously about finding a cure. His only thoughts of Alicia had been selfish. He missed her, but he felt no remorse over killing her, betraying her. He was betraying her again now by not seriously seeking out a cure. She had come with him to Seattle because she had believed he could cure the terrible thing growing inside him, but he had now given in to it. He now thought of the disease, the curse, as an indivisible part of him. The monster. It wasn't an alien presence or an alter ego living inside of him. It *was* him. It was who and what he was. Joe had let himself become this loathsome, destructive, violent, evil thing. Alicia would not have recognized him now. She would not have loved him. He hadn't fought the curse hard enough. Joe had let his regret over the loss of Alicia sap him of all hope. He had given in to the horror that lurked inside him, worse, he had come to enjoy it. He had nurtured it with rage and self-pity, allowed it to grow out of control. Every move he'd made the last several weeks had been calculated to get him out of prison and access to more victims. Finding his grandfather had been a peripheral concern at best. Even if he found the man and killed him, his confidence that it would change anything was almost nil.

Joe wiped the tears from his eyes and opened the next letter. It was from the woman who used to run his Sex Addicts Anonymous group. She was still trying to fuck him after all these years. Joe chuckled and tore it to shreds. The next letter was from his cousin Dirk. It was dated a week ago; the day after Joe called his cousin and told him to contact Selene.

Yo, Cuz!

I found out some more information about your real grandfather. Remember when I told you he went to prison for trying to kill his wife? Well, I did a search on the case and turned up a whole bunch of crazy shit. I guess the case was a big deal back in the sixties. It was in all the old detective magazines. They even had pictures of him. He looks just like you. Crazy. I attached a photo. He looks like a 1950s Clark Kent! Anyway, he didn't just try to kill his wife, he cut her tits off! Wild, huh? The detective magazines said he tied her up, cut her tits off, fried them in cornmeal, and ate one and fed the other one to her. She escaped to a neighbor's house and they took her to a hospital. That's how he got caught. She almost bled to death and wound up going crazy and spending the rest of her life in an asylum. He ate her fucking tits! Don't that sound familiar? I think you're on the right track with this one. This dude was sick! You were looking for the guy who started all this, well here he is. I hope you find that old fuck and fuck his shit up good. Take care, Cuz.

See you soon ;)
Dirk

P.S. I found the hotel where Selene is staying in town. I'm going to meet up with her tonight.

Tonight? That would have been a week ago, but Selene hadn't mentioned seeing him. Joe remembered the smell of death wafting from Selene's skin. She smelled like she'd been drenched in blood.

No. She wouldn't.

But Joe knew it was true. He played the scenario over in his head. He could imagine Dirk meeting Selene, her seducing him, bringing him up to her room, drugging him, and then … drunken shrimp. Dirk had been her kill, her drunken shrimp. Joe stared at the letter for a long time, knowing it would be the last one he'd ever see from his cousin. His last link to his family was gone. He was losing everything.

Joe was dangerously insane. He knew that and had known it for many years. He had fought his own madness, had often given into it, but he had always been aware of it. What he was only now becoming aware of was the destructive insanity he had surrounded himself with. Selene, Nathan, even Dirk himself. He attracted perverts, sadists, and psychotics. He lived in the company of lunatics. They wrote letters to him every day. He had let them into his life and now one of them had murdered his cousin. His life had gotten far out of control. It was time to take that control back, to take his life back. He still needed them to get him out of prison, but that was where it had to end. He could not cure himself while surrounded by people who enabled and encouraged his illness. He had learned that years ago in Sex Addicts Anonymous. Staying with Selene was a recipe for relapse. More than that, he needed to avenge his cousin's murder. Dirk had not deserved this. He had been a good and loyal friend to Joe and it had cost him his life. Someone had to pay for that.

Joe began composing a note for Professor Locke. The man had believed in him and Joe felt he owed him an explanation before he disappeared. He had just begun putting pen to paper when Joe spotted a familiar face staring at him from across the room. He sighed and rolled his eyes as he recognized Officer Belton's characteristic scowl. Belton locked eyes with Joe in what was clearly a challenge, more of his chest-beating, macho bullshit. Belton still could not stand the idea that there was one inmate in the penitentiary he couldn't humble. The big, angry corrections officer lifted his chin and smirked. It looked more like a sneer. If Belton was stationed anywhere near the infirmary this evening, it was going to be a problem. Joe had no intention of letting the man get in the way of his freedom.

The day crept by like all days in the penitentiary, one sluggish second loping lazily after another in a painful, crushing monotony. Joe went for several naps between walks. He had one last trip to the physical therapist.

"I think you're ready to get out of here. Your stitches have healed and you seem to have your strength back. We need that bed for the sick patients," said Mrs. Apley, a portly, black corrections nurse who also served as the hospital's only physical therapist.

"The only reason they let you stay here this long is to make certain you didn't just wind up right back in here. The warden wanted to make sure you healed enough to be able to protect yourself. It was either the infirmary or solitary or back to supermax."

"Then I'm glad he chose the infirmary," Joe said trying a smile that failed miserably. Joe still had a hard time with normal human interactions. His only comfortable, natural relationship with humanity was one of predator and prey. Relating to humans as peers had always been a problem.

"I hear he had help making the decision. Rumor is there's someone giving him some monetary inspiration where you're concerned."

She studied Joe's face, obviously waiting for a comment or facial expression to confirm or refute the rumor. Neither was forthcoming. Joe merely stared back at her, returning her inquisitive stare with one full of threat. She turned away.

"Anyway, I'm putting in your release papers. Tomorrow you go back to your cell."

"Home sweet home," Joe replied with a smile. He'd begun filing his teeth again. They were as sharp as ever, like a mouth full of tiny, white arrowheads. Nurse Apley turned away with a shiver.

"Thanks for everything, Nurse Apley. I guess I'd better go get ready to leave."

"Goodbye, Joseph. I hope I don't see you back here any time soon."

"You won't. I promise you that."

Joe smiled again. The expression had never fit comfortably on his face, not since he was a child, before he'd been assaulted, before he became a monster. Now, with his teeth filed to sharp points, his smile was absolutely terrifying. He remembered how threatening it had looked on Devon and even on Luscious and felt sorry for the nurse, but there was no way to make it look any less monstrous. He shut the smile down and turned away.

"Goodbye," he said as he wandered back to his bed.

Fausto was there when he returned.

"Hey, hermano! You look good! You heal pretty quick, huh, right?"

"I guess so."

"Listen, homes, there's rumors going around that Devon and Luscious are going to fuck your shit up when you get back to genpop. You want me to say something to the warden for you? See if they can get you moved to another cell block?"

Joe shook his head.

"I'll be okay, Fausto. Thanks for the warning."

Fausto nodded.

"Okay. I know you's a bad motherfucker and all, but you sure you don't need help?"

Joe patted the big Mexican on the shoulder. Fausto flinched. Inmates didn't touch each other much unless they were gay. Joe pulled his hand quickly away, seeing how uncomfortable it made his cellmate.

"You know what's funny? Until I saw what you did to Devon, I was planning on raping your ass one night. I know you're tough and shit, right? I mean, you fucked up Luscious and Armondo, right? Yeah, I knew about Armondo and I know you were trying not to say nothing, but my homies, they wanted you fucked up for that shit, right? And they wanted me to do it. They wanted me to rape you and then cut your loco ass up. You know, right? But after seeing you handle yourself, I knew you would have killed my ass if I tried some shit. Besides, you're a pretty cool dude and Armondo was an asshole. It was only a matter of time before he fucked with the wrong dude. Plus, I know the screws made you fight him. It wasn't like you just picked him out of a crowd and decided to rip his face off, you know, right? You ain't have no choice. Anyway, I told the homies to just let it ride, so you don't have to worry about no beef from us."

Joe nodded.

"Thanks, Fausto."

"You take care, hermano. Stay safe and I'll see you back in the cell."

Fausto held up a bottle of pain killers so Joe could read the label. It was a bottle of percocets with Joe's name on it. Fausto placed them in his pocket.

"I swiped them from one of the nurses. Last week. I figured you were tough enough you didn't need 'em anyway, huh, right?"

"That's fine. You take 'em. Consider it payment for Armondo."

Fausto smiled and nodded enthusiastically then and stuck out his fist.

"Huh, right?"

Joe bumped fists with him.

"Right."

"One more thing, hermano. You're gonna need something besides those teeth to protect yourself with. Here—"

He handed Joe a little toothbrush with a razor blade embedded in it. The bristles had been melted and the blade was stuck in the wax, then glued down with something, and wrapped in duct tape.

"It works, homes. You'll see. You might need it."

"Thanks again, Fausto."

"No problem, hermano. I mean, I was planning on raping you. I guess this is the least I could do, huh, right?"

Joe smiled.

"Right."

"Those teeth of yours are fucking crazy! You're fucking loco for real, huh, right? You take care of yourself and I'll see you back in the cell."

Fausto left and Joe sat silently on his bed. He thought about his mother for the first time since her last visit. He wondered if he should try to see her again when he got out, but knew the Federal Marshals would have her place staked out for sure, expecting him to try to make contact. In all likelihood, her last visit was the last time he'd ever see her. Joe sighed deeply and tears welled up unexpectedly in his eyes.

His life had changed so much in the last few years. He'd fought so hard to maintain some semblance of normalcy when he first felt the psychotic urges overwhelming him. He'd done everything he was supposed to do. He went to counseling. He tried to lose himself in his art. He even spoke to his professor about it before taking the matter into his own hands and seeking out his own cure. Now, his entire life had changed. Before he'd been afraid he would grow fangs and fur and turn into some sort of werewolf or vampire. Ultimately, he had fashioned his own fangs and become something as bad or worse than the mythical creatures whose legends he'd looked to for a solution to his problem. His life had now changed in ways he would have never been able to imagine. The idea that it might all be over soon was exhilarating. He only wished Alicia was still around to share it with him. He missed her so badly it was like physical pain. Again, his thoughts drifted to Alicia's sister, Lana. She was so different from Alicia in so many ways, but so similar as well. If he could make her love him, his life would be complete. But he knew that was impossible. And what about Selene and his grandfather? They both had to be handled before he could even think about loving anyone or being loved. Even after he escaped, Joe knew the myriad obstacles in his life would be far from over.

Joe sighed deeply, overwhelmed by the magnitude of his problems. Nothing was ever simple, but Joe was resolved to getting his life back. Anything or anyone that stood in the way of that was in for a very short life. When Joe looked up and casually scanned the room, noting his fellow patients, the stern nurses who seemed to double as corrections officers themselves, two of the less than half-dozen full-time doctors the prison employed, Fausto busily mopping up some mess caused by one of the other patients while glowering at the patient murderously, Nathan helping transfer a coughing older inmate who looked to be in his seventies or eighties from a gurney to one of the beds, he spotted officer Belton standing outside the infirmary again, peering in at him and scowling. Belton was definitely going to be a problem. And Joe couldn't allow any problems. Not when he was so close to regaining his life.

PART FIVE

Ikizukuri

One small adult
One large lemon
Soy sauce to taste
Two bottles of saki

When eating raw long pig, just as in sushi, freshness is critical. Refrigeration hardens and dries the meat. The fresher it is when served, the juicier, more succulent, and softer the meat will be. Ikizukuri literally means "prepared alive." There is no fresher meat than one that is still twitching, moaning, and screaming.

To begin, prepare the meat by getting the long pig to imbibe both bottles of saki. This is preferable to drugging the victim as certain narcotics can interfere with the taste of the meat and the saki will add flavor. Restraints will still be necessary.

Surgically slice off the flesh of adult long pig, avoiding all the vital organs and major arteries to keep the long pig alive. Cut the flesh into paper-thin sheets. Drizzle with lemon and soy sauce. Reassemble it in the long pig's body and serve with wasabi and soy sauce.

42

Cindy came for him exactly at midnight. There were other inmates still awake. He could hear them mumbling, whispering, and moaning in pain in the dark all around him. They all knew better than to say shit about his visitor. Ratting out a CO was a good way to get yourself killed. Ratting out the most dangerous inmate in the penitentiary and a CO was a guarantee of certain death. Cindy held up a finger, a needless reminder for Joe to be silent as he slipped from beneath the cover into his prison slippers.

There were no nurses on the floor when Joe and Cindy crept out of the infirmary and down the hall. Joe's excitement was at a fever pitch. They turned down another hall and started toward the stairs leading down to the prison morgue. That's when Joe heard the first footsteps and smelled the familiar testosterone musk of his old friend, Officer Belton. He was following them.

There were cameras in every hall and room except the morgue. Evidently, Belton was looking for something more than just proof of Joe's romantic involvement with Cindy. He wanted to catch them red-handed and make some sort of scene. Joe was having a hard time figuring out the man's angle. The number of people Joe was going to have to kill before he could be free of this place was continuing to grow. Unlike what he had to do to Cindy, killing Belton was something Joe knew he would never regret.

Joe's predatory instincts were now fully engaged. The monster was awake and in a fury. It hated being pursued. It wanted to taste blood. Joe took note of the security cameras he passed, looking for a blind-spot where he could end the pursuit. They passed a room meant for temporary solitary confinement and the door was ajar. Joe paused and peeked inside. There were no cameras.

"You want to go in there?" Cindy asked.

"No. I was just curious. Let's go down to the morgue. Do you mind if I stop to take a piss? I'll catch up to you."

Cindy stood her ground.

"I'd better stay with you in case somebody finds you."

"I'll tell them I came down here on my own. It's better than them finding us together. That would be harder to explain."

Cindy thought about it and nodded.

"Okay. Be quick though."

"I will. I'll see you down in the morgue. I know the way."

Joe watched Cindy enter the stairwell and listened for her footsteps fading away down the stairs and the door at the bottom opening and shutting before turning to focus his attention on the stealthy footsteps advancing from the opposite direction. He slipped into the isolation cell and waited, peering through the crack in the door. It wasn't long before he saw the bald head and wide shoulders of Officer Belton slip past the cell door. His radio was turned down low, but Joe could still hear it squawk. Belton whispered a curse then turned the radio volume down even lower. Joe flung the door open and dragged Belton inside before he could so much as scream. Belton was built like a football player, heavy and muscular, but he was still no match for the enormous super-predator. Joe's body was built for killing. His arms were thick as pythons and his body was like a suit of armor—hard, unyielding, and nearly impervious. Belton fought his way free, twisting and throwing punches and elbows, but not before Joe stripped him of his radio and pepper spray. He turned off the radio and dropped it to the floor. Now, the only sound in the room was their combined heavy breathing.

Joe could almost hear the man's heartbeat like a powerful pneumatic piston pounding in his chest. His heart sounded like it was about to come right through his ribcage. Belton's eyes widened, taking in the six-foot-six, two hundred and sixty-pound cannibal with muscles that seemed to have been chiseled out of iron, as if seeing him for the first time. Joe could see the exact moment when Belton realized he was about to die. He heard him swallow hard and struggle to catch his breath. He was almost hyperventilating.

"Come on, mutherfucker! I ain't afraid of your crazy ass!" Belton yelled, raising his fists in a boxer's stance. Joe lifted his knee to his chest and brought the heel of his foot up into Belton's chin, putting his back and hips behind the kick like he was breaking down a door. Teeth cracked and spilled from Belton's lips. He held his bleeding mouth and staggered backwards. Joe dropped down onto one knee and grabbed the officer's groin, hooking his fingers into claws and seizing Belton's cock and balls in one massive hand, just as he'd been practicing for months. He twisted and jerked and felt something give and tear. Blood and urine poured into Joe's hand and trickled down his arm. It stank of ammonia and raw meat.

Belton screamed and collapsed, writhing on the floor in agony and holding his bleeding genitals.

"AAAAAAAAAaaaaaah! Aaaaaaah! FUUUUUUCK! YOU RIPPED OFF MY FUCKING BALLS!"

Joe dove on top of him, mounting the big CO and straddling his chest. He began pummeling Belton with elbows, dislodging more teeth, shattering and pulverizing the man's nose, smashing his cheekbone and orbital eye socket, reducing his face to a bleeding ruin. Joe was in an ecstasy of raw carnage, delighting in the violence, feeling all his pent-up frustrations flow down his arms, lending more ferocity to every blow.

He could hear the officer moaning and gurgling through

a mouthful of blood as Joe continued hammering him with elbows, twisting his waist and shoulders into every blow, determined to crush Belton's skull and end this before Cindy came back upstairs looking for him. He felt Belton's skull crack like a pumpkin and spill blood and brain matter. The next elbow met less resistance, and the next sank into something squishy. Finally, Joe leaned down and tore a huge avulsion in the officer's hamstring, jerking his head back and forth as he lacerated Belton's tendons and tissue like some voracious beast, no longer thinking, all instinct and appetite. Blood sprayed from Belton's femoral artery, painting the walls red, emptying the officer's body of vital fluids with each pump of his heart.

The blood lust was now a frenzy. Joe bit deep into Belton's throat, ripping out large chunks of his esophagus and spitting them on the floor. He chewed through to the man's vertebrae and crunched down on that as well, thrashing his head from side to side, snapping Belton's spine and nearly decapitating him.

He didn't eat any of the meat this time. This kill wasn't for enjoyment, but necessity. He'd have had plenty of time to enjoy himself with Cindy before the mortuary van came in the morning to take his coffin away.

Joe walked away, leaving Belton's head a misshapen pulp bleeding out on the floor and his head connected to his body by a few stubborn tendons. After months of abuse from the man, killing him had been anticlimactic. He wished he'd had time to get creative and savor the man's death. Luckily, there would be many others in the next twenty-four hours. Of that, he was certain.

Joe wiped Belton's blood from his face and hands with his shirt, then tossed the shirt aside, and dashed down the stairs. Cindy was just opening the door and stepping out into the stairwell with a concerned expression scarring her painfully cute face when Joe ran down into her arms.

"Is everything all right?" she asked.

"Everything's perfect except ... well ... you're still wearing your clothes."

"We can fix that," Cindy replied with a smile.

Cindy pulled her shirt tails from her pants and began unbuttoning it. Joe leaned in and kissed her, moving Cindy out of the stairwell and into the room where the prison kept its most successful escapees, the ones who would never return to their cells, the ones that were finally free. He pulled her Sam Browne belt from its loops and tossed it, along with her radio, handcuffs, and pepper spray, onto a stainless steel gurney, one of the few unoccupied ones in the room. Joe was struck by how much the morgue resembled the infirmary above it, except that the bodies filling the tables in this room were no longer moaning, fidgeting, and complaining. There was also the ominous bank of steel cabinets that lined the walls, where the bodies were stored post-autopsy.

Already entwined like two mating serpents coiled around one another, Joe and Cindy fell atop one of the few empty tables, kissing and hurriedly undressing. Cindy's lips kissed their way down the gigantic killer's sinuous neck to his massive chest, his chiseled abdominal muscles, the trail of hair that led to his groin, and down to the root of his manhood, where the monster lived ... and it was happy to see her. Joe could hear the blood rushing in his ears. He could hear his own heartbeat, smell Cindy's musky pheromones, and he could still taste Belton's blood and flesh on his tongue. He wanted more. His lust for the flesh was voracious and Belton's death had only increased his appetite.

Right up until he'd murdered Belton, he had been considering letting Cindy live. She might have been able to cover his tracks if he could convince her that escaping was the only way he would be safe and they could finally be truly together. But now it was too risky. He had murdered a CO and the manner of Belton's death and all the DNA Joe left behind on the carcass would leave no doubt who the killer was. Cindy would be questioned and she'd spill everything. He reached down and removed the shank Fausto made for him from his pants pocket before stepping out of them and kicking them aside.

"I love you, Joe."

He felt bad lying to her. Cindy really was a nice woman, but telling the truth was inefficient. The truth would not set him free.

"I love you too, Cindy," Joe said as her tongue trailed along the underside of his cock. All the affection he felt for her was summarized in his craving for her flesh. He'd kept it in check for weeks to avoid freaking her out, but now the monster wanted to feed and there was no reason Joe could find to deny it sustenance. His stomach growled and his erection swelled. A pearl drop of pre-cum dribbled from the head of his massive cock and Cindy lapped it up. She eased all eight inches down her throat, sending tingles of pleasure through Joe's tumescent sex organ.

Joe seized the back of her head and began slowly fucking Cindy's throat. He felt the head of his cock slide past her tonsils. She gagged once and pulled away slightly, then swallowed and coughed several times, blinking tears from her eyes, before taking his erection in her mouth again and slowly easing it back down her throat, grabbing Joe's muscular buttocks as she forced him to thrust deeper. She had gotten so good at sucking cock Joe could already feel himself missing her, but there were other things he wanted far more than a good blowjob. Just as he neared orgasm, he withdrew his cock from her mouth and stroked himself as she stuck out her tongue to take his seed like a sacrament. Her lovely, cherubic face with the pudgy cheeks, dimples, and puppy dog eyes, stared up at him as he came with a roar that emptied his soul. He ejaculated onto her tongue, lips, cheeks, chin. She smiled appreciatively and licked his seed from her lips. It was such a beautiful sight, he felt a tug at his heart. It was easy to imagine himself falling for a woman like Cindy. But that would have to wait for another life— one without monsters.

Lifting her up from the floor and onto his shoulders so that her legs hung down his back and her sex was pressed firmly against his face, Joe began licking her labia and clitoris gently at first, then more aggressively as the taste of her transported him out of himself. He became a part of her where his lips joined her sex, feeling her kegel muscles contract around his tongue as he thrust it deep inside her and licked her vaginal walls. She grabbed the back of Joe's head and ground her clitoris against his mouth, moaning and thrusting, fucking his face the way he had so often fucked hers.

"Oh God, Joe! That feels amazing! Oh my God! Keep going! I'm going to cum!"

Joe flicked his tongue across her engorged clitoris faster than a hummingbird's wings, feeling it throb and pulse as he sucked it and swirled his tongue around it. Her orgasm, when it finally came in a screaming, hissing, scratching fit was like an avalanche. Wet warmth spilled into his mouth. Her body bucked and convulsed and Joe's muscles strained to hold her in place on his shoulders. Her juices cascaded down over his tongue as he continued licking and sucking the tiny nub of sensitive nerve endings. She tasted marvelous. Like blood and honey. It was the taste of blood that brought the monster forth.

He bit deep, tearing into her delicate flower with a savagery born of years of abstinence. He'd been imprisoned for five years, and all his fantasies had been about the moment he would once again consume a woman's flesh. Man flesh was tough and chewy, but the taste of woman was heaven, an extravagant confection that melted on his tongue like warm pastry.

"AAAAAaaaeeeeiiiiii! Aaaah! AAAAaaaaaahh! NO! OH GOD, JOE! STOP! NOOOoooooo!" Cindy screamed.

From the first bite, a wave of ecstasy rushed through Joe's loins followed by an explosive orgasm. His swollen cock spat its seed into the air as he bit large avulsions in Cindy's succulent loins, rending her sex with his saw-like teeth. He almost dropped her, overcome by the most profound rapture he'd felt in half a decade.

Cindy punched at Joe's head and screamed again and again. If he didn't silence her, Joe worried, someone might come to investigate the commotion. He pulled her from his shoulders and she fought him harder, scratching and biting. Joe palmed her entire face in his massive hand, tilted her head back, and slashed her throat with Fausto's shank.

Blood spurted from her severed arteries and rained down her chest, streaking her tiny, milk-white breasts red. She continued to scream, louder, shriller now. Joe cut deeper, sawing through her esophagus, through her larynx, choking off her screams. He leaned down and drank the gouts of warm blood as it spurted from her severed arteries, intoxicated by the taste of her life flowing forth in a river of red down his gullet. He laid Cindy down on the table and continued to lap at the fountain of blood pouring from the ear-to-ear gash in Cindy's throat.

Joe leaned down and tore off her tiny breasts with his serrated teeth, chewing and swallowing the fatty meat in a frenzy, exposing her ribcage as he cannibalized her diminutive mammary glands. Cindy was still fighting, punching and scratching at him even as her strength dwindled. Joe was impressed, but the curse pumping through his veins demanded more. He could see her heart beating behind her ribcage and he wanted to consume it as well, to rip it still beating from her chest. The monster was ravenous tonight.

He climbed up onto Cindy's chest and looked down at her. Her eyes rolled in her skull, unable to focus. She made gargling sounds deep in her brutally savaged esophagus, as blood gurgled from the wound and she drowned in her own blood. Joe brought the shank to her throat again and cut completely around to the back of her neck then began peeling the skin off her throat like he was removing a ski mask. He jerked the skin free of the bubbly, popcorn-colored fat and striated muscle tissue beneath it and peeled it over her chin and up over her cheek bones. Her head was now a mere living skull wrapped in an intricate lattice of glistening facial muscles. She began to convulse, thrashing on the steel table.

Her body was in shock and was shutting down. Joe rolled her over onto her stomach, and stared down at her magnificent ass. He had to have it one last time. He took himself in hand, lubricating his erection with Cindy's blood before easing it into Cindy's puckered anus. He fucked her hard, beyond all mercy or compassion, no longer even thinking of her as Cindy, no longer even regarding her as human, just flesh to be fucked and consumed to assuage his ravenous hunger.

It was so different than it had been with Alicia. With Alicia, he'd felt his love for her, her love for him, with each bite he'd consumed. With Cindy, all he felt was her fear and pain and his own psychotic, gluttonous rapture. He tugged on the skin covering Cindy's skull, peeling off her face with a wet, sticky, ripping sound that he found oddly erotic. His rhythm increased, pounding deep into the dying woman's rectum, watching her marvelous ass bounce and jiggle. He came again with a roar that shook the room, emptying his testicles into Cindy's salacious ass as he pulled her entire face off, wrenching it up over her forehead and then cutting around her skull to leave her scalp still attached to her head. He climbed off of her, leaving Officer Cindy Addison's body twitching on the table as her life escaped her. He leaned over and placed a loving kiss on her beautiful buttocks then bit into it and tore off a large piece, quickly swallowing the chunk of muscles and adipose tissue like he was slurping down a raw oyster.

Joe stared at Cindy's disembodied face. It did not look as pretty detached from her head. He rolled it up and began eating the supple flesh like a burrito. He stared down at Cindy's silent corpse, still leaking a dribble of blood and semen from her plundered rectum. Joe felt wretched as he began stroking his stiffening cock while taking small bites from Cindy's facial tissue, chewing slowly, savoring the soft, delicate taste and texture. It reminded him of barbacoa, the most tender meat he'd ever tasted.

He rolled her over and used the shank to cut open her stomach. Cindy's entrails spilled out of her, ropes of steaming purple intestines like a nest of eels. Joe reached inside and tore out her liver. He crammed it into his mouth, barely chewing as he gobbled it down along with the rest of her face.

"Good bye, Cindy, and thanks," Joe said as he took the last bites of the face he'd kissed and caressed for more than a month, the face he'd professed his love to, the one he'd lied to. A tear rolled from one eye. He wiped it away and it was quickly replaced by another.

"I'm so sorry, Cindy."

He dropped to his knees and vomited again and again. It felt like it would never stop.

43

There was little left of Cindy when Nathan arrived the next morning.

"Jesus Christ, Joseph! What did you do?"

The room was an abattoir. Blood covered the floor in a tacky, red pool, the aftermath of the rapacious murderer's psychotic passion. Cindy's dilacerated corpse lay across a stainless steel dissection table in pieces. The gigantic cannibal sat on the floor naked and covered in blood and gore from head to toe. The room reeked of vomit and fetid blood and organs.

"I—I couldn't stop myself. I was hungry," he replied, wiping dried blood from his lips as he climbed from the floor, his belly distended, looking like a blood-gorged tick.

"Shit." Nathan said in awe, surveying the carnage with a smile. He appeared more impressed than horrified. He looked at Joe and nodded, still smiling. His expression looked almost honored.

"We need to clean it up."

Nathan held out his hands, turning in a small circle and looking at the chunks of meat and pools of blood scattered around the table.

"Where do we start?"

"Help me lift the body."

Together, they found an empty drawer for Cindy's body and began mopping the blood from the floor and dumping piles of masticated meat into trash bags. An hour later, the room looked reasonably clean.

"I can't believe you tore her apart like that. It must have been fucking cool! I wish I could have been here to see it,"

Nathan said, smiling enthusiastically.

Joe stopped and turned to face Nathan, pinning him down with eyes as cold and unfeeling as a shark. He took a step forward and Nathan took two steps back, bumping against the table where Cindy's dismantled corpse had lain for most of the night. Nathan's bottom lip trembled and his eyes began to water.

"I-I just meant, you know, that you must have had a good time with her."

Joe shook his head.

"You want to know what I did to her? I tore off her face while she was alive and I ate it. I ripped out her liver and ate that too. I did it because I can't control myself. It wasn't cool. It was fucking terrible. And, if you had been here, you'd probably be dead right now too."

For a moment, Joe considered murdering the man right there. The monster liked that idea. It was always hungry, never sated. But Joe was not in the mood for any more bloodshed. He would probably have to kill more people when they got where they were going, the truck drivers at the very least. But now he was tired. He was looking forward to resting in the coffin for a few hours. He wished it was more than just a pine box. A satin-lined casket sounded like the most comfortable thing in the world right now. The monster stiffened. Nathan's eyes dropped to the thick, blood-encrusted organ and he let out a whimper. Joe closed his eyes and took a deep breath, exhaling to the count of ten, putting the monster back to sleep. When he opened his eyes, he had regained control.

"What do we need to do now?" Joe asked.

Nathan exhaled, closed his eyes, and swallowed hard. He wiped a sheen of sweat from his forehead.

"Th-the truck will be here soon. We-we need to grab the coffins and put them on the loading dock. I usually help the guys from the mortuary load the truck. They'll be pissed when they see they have to load them by themselves, but it wouldn't be the first time."

The "coffins" were simple, unadorned pine boxes. There was a room full of them piled nearly to the ceiling.

"I make the coffins too," Nathan said with obvious pride.

Joe grabbed one and carried it with ease out of the room and onto the adjacent loading dock. When he returned, Nathan was wrestling one of the large crates out the door with obvious effort. He was already perspiring heavily as he dragged the box through the doorway.

"Need some help?" Joe asked.

"Uh, yeah. If you don't mind," Nathan answered.

Joe reached down, picked up the box, and slung it up onto his shoulder.

"Wow. You are strong, huh? During your trial, the court reporters kept talking about your muscular physique and how you looked like Christopher Reeve on steroids."

"I never used steroids."

Nathan held his hands palms out and did a sort of deferential bow.

"Oh, oh I know. I'm just telling you what they said. They kept bringing up the screen name you used on that cannibal website, 'Superpredator', and speculating on whether it had something to do with you looking like Superman."

Joe lifted the coffin from his shoulder and placed it down beside its twin. When he looked up, Nathan was looking at him expectantly.

"Well, did it?"

"Did what?"

"Your screen name. Did it have something to do with the whole Superman thing or what?"

"I chose that screen name before I came up with the theory that I was affected by a disease. At the time I had a different theory."

"What was your theory?" Nathan asked, eyes wide with enthusiasm.

"I believed that serial killers were the next stage in human evolution, an evolutionary mutation. It was my idea that serial killers had evolved to curb the exponential growth of humanity, to cull the herd."

"That's pretty cool. I like that idea."

Joe's face was solemn.

"I don't. If it's true then there's no hope for me to change."

Nathan raised an eyebrow and screwed his mouth into an awkward sneer.

"Change? Why would you want to change? You're fucking awesome, man!"

Joe snorted and shook his head.

"Let's get in the coffins before the guys from the mortuary show up."

"You get in first and I'll nail it shut."

There was a moment of hesitation and fear at the prospect of Nathan nailing him into a coffin bound for the crematorium. Joe studied Nathan's eyes for any telltale sign of his intentions. What he saw was the same honest, somewhat fanatical reverence that had always been there. He knew the man was crazy. He even suspected he had killed a few times trying to emulate his murderous heroes, but was he a threat to Joe himself? He couldn't see it. Joe grabbed Nathan's arm and glared at him.

"Okay, Nathan, but if you drive one extra nail in the lid of this coffin, if I think for a moment that you're trying to fuck me, I'll make you hurt in ways you could never imagine."

"Whoa, man. It's cool. I wouldn't try to fuck you. I promise."

Joe was still staring hard into Nathan's eyes. He could see the man quiver under his gaze. Nathan was terrified and that was good. Joe could trust fear. It was honest and real.

"Okay. One nail in each corner and one on each side. You put in anymore and I smash this box to kindling and tear you apart."

"I promise, man. I'm cool. I'm on your side."

Joe nodded.

"Okay. Now, how do we nail your coffin shut?"

Nathan held up a staple gun.

"We don't. I'm going to staple myself in from the inside."

"Clever. Let's do it."

With his face, teeth, and clothes still stained with the blood of his ex-lover, Joe lay back in his coffin and watched as Nathan put the lid on and began pounding in the nails. Almost free.

44

Joe heard a loud clang and a prolonged squeaking as chains and pulleys slowly raised the loading dock door. Moments later he heard two voices cursing and complaining as his coffin was lifted, carried, and then slid. Soon he was being bounced and jostled as the truck drove away from the prison. When Joe heard the sound of highway traffic and felt the vehicle pick up speed, there was a moment of elation. He inhaled deeply, smelling exhaust fumes and the moist, morning air. It smelled like freedom.

Time stretched and warped around the casket. Joe could feel his own breath steaming off the coffin lid back into his face, adding to the claustrophobic feeling of entombment. Every minute felt like an hour. When the truck finally came to rest, Joe wasted no time extricating himself from the pine casket. He pushed against the lid. His powerful triceps slowly forced the nails free. After tossing the lid aside, Joe hurried out of his casket and found the one containing Nathan. He could hear Nathan struggling inside his wooden coffin, trying to free himself. Joe considered for a moment leaving the man to be either discovered by the mortuary assistants and returned to the prison or to remain undiscovered and be immolated in the crematorium. Being roasted alive was his fantasy, after all. There would be some poetic justice in that.

The doors of the truck opened and slammed shut. Footsteps walked along the edge of the truck, crunching gravel as they made their way to the door of the vehicle. It was now or never. Joe reached down and wrenched the lid off Nathan's coffin then lifted him to his feet just as the truck's rear door raised and the harsh morning sun cut through the darkness of the truck, blinding them both temporarily.

"Hello, lover," said a familiar voice. Selene's voice.

"Holy fuck," said a strange voice, a man's voice—deep, harsh, scratchy, like he'd been smoking cigarettes for decades. "He's covered in blood!"

There was a man standing beside Selene holding a gun. He was an older Italian man, with curly, salt-and-pepper hair slicked back into a ponytail that hung down between his shoulder blades. His eyes were small, almost beady, with a web of hard lines radiating from the corners. His mouth was a stern line slit into a face that looked as hard as tanned leather. He looked like an iconic Hollywood Mafioso, the silver screen's image of a mafia capo. Joe could only assume he was the same man Selene had used to dispose of Dirk's body.

Selene was wearing tight shorts that showed off her thick thighs and hips and a tight baby-t-shirt that made her breasts look enormous. Joe felt the monster stir. She looked delicious.

"There's two of 'em," the Mafioso said.

"Who's your friend, Joseph?"

Joe stepped forward, shielding his eyes from the light.

"Where are we?"

"We're on the I-5 South almost to Tacoma, Washington. Well, we're not on the I-5 now, obviously. We're in a fucking parking lot holding our dicks," said the old guy with the ponytail and shrew-like eyes. Joe towered above the man. Still caked in Cindy's blood, Joe looked like a zombie or a Halloween ghoul fresh from the grave.

"Who are you and why are you carrying a gun?" Joe asked.

"Yeah, what the fuck's up with that?" Nathan added from behind him, peering over Joe's shoulder.

Selene reached out and placed her hand on the weapon in the Mafioso's hand, lowering it so it was facing the floor.

"This is Mario. He's a friend of my father's. He's here to help us."

Joe hopped out of the truck and looked around. The only building nearby was a furniture warehouse with a "going out of business sale" sign on it that looked abandoned. The parking lot was empty except for a handful of scattered automobiles. The vehicles were all empty. The only activity was at a fast food restaurant across the street. Joe held out his hand.

"Pleased to meet you, Mario."

Mario put the gun back in its holster and accepted Joe's hand. Joe grasped Mario's hand and abruptly jerked him forward. He seized the Mafioso's ponytail and snatched his head back, exposing the man's throat which Joe promptly ripped out with his sharpened teeth, leaving a yawning, ragged hole where the man's trachea had once been. Mario dropped to his knees, blood pouring from his lacerated throat like a fountain, making wheezing and bubbling noises as he gasped for breath and groped for his gun.

Joe seized the dying leg-breaker by the wrist and jerked his hand away from his holster. He brought Mario's arm to his mouth and bit into his forearm, tearing his brachioradialis from the bone with a quick jerk of his head that sent blood spraying across the parking lot, spattering Selene's face like dark red freckles. She wiped the blood away, in disgust. Joe chewed the dripping red muscle and sinew, shuddering, eyes closed as if in the midst of some deep, all-consuming rapture. His head jerked back and the veins and cords in his neck bulged as waves of ecstasy buffeted his nervous system. Joe struggled to maintain control of himself, to resist the urge to feed, to tear the man apart and consume his organs, wash in his blood. There wasn't time for that. They needed to get on the road.

Mario punched at him with his other hand, eyes glazed in horror. Joe released the man's half-eaten limb and let it fall limply at his side. The huge, six-foot-six, two hundred and sixty pound serial killer snarled like a wolf, baring his gore-streaked teeth as he seized Mario's other arm in mid-strike. He shoved Mario's hand into his mouth and bit down hard, crunching through the tiny bones and severing two fingers. Another voluptuous wave of pleasure rippled through Joe's body. He closed his eyes and moaned softly. It sounded like the purr of a large jungle cat. When he opened his eyes, both Nathan and Selene were staring at him wearing expressions of shock and fear.

Mario fell over on his side, twitching and bleeding like a slaughtered calf. Joe reached down and pulled the gun from the dead man's shoulder holster and tossed it into the back of the truck. He lifted Mario onto his shoulders then and tossed him up into the truck as well, into the casket Joe had occupied scant minutes before. Joe climbed up into the truck.

He put the lid on the casket then and held out his hand toward Nathan, who handed him the staple gun. Joe stapled the lid shut before jumping down from the truck and lowering the door.

"What? Why did you just do that? Why'd you kill him like that?" Selene asked, wide-eyed with shock.

"I didn't trust him. Is that a problem?"

Selene's face softened slowly.

"No, Daddy. It's not a problem. He kinda scared me anyway. He reminded me too much of my father."

"Good. Did you get the SUV?"

She pointed over her shoulder at a large, black Lincoln Navigator parked nearby.

"Your chariot awaits."

Joe wiped the blood from his lips with the back of his hand. His body quivered, tingling all over with sexual excitement.

"Let's go," he said. His voice was a low, rumbling growl that barely sounded human. This was his third kill in fewer than twelve hours. The monster was enraptured, glutted on meat and blood.

Selene led them to the vehicle.

"Is he coming with us?" she asked, gesturing toward Nathan while she climbed behind the wheel of the big SUV and slid her key into the ignition.

Joe looked over at Nathan and cocked his head to the side, silently appraising the man, deciding his fate. Nathan pushed his glasses up on his nose and swallowed hard. His eyes were wide. His mouth worked soundlessly, forming some silent plea. Joe nodded without saying a word and climbed into the vehicle. Nathan joined him on the backseat.

They drove out of the parking lot and back onto the freeway headed toward San Francisco. They had driven less than a mile when Joe heard muffled screams coming from the back of the SUV.

"Um ... there's somebody tied up back here."

Joe looked at Selene and narrowed his eyes.

"It's a present. For you."

"Pull over," he pointed to a small dirt road just off the freeway that led to a large thicket of shrubs and trees. "There. Pull over there."

"We don't have time. We need to get out of the state."

"Pull over now, Selene. Now!"

She piloted the vehicle off the freeway and over to the copse of thick vegetation. Joe hopped out as soon as the vehicle stopped. He walked over to the back of the vehicle and raised the rear hatch. A nude woman lay in the back of the vehicle with duct tape wound tightly around her wrists, ankles, and mouth.

The woman had thick hips and thighs. Her breasts were enormous but looked artificial, too round, too firm, like the work of a surgeon. Her ass was large and round as well and clearly natural. It reminded him of Alicia's. Joe's breath caught in his lungs as he reached out and caressed her thighs, running a hand along her curves while she quivered and wept and screamed against the duct tape around her mouth.

"Shhhhhh," Joe said. "It'll be all right. No one's going to hurt you."

Joe rubbed her back, running his fingers down her spine and over her voluptuous ass.

"I got her for you. I knew she was your type," Selene said.

And she was. Joe wanted her so bad, even with all the meat he'd consumed, Cindy's flesh still digesting in his belly, he wanted more. He wanted to rend the woman's curvaceous body to ribbons and gobble up every ounce of her. But it had to end somewhere. The killing had to stop sometime or it never would and there was still more killing that had to be done before he would be free. This woman's death would be a needless indulgence, but he'd been deprived for so long in prison. Joe wanted to indulge every impulse, to greedily consume until he was beyond sated, glutted. He wanted to stuff himself full of flesh and blood, to fuck and kill until his senses were numb, but that was a step in the wrong direction.

The more he killed, the less human he became. Killing Belton, Cindy, even Mario, could be justified. Those murders had been necessary. But killing this woman would be for simple pleasure. Joe remembered something Alicia said to him years ago when she saw Frank roasting over a pit of hot charcoal:

"How the hell are you going to cure yourself if you keep giving in to the curse and killing people? Every time you eat somebody it'll only get stronger and harder to quit."

Alicia was right. Every time he killed, the desire to kill again grew stronger. He caressed the woman's breasts, gently squeezing each one and pinching the gumdrop colored nipples. The monster strained against his prison issue briefs, hungry for her flesh. The woman trembled and her eyes welled with tears. She shook her head back and forth as tears traced the contours of her face.

"Let her go."

"What?" Selene and Nathan asked in unison.

Joe grabbed one of Selene's suitcases and pulled it out onto the ground. He opened it and rummaged through it for clothes.

"What are you doing?" Selene asked.

"I'm finding her something to wear."

"You're really just going to let her go? Right here? Wearing my fucking clothes?"

Joe paused and turned to look at Selene. She was pouting like a spoiled child.

"Yes."

"Joseph, what's wrong with you? Why are you acting like this? First you kill my driver and then you want to let this bitch go? I know you want her. I can see it in your eyes. So take her! Fuck her, kill her, eat her! Tear her the fuck apart! You know you want to. I want to see you do it. I want to watch you take her."

Selene reached down and grabbed the woman by the hair, lifting her head so her face was pointed skyward. The woman was sobbing. Selene reached down and grabbed one of the woman's massive breasts, squeezing it so hard her fingers left little red indentations. She let it drop then and grabbed the woman's other tit, squeezing it even harder and shaking it. He had been wrong. They were real after all.

Joe's erection throbbed painfully. He wanted the woman and Selene knew it. He imagined biting into those succulent mammary glands, chewing them slowly, devouring them bite by luscious bite. A shiver went through him. He closed his eyes and took a deep breath, trying to chase the gruesome fantasies from his mind.

"No. It's not right. I can't. Just let her go."

Selene looked around like she was in some sort of nightmare, trying to find a way to wake up.

"What? What? What the fuck is wrong with you, Joe? This isn't you!"

276

"You don't know what I am, Selene. And neither do I." He thought about what he'd done to Cindy. He had told her he loved her one day then slaughtered her the next. He thought about what he'd done to Alicia, what he was planning to do to Nathan. It had to stop. "I don't know what I am. I just know I can't do this. Let her go."

"Okay, then take me."

"What? Don't be crazy, Selene."

"I'm not CRAZY!" Selene shouted. Her eyes were wild. There was a desperation there, but also a fire. Her soul was like an inferno blazing within her flesh. Joe wanted to tear his way to it, to devour that fire.

"I'm not eating you, Selene."

Joe turned back to the captive, weeping in the back of the SUV. He peeled the tape from the woman's legs and wrists and helped her out of the van. He handed her one of Selene's dresses. She pulled the tape from her mouth, snatched the dress from Joe's hand, and backed away, covering herself with both arms, trying to hide her nudity.

"You're both fucking crazy! Help! Help!" She jabbed a finger at Selene. "You were going to kill me, you crazy bitch!"

"I still might," Selene answered, stepping forward. The woman took several quick steps backwards and almost fell when her heels hit an indentation in the road.

"Get back in the car, Selene," Joe said.

Selene began to weep.

"No! Why are you doing this? Why aren't we killing this bitch? Why are we letting her go? Don't you want me anymore? What's wrong with you, Joseph?"

"We have to go."

He turned, and shut the SUV's hatch, then took the keys from Selene, and walked to the driver's side. Joe climbed behind the wheel and started the engine. Even in the huge vehicle he looked enormous. Selene walked slowly around to the passenger side and slipped inside.

"You're just going to leave me here on the side of the road? You crazy pieces of shit! I'm calling the police!" The woman shrieked in a voice full of anger and fear. She was struggling to slip into Selene's dress without falling over or exposing any more of herself to passing vehicles.

They drove off, leaving the woman behind. Joe could see her running toward the freeway, waving her arms for someone to stop and help her. He stepped down hard on the accelerator, watching for police as he put as much distance as he could between himself and the woman Selene had kidnapped as a present for him.

45

"Tell me about the curse," Selene said. They had been driving for several hours, only stopping to use the bathroom and refill the gas tank. Joe had changed clothes in a rest stop bathroom and washed all the blood from his face and hands as best he could. He left the blood-soaked clothes in a trashcan outside the restroom and climbed back into the car smelling like lemon hand soap. None of them had spoken much since leaving the naked woman by the side of the road.

Nathan had fallen asleep in the back of the SUV. He was curled up in a fetal position with both hands pressed together palm to palm as if in prayer and tucked under his cheek. He was sleeping like a baby despite all the horror and murder he'd seen today. He didn't seem to have a care in the world.

Joe and Selene were taking turns driving. It was almost time to switch. Joe's eyes were feeling heavy.

"It's a disease."

"So tell me about it," Selene said. "What do you think it is?"

"Like I told you in my letters, I think it's a genetic retro virus, like HIV. It carries DNA material with it from host to host. My guess is that whoever the original host was had something in his DNA, some genetic trait, that gets passed onto whoever the virus infects. A murder gene. So, instead of making you ill or killing you, this virus makes you kill."

"So, it's transmitted by body fluid like AIDS?" Selene asked.

"Blood, semen, maybe even saliva. I don't know. I think it has to be transmitted violently, a bite, sex. Maybe it takes both. Maybe only blood does it or blood and semen combined. I'm not sure. Maybe it's a combination of the emotional trauma of being assaulted and being infected with the virus that makes it happen. I'm not sure how it works, but I know it's real. I can feel it inside me."

"Do you know how you got it? I mean, have you figured out who patient zero for this thing is?"

Joe nodded.

"I thought I got it when Damon Trent attacked me when I was a kid. But I don't think that anymore."

"Because killing him didn't cure you? That whole vampire/werewolf thing, right?" Selene asked.

The hulking serial killer nodded, obviously enthused by Selene's interest in the topic. It was the first time he'd talked about it with anyone in years, except Professor Locke.

"If the myths are true, then killing the source of the original infection should have cured me."

"But it didn't."

"No. But I think that's because Damon Trent wasn't the original source of the infection."

"Your dad?"

Joe nodded.

"I think I was born with it. I think my father had it and his father before him. That's why we have to go to San Francisco, to stop the disease at its source."

Selene stared at Joe then rubbed his face. He kept his eyes fixed on the road.

"Joe?"

"Hmm?"

"What if the vampire legends have nothing to do with it? What if it is a disease like you said, but all the myths are wrong? What if killing your grandfather doesn't do anything?"

Joe's fingers tightened on the steering wheel. He continued staring straight ahead.

"That won't happen."

"But if it is a disease, a virus like HIV, then there's no

reason to think there's anything supernatural about it. You might need a doctor."

"I went to a doctor. He couldn't cure me. He wanted to keep me drugged up on ketamine."

"Ketamine? Special K?"

"Yes."

"Wow. Do you have any left?"

Joe shook his head, still without looking at her.

Selene looped an arm around Joe's arm and snuggled up against him.

"I missed you, Joseph. Your letters were so beautiful. I couldn't wait to see you."

"I missed you too, Selene."

"So, what's going on with the guy in the back seat? Who is he?"

"That's Nathan. He's a fan. He helped me escape."

Selene nodded.

"So, is he going to stay with us the whole trip?"

Joe shrugged.

"I don't know, Selene. I haven't thought that far ahead."

Selene let the matter drop and changed the subject.

"I'm sorry about what happened at the prison. I just wanted you so bad and when you didn't give me what I wanted, I guess I got a little spoiled."

"It's okay."

"So, whose blood was that all over you?"

Joe's hands tightened on the steering wheel again.

"I had to kill someone to escape. Two people actually, guards."

"That's a lot of blood. I guess they didn't go quietly."

Joe shot her a warning look but Selene ignored it. She unzipped her shorts and pulled them down along with her panties. Then she pulled her shirt over her head and took that off as well. She put her hand between her legs and started fingering her clitoris.

"Tell me how you killed them. Tell me everything."

Joe didn't speak. He looked Selene over from head to toe. She had filled out so nicely, but he wanted to forget all about what he'd done to Cindy, his betrayal.

Selene slid her hand into his lap and unzipped his pants. She took his cock out and was only slightly surprised to see that it was covered in blood too.

"Oooh! This must be a good story." Selene continued fingering herself. She was wet now. She slid two fingers into her pussy, fucking herself while still rubbing her clitoris with her thumb, then she withdrew her fingers and rubbed them on Joes lips. Her scent was feral, animal. She slid her fingers into Joe's mouth and he sucked them clean. His cock immediately swelled. She began stroking his cock. It crackled with dry blood.

"I'm sorry. Let me moisten that for you." She leaned down and dragged her tongue down one side of his cock and up the other, tasting Cindy's blood.

"She was a sweet one, wasn't she? I have to hear all about it." She slid his erection between her lips and began bobbing her head up and down on it while swirling her tongue around the head. Joe let out a moan and tried his best to focus on the road.

Selene slid his cock out of her mouth and looked up at him.

"MMMmmm. Tell me how you killed them, Daddy."

Joe hesitated. Selene flicked her tongue along the head of his cock.

"Tell me how you did it, Daddy."

She was furiously masturbating now. Her voice was low and sultry.

"Uh, um. She was sucking my cock, just like you are now and then I cut her throat and peeled her face off and ate it."

Selene moaned as if she was the one getting the blowjob. Imagining him eating some poor woman's face was turning her on. Remembering the experience evoked a disturbing confusion of emotions within Joe—remorse, disgust, and intense sexual arousal. There seemed to be no confusion in Selene. She was panting like a hungry beast, moaning deep in her throat as she tried to suck the life out of Joe through his hard cock.

Joe almost crashed, jerking the wheel to the left to avoid drifting into oncoming traffic, when Selene climbed into his lap, impaling her sex on his tumid flesh and bouncing her voluptuous ass up and down the length of his shaft. She produced a small razor and began cutting her breasts, slicing her one remaining nipple and bringing Joe's mouth to her breasts to lap up the blood.

"Suck it, Daddy! Oh, fuck me, Joseph!"

Unable to contain the monster any longer, Joe lapped at the blood then and sucked the erect nipple into his mouth. He bit down, eliciting a gasp from her as he nearly severed it from her breast. Fireworks went off in Joe's head as he imbibed Selene's essence. It tasted richer, fuller, wilder than he remembered from the small taste she'd given him before. Her blood was white lightning and blue flame. Joe felt electrified. Selene's kegels contracted around his cock and he struggled to keep the vehicle on the freeway. He heard the bumpity bump of the big SUV tires hitting the road reflectors along the median line and steered it back onto the road, overcorrecting and crunching the gravel along the breakdown lane before managing to straighten the vehicle.

"That's it! Bite me, Joe! Bite me! Oh, God! Oh, fuck! It feels so good! I think I'm going to cum!"

Joe bit through her nipple and ripped it off her chest, chewing the tiny morsel of salacious flesh like meat-flavored bubble gum before swallowing it. Selene grunted in pain and sped up the motion of her hips. Joe roared and came, thrusting deep in Selene's sex, emptying his seed inside her. Selene raked her nails up his back and across his neck, flensing away skin then leaning down to suck the blood. It was too much. Joe didn't like it. It reminded Joe of what Damon Trent had done to him. He felt vulnerable again like he had back then. Helpless. Victimized.

"Stop."

"Oh, Joe! I think I'm going to cum! I think I'm really going to cum! Fuck me harder! Harder, Daddy! Harder!"

"STOP!"

Joe grabbed her by the hips and tossed her back into her seat. He was too late. He'd been distracted from the road too long and the SUV angled off the road and down an embankment. It went up on two wheels, and for a moment, Joe thought it was about to flip. Then it righted itself and came to rest with its front wheels in a ditch.

"Dude! That was fucking wild!"

Joe had almost forgotten about Nathan. He looked over his shoulder and Nathan was still strapped into his seat belt. His pants were around his ankles and he had semen splashed on his stomach. Nathan had been watching Joe and Selene the entire time, masturbating to the show. And from the position Selene had been in while she straddled Joe's cock, there was no way she could not have seen it. She had been putting on a show for both of them, getting Nathan off as well as Joe.

The vehicle was surprisingly undamaged. Selene had a bruise on her forehead from where she must have struck the windshield. Other than that, she seemed fine, though somewhat perturbed.

"I almost came. Why'd you stop me?"

"We almost died, Selene. Did you miss that part?"

Selene shrugged her shoulders.

"Can you think of a better way to go? That would have been one hell of a climax."

Her lips were stained with Joe's blood and his seed dripped from her neatly shaved snatch. If the virus was real, there was no doubt she had it now, and Joe was certain she had intended it that way. She had wanted to get infected. Joe remembered Luscious and Devon back in the penitentiary with their teeth filed like his, eyes vibrant with the same predatory lust. He had left them alive and now they carried the infection. Human predators like him. If he left Selene alive, she would become a murderer too. *But she already was, wasn't she?* Joe thought.

He looked over at her. Despite her injury, she was still rubbing her clit, grinding her hips against the air in a circular motion, frustration writ large in her expression. She still wanted to fuck. Joe had left her unsatisfied. She licked the blood from her lips then slid a finger up inside her, stirring the creamy soup of semen and vaginal fluids. She scooped the frothy custard cocktail of juices from her pussy, brought her fingers to her lips, and licked them clean. Joe turned away. He put the SUV in reverse and pulled them out of the ditch. That was the beauty of four-wheel drive.

"MMmm. Why did it have to end? I was so close. I think we need to stop for a while. I'll rent us a room. Drive to the nearest motel," Selene said.

"Maybe we should keep going? We've got a long way to go," Nathan interjected and the look Selene gave him would have melted steel.

"I need to rest. We all do. Just for a couple of hours."

Joe did feel tired after the orgasm and the near-death experience. He'd been fucking and killing since late the previous evening. His body was on overload. The meat he'd eaten weighed heavy in his belly. He hadn't eaten real food in almost a full day. His belly was still fat off Cindy's flesh.

"Okay. We'll stop at the next hotel."

"I need to stop at a pharmacy or a gas station first. I'm still bleeding."

Selene's breasts were awash with red where Joe had bitten off her nipple. Blood dripped steadily from the wound.

"Wow. You guys make quite a couple, you know that? I've never seen anyone fuck like that. I thought you were going to tear each other apart. That was pretty fucking intense. You had the car going over a hundred and ten miles an hour at one point, just before you came, Joe," Nathan said. "I really thought we were all going to die. It's funny, but I was cool with that, you know? Weird, huh?"

Joe nodded, still staring at Selene's breasts as he tucked his own cock back in his pants. He was getting hard again. He'd had so many orgasms in the last twenty four hours that getting an erection hurt. The monster throbbed in pain and Joe had to tear his eyes away from Selene's blood-soaked globes to keep from attacking her again. He stared at the road and forced his mind to avoid thoughts of cannibalism.

Her breasts were so much fuller now. Cindy's tiny bosoms had been wonderful, but barely more than a snack. Selene's would be an absolute feast. He remembered the white hot fire that coursed through her blood stream, the taste of her passion that had nearly scalded his tongue and seared his brain as it ignited inside of him. He wondered if his blood tasted the same to her; the blood of a kindred monster.

Selene managed to get the bleeding under control by putting pressure on the wound with a rolled up sock. She slipped back into her shorts and T-shirt. Joe felt a pang of regret as her breasts were once again covered. They passed a sign that announced a rest stop at the next exit.

"We'll stop here. You should probably go clean up," Joe said.

"Pass me my bag, Nathan. I need a change of clothes."

Nathan hefted a small suitcase into the front seat and Selene quickly rifled through it for new underwear and something to wear. Blood was already beginning to leak through the one she was wearing. Luckily, she wasn't bleeding half as bad as she had been.

They pulled to a stop in front of a gas station that was

also a restaurant and general store. Joe pulled up in front to let Selene out.

"Does anyone else want anything? Something to drink?"

"Can you get me a soda?" Nathan asked.

"Sure. What about you, Joe?"

"I could use some milk and maybe an energy drink. We've still got a long drive ahead of us. I need something to keep me awake."

Selene frowned.

"I thought we were going to stop at a motel."

Joe shook his head.

"I think it's best if we drive straight through to San Francisco."

"That's still five hundred miles away. It'll take us another seven hours to get there. You can't drive that long."

Joe shrugged. "I can try."

Selene walked off in a huff, leaving Joe sitting in the car in a cloud of confusion. He had originally planned to kill both Nathan and Selene, but he was finding their company enjoyable and he feared now that killing anyone else would curse him forever. He hadn't felt human in years and he longed to rejoin the society of man. Sitting in the bloodstained SUV with the taste of Selene's blood and flesh still fresh on his tongue, he felt anything but human.

Joe reached into his pocket and took out two small pills wrapped in cellophane. After his last meeting with Professor Locke, the professor had given him Riluzole pills to try instead of the ketamine injections. They were designed specifically to modulate glutamate in OCD patients. Joe hadn't taken them, but had palmed them instead to save for later. He'd known he would be escaping the next day and didn't want anything blunting his aggression. Now, he needed something to quiet the monster. It was the only way he could resist the urge to eviscerate and devour his two traveling companions. Joe looked back at Nathan.

"Nathan, after we get to San Francisco, I think we need to part ways. You've been a great help. Really, I can't thank you enough for helping me get out of that place, but if you stay with me, I'm afraid it's going to end badly for you."

Nathan was silent, but Joe could sense the man wanted to interject something. Joe waited, but nothing was ever spoken. Minutes went by in complete silence. Joe's thoughts drifted back to his mother. After their last meeting, Joe had partially blamed her for what was wrong with him because she had known what her husband was up to or at least suspected. Now, he found himself forgiving her, understanding her more. There was something charismatic about murderers, something magnetic and attractive. From John Dillinger to Ted Bundy, society has long been fascinated by them, women in particular. Joe suspected it was the instinctual attraction to the alpha male. Females of all species were wired to seek out the strongest mating stock available and the man who hunted other men naturally stood out as a powerful mate as proven by his dominance over other members of his species. Even other men were programmed to follow the leader, the alpha male, the one who was the most violent, the most powerful. It was a genetic predisposition of social animals. Men like Nathan and women like Selene, Cindy, Alicia, and even his own mother may have had no choice in the matter. The more they were in tune with their primal instincts, the more those instincts would lead them to men like him. Nathan's pull toward Joe undoubtedly came from the same dark, primal place, from his Neanderthal, primate brain. Either that or he was just a sick fuck getting off on the carnage. Maybe they all were.

Joe thought back to how his mother had been before his abduction by Damon Trent, before the monster had begun to emerge. He never had any clue there was anything wrong with his family. His mother had always been loving and affectionate. His earliest memory of his mother was of pies.

288

It seemed she was always baking. The house smelled of fresh pastry. He still associated his mother with the taste of cherry pie. He remembered her hugging him and mussing his hair when his father wasn't looking. Joe's dad didn't think boys should be hugged too much. He was of the opinion that too much affection turned boys into homosexuals. So, Joe's mother always hugged and kissed him secretly.

The clandestine nature of his mother's affection had almost made it feel dirty, wrong. As he got older, Joe often wondered if perhaps he'd been molested and just couldn't recall. He just remembered the way he would stiffen and feel uncomfortable whenever his mother touched him, expecting his father to come around the corner and punish them both. After joining Sex Addicts Anonymous, he had considered that his lust for the flesh may have been partly due to love and affection being a dirty secret in his home. He never saw his parents show each other affection and his father had never hugged him that he could recall. So, he had grown up starved for human touch, sensual love. Perhaps it was as simple as that. Perhaps his lust for the feel of human flesh had simply morphed into a lust to consume it. He had to at least consider the possibility that his psychosis was strictly a mental illness and that there was no viral component to it at all.

During their last few sessions, Joe had gotten the distinct impression Professor Locke was no longer pursuing the viral theory of signature sex murderers. When Joe was first incarcerated, the professor had hired a virologist and a geneticist to study Joe's blood for signs of infection. That lasted only a few weeks. The last few years, he'd mostly employed a neurologist, studying Joe's brain for physical and chemical abnormalities. If the professor didn't believe him, perhaps it was all a fantasy Joe had concocted to justify his psychosexual rampages. And if that was the case, killing his grandfather wouldn't do anything but end a man's life and make Joe's addiction that much stronger.

"No more killing," Joe whispered. Hearing himself say it made it more real for him. "No more killing," he said again. From the backseat, he heard Nathan clear his throat to speak but seemed to think better of it and fell silent again. Moments later, Selene returned, looking refreshed in a canary-yellow summer dress and Birkenstocks. The dress seemed to hug her curves in all the right places and Joe wondered how she could make even such a formless garment seem sexy. Her bloody clothes were rolled into a bundle and tucked under her arm. She carried a bag full of drinks.

"You look good," Joe said timidly.

Selene beamed.

"Thanks. I feel a lot better. I took a bit of a whore's bath in the women's room. It was hard cleaning all the blood off my skin. Here, I bought you an energy drink. And I bought you a cola," Selene said, handing a fountain drink over the backseat to Nathan. Joe noticed the drink had no lid and thought it odd, but couldn't quite put his finger on it. He popped the tab on his energy drink then and tore open the little package of cellophane-wrapped pills.

"What are those?"

"It's Riluzole. It's to control my compulsions."

Selene frowned.

"You mean it's to chemically neuter you. You still want to change what you are? How can you still think about that after what we just did together?"

Joe shook his head and looked down.

"I can't do it anymore, Selene. I never wanted to be a monster. I never wanted this. I just want to be normal and I feel like I've gotten worse since they locked me up. I've forgotten who I am. I let them make me into a monster. That's not who I am, Selene. That's not who I want to be."

Selene sneered. Her face turned a deep red. She looked like she was about to attack him.

"I thought we would be together, Joseph."

Joe struggled to make eye contact with her. Her fury was so evident it was like a fiery wall between them, like staring into a hot oven.

"We *can* be together. But, if I don't change, every second you're with me your life is in danger. If I hadn't already eaten, do you think I would have stopped at just biting off your nipple? I would have killed you, Selene." Joe gestured toward the backseat. "I would have killed both of you."

Selene nodded. Her face relaxed and her shoulders slumped.

"Okay. Okay, Joe. We can do it your way. Here, I bought you some milk like you asked for. You should probably take it with this instead of the energy drink. You never know about chemical reactions and stuff."

Selene handed Joe a small, quart-sized carton of milk. It was opened. Joe thought about it for a second and then figured it was just her way. Nathan's container had been open too. Joe didn't notice that Nathan had not moved since he drank the cola. He popped the Riluzole and chased it with milk, chugging down the entire container.

"All right," Joe said, shifting the car into drive. "Let's get back on the road. I think I can drive straight through."

Joe fastened the seatbelt and turned the steering wheel. His arms suddenly felt weak and the road blurred. He never made it out of the parking lot.

291

46

The smell of frying meat was the first thing Joe noticed, before he opened his eyes. The smell and the screaming. The next thing he noticed was the man in the shiny, dark-gray, pinstriped suit. He had an oily ponytail, just like the last guy, only he was balding in the front and the gray had clearly been dyed out of his hair. He had a scar in one corner of his mouth as if someone had tried to widen his smile with a knife. His eyes were the same beady, black orbs, staring out of a face hardened by life. Joe guessed there was probably a line in the man's face for every cruel thing he'd ever done or bore witness to. It looked like a roadmap.

Joe tried to move but his arms and legs had been duct-taped to his chair. His clothes were missing. He was naked and helpless. He looked around, surveying his surroundings. They were in some sort of warehouse. Dust-covered machinery sat in shadows just beyond the glow of a naked incandescent light bulb. Beneath the cone of light emanating from the bulb, Nathan lay duct taped to a wooden table, crying out in mortal anguish. He was bleeding from what looked like a dozen or more wounds. Pieces of him were piled in a foil container on a small table. Selene stood beside him, sticking the poor man's arm into a big, stainless steel fryer. His arm was covered up to the shoulder in a thick cream. It took Joe a few seconds before he realized what it was— batter. Selene was deep-frying him … alive.

Nathan was already missing one arm. Joe looked around and found the missing appendage sitting beside him on a platter, roasted to a flaky golden brown. It smelled marvelous. Nathan's fried limb was the scent that had greeted him when he first awoke.

Selene stood beside Nathan wearing nothing but a pair of thick, blue, rubber gloves rolled up to her elbows. Two empty gallon containers of peanut oil lay overturned on the floor. Two more unopened containers sat beside those. Joe assumed those were for him. A five-pound bag of Bubba Jake's Fry Batter Mix sat beside a large stainless steel bowl. Joe had been correct. She had batter-dipped Nathan. Despite himself, Joe's mouth began to water.

"What are you doing, Selene?"

She didn't hear him. She was too preoccupied with Nathan. He was thrashing about and the duct tape had begun to loosen, splashing hot oil everywhere. A few drops landed on Selene's naked flesh and she danced away, cursing in pain. The guy with the ponytail ran over to help restrain Nathan so Selene could continue to cook him.

"WHAT THE HELL ARE YOU DOING?"

This time she heard him. She turned toward him with a smile that looked like a horror show. She had obviously started eating without him. She walked over to Joe, carrying a large buck knife in one hand and what looked like a half-eaten pectoral muscle in the other. It too had been batter-dipped and fried.

"I'm making dinner for us, lover. I promise you'll love it."

Ponytail pulled Nathan's hand from the deep fryer. The fingers looked like fried chicken strips. Nathan made eye-contact with Joe and his pitiful expression was absolutely heartbreaking. Joe could not imagine his pain. It made him think of what he'd done to Cindy. She hadn't deserved to suffer. Neither did Nathan.

"Why are you doing this, Selene?"

She smiled and took a bite of the fried meat. It was tender and moist. Grease drooled from the corner of her mouth as she chewed. She swallowed and licked her lips and then her fingers, one by one.

"Because I want to. Because it gets me off," she finally replied.

"You're just a spoiled little girl, Selene. You want it all. Your daddy's money. Me. But why Nathan?"

She shrugged.

"He was there. I wanted it to be the bartender, but you had to go develop a conscience and let her go. You didn't really leave me with a choice, Joseph."

"Who's your helper?"

"He's the guy who helped me clean up the hotel room after my little meal. That poor piece of shit you killed was just a chauffeur I hired."

"So what happens now, Selene? You going to fry me up too?"

Selene frowned and shook her head. "No! Of course not."

"Gaining all this weight to look more like Alicia, giving me that taste of your flesh, hiring a lawyer for me, getting me moved to general population, helping me escape. It was all so you could get the curse? Just so you could get off, you spoiled, over-privileged, little slut! You did all this for pleasure? Well, it's bullshit, Selene. There's no curse. You did all this shit for nothing. There's no werewolf or vampire virus. I'm just fucked up! I'm crazy, just like they said I was and so are you. We're both a couple of psychos!"

Selene scowled. Tears welled in her eyes. She shook her head vehemently.

"No. No! Why would you say that? Why are you being like this? I love you! I just want us to be together. I want you to be like you were!"

Joe shook his head.

"That's not going to happen, Selene. I'm done with all this."

Selene slapped Joe hard.

"Stop saying that! You think you're not a killer anymore,

just because now you conveniently feel remorse? Now that you're free? Did you feel anything but your own hard dick and that bitch's meat when you were fucking and eating her? A lot of good this conscience of yours did her. Now that she's dead and you've already cum. Just like a fucking man.

"And what about all the people you killed to get out of prison? Don't tell me you wouldn't do it again given half a chance. You're not rehabilitated. You're not fucking cured. You're not sensitive or misunderstood. You're not the hero, Joseph. You're the fucking monster! All those people you murdered, you think there's redemption for what you did to them? You think it matters one bit that you're sorry for what you did? You did it because it gets you off, the same reason I'm doing this. It's okay for you to treat women like a piece of meat, but when the roles are reversed then I'm the bad guy? Fuck you, Joe!" She slapped him again and wagged her finger in his face.

"You don't get to sit there acting all morally superior! You're the bad guy, Joe! You! Not me! You talk about how much you loved Alicia, but you didn't love her, Joe. You objectified her. You used her like you use everyone. I've never heard you mention a single conversation the two of you had. All you talk about is her ass and her tits and how wonderful she tasted. You loved her pussy, not her mind. Don't you get it, Joe? You're not some romantic hero. You have no idea what love is. All you know is lust. I just want to know it too."

She sighed and covered her face with her hands, looking up at the ceiling as if expecting some bloodthirsty deity to come to her aid and force Joseph to kill again. "Can't we just be bad together?"

Joe looked away. His face twitched and he closed his eyes several times and took deep breaths. Her words had wounded him.

"I'm done, Selene."

Selene's face hardened again.

"No, you're not."

Selene reached out and took Joe's limp penis in her hand. She began stroking his manhood, languidly at first, and then faster and more aggressively, commanding his dormant flesh to rise. It responded immediately, lengthening to its full eight inches under her impatient yet talented ministrations. When he was fully erect, Selene straddled his cock, easing it up inside her sopping wet pussy. Her juices flowed down her thighs in a honey sweet cascade, dampening Joe's lap. He had to admit, it felt like heaven inside her.

There were goose bumps on her arms and legs. Her body trembled as she pressed herself against him. She was practically vibrating with sexual arousal like a high-voltage battery.

"Oh, Daddy, I love the way you feel inside me. Your dick is fucking amazing." She contracted her kegels in rhythm with her hips as she rode his cock.

Joe closed his eyes, lost in sensation, his own flesh betraying him, unable to resist the feel of Selene's voluptuous body. She leaned over and lifted the crispy fried arm from the plate on the floor, brought the meat to his lips, and placed the buck knife against Joe's throat.

"Eat!"

The knife wasn't necessary. The smell of the meat, Selene's luscious body, had already roused the monster. He bit down savagely and tore a chunk of the meat off the bone. Selene took a bite as well, trying her best to duplicate the moment Joe had once shared with Alicia in the woods outside Tacoma, Washington. Joe knew what she was doing and it was reminiscent of that long ago evening, but it wasn't the same. He didn't feel the same way about Selene as he had about Alicia and Alicia hadn't tied him up and practically raped him. Still, the moment was no less exciting. Selene impaled herself on his hardened penis, bouncing wildly up and down, desperately racing toward orgasm as she ate Nathan's severed arm. Joe responded, meeting her thrusts with his own.

They finished the hand and forearm, but Joe was in a satyriacal fervor. The monster was off its chain and it was insatiable.

"I want more!" Joe growled and Selene leaned down and kissed him.

"That's my Joe! Welcome back, my Cannibal Cassanova."

Hearing that corny tagline repeated almost took him out of the moment. He looked over at Nathan, who still lay on the table, eyes glazed with shock. It looked like he was watching them and Joe thought he saw the man smile.

The old, Italian leg-breaker took a knife and cut off the arm he'd just fried. Nathan screamed again and then went silent. Selene's hired muscle brought the arm over to her. She quickly took a bite then and fed the rest to Joseph. She leaned over and bit off one of the fingers. Her eyes rolled back in her head and her breathing sped up. She was almost hyperventilating. Her legs began to shake and she threw her head back and let out a scream. Selene's entire body tensed and shuddered and her nails dug into Joe's chest. Her pussy contracted so hard it felt like it would snap Joe's cock like a carrot.

"I-I'm coming! Oh God, I'm coming! I'M COMING!" She thrashed and convulsed as seismic tremors rolled through her body like a series of earthquakes. Tears rolled down her cheeks and she began to laugh before falling against Joe's chest and sobbing uncontrollably.

Nathan was still staring at them and Joe was shocked to see the gravely wounded man's own erection swell. It wasn't exactly an oven, but Nathan had gotten what he asked for. He'd been eaten alive by his hero.

"I love you, Joe. I really do. That was incredible. I want to do it again."

"Untie me first."

She paused and looked over at the old Italian with the ponytail and the pinstriped, sharkskin suit. He held up his hands and shrugged, and then gestured to her, indicating that it was her call. This was her show.

"Uh—I—you won't hurt me, will you?"

"Do you love me, Selene?"

Fresh tears rolled from her eyes and she nodded. "I do. I love you so much, Joe."

"Then you have to trust me or you're going to have to kill me."

She nodded again then and waved Ponytail over to untie Joe. The big cannibal rose, with Selene still straddling his cock. He wrapped his arms around her waist and she wrapped her legs around his. Joe walked over to the table where Nathan lay breathing rapidly, clearly in shock. He took the knife from Selene and used it to cut off Nathan's other chest muscle. It was pale and blubbery with excessive adipose tissue. It felt soft to the touch, like a woman's flesh. Joe held the bloody meat up to Selene and she turned up her nose.

"Fry it first. I don't like it raw."

"You will. You'll come to love it." Joe laid her across Nathan's belly. It rippled and jiggled beneath her. Joe lifted her legs up onto his shoulders, thrusting harder as he offered her the meat again. This time she took it. She bit off a small piece, chewed it slowly, then swallowed it, and bit off another. Joe grabbed her by the chin and turned her head so she was looking down into Nathan's eyes while she ate a piece of him and Joe fucked her hard using Nathan as a mattress. She came again, just as Nathan stopped breathing. Joe withdrew his still-erect cock and left her lying on top of Nathan's corpse as he walked over to Ponytail and shoved the knife into his stomach.

Ponytail reached for his gun, but Joe easily knocked it

from his hand and grabbed him by his throat, crushing the man's windpipe in his powerful grip. Joe ripped the knife upward, opening the old Italian from his belly to just under his chin, bisecting him like he was gutting a hog. Ponytail's intestines spilled out onto the floor. Joe reached a hand inside the gaping wound in Ponytail's torso, fishing through his organs and pushing aside his stomach, bladder, and lungs until his fingers found Ponytail's beating heart. The heartbeat was rapid. The tiny muscle was doing its best to keep blood flowing to the dying man's organs, succeeding only in hastening his exsanguination. The heartbeat stuttered when Joe's fingers closed on it. He met the man's eyes and smiled at the shocked and appalled expression, the rictus of horror and agony twisting Ponytail's face before Joe wrenched his heart from his chest along with much of the old Italian's internal organs.

Joe walked back over to Selene, knife in one hand, her accomplice's twitching, pulsating heart in the other. Selene lay with her mouth hanging open where he had left her, draped across Nathan's belly. Her eyes were wide with terror, watching Joe walk toward her, drenched in blood and viscera. Joe seized her by the hair and rolled her over, bending her over Nathan's corpse. He let go of her hair and lubed his cock with the dead Italian's blood. He lifted Ponytail's heart to his mouth and took a bite, silencing the still- twitching organ. He spread Selene's ass cheeks and spit in the crack of her ass then and slid his cock in her anus.

Selene gasped and tried to inch away from him. He grabbed her by the hip with one hand and thrust, driving his cock balls-deep in her asshole. She cried out and closed her eyes and bit her bottom lip. Joe fucked her savagely, mercilessly, plundering her rectum with his mesomorphic sexual organ while he cannibalized Ponytail's heart.

The monster roared and so did Joe. His muscles locked and trembled as he ejaculated in Selene's bleeding anus. Just as Selene had done after her orgasm, the notorious sexual sadist and cannibalistic murderer, Joseph Miles, wept. He wept for his humanity, which was now forever lost.

Selene was panting heavily, completely spent, when Joe leaned down and whispered in her ear. "I know you killed Dirk."

47

They were back on the road. The radio was tuned to National Public Radio and updates of their recent escapades dominated the news. The bodies of escaped inmate Nathan Fillizi and multiple convicted felon with suspected mafia ties, Vincent Damiano, were found in an abandoned warehouse. Earlier, NPR reported on the brutal killings and mutilation of two corrections officers at Seattle's Maximum Security prison. They had even interviewed Fausto.

"What was Joe like? Well, like, he was a cool dude. He never tried to eat me or nothing, you know, right? He just seemed like a regular guy trying to do his time, but dudes were always tryin' to mess with him, you know, right? Like the guards, other inmates, and stuff, right? He didn't start fights with nobody, but people were always starting fights with him. I think they were just trying to make a name for themselves, you know, right? The screws included."

Joe smiled. It was funny that none of the reports mentioned the bodies had been partially eaten. They probably didn't want to frighten the public, which was stupid. Everyone knew who he was and what he did. The name Joseph Miles had recently become as widely associated with human cannibalism as Hannibal Lecter and Jeffrey Dahmer. Just because they didn't come right out and say it, that wasn't going to fool anyone.

They pulled up in front of an all-you-can-eat sushi restaurant on Divisidero Street in the Lower Haight Ashbury district called *Barracuda Sushi*. The head chef, Jiro Saggawa, had often written to Joe while he was in prison, asking for details of his crimes and suggesting new recipes for the preparation of human flesh. There was one Joe was particularly interested in. A technique called "Ikuzukuri."

Selene didn't protest at all when Joe lifted her from the SUV. The duct tape secured around her mouth had seen to her silence. She squirmed a bit, but the duct tape wrapped around her legs and arms up to her knees and elbows held her firm. Joe greeted Jiro at the backdoor.

"Joe?" asked a diminutive Japanese man in his mid-fifties with long ,wild, black hair like a rock star and delicate hands with long, slender fingers like a pianist. Joe had never met the man before, but he looked just as Joe would have pictured him.

"Hello, Jiro."

Jiro's smile was quick and genuine and instantly infectious. Joe felt his spirits immediately lighten. Jiro patted Joe's chest and looked up into his ice blue eyes, still smiling.

"You really big man. Like a giant to me. Oh! And you brought us some fresh meat. We'll prepare her together. Okay? Come in! Come in!"

Joe carried Selene through the back door and into the empty kitchen. The place was remarkably clean. Stainless steel implements shined, as did everything from the newly polished tile floor to the pots and pans and even the stove and the oven. Jiro cleared a table and Joe laid Selene down gently, careful not to bruise her skin.

"I am so excited! This is great honor for me," Jiro said, beaming like a kid on Christmas morning as his eyes crawled lasciviously over Selene's nude form.

"I am the one who is honored, Jiro. I have wanted to try this ever since you sent me your letter. Have you done this before?"

"Many time, with carp and lobster, even octopus, but never with human."

Joe smiled and patted Selene on her well-rounded ass. It was beautiful. It reminded Joe of Alicia's so much he felt a

302

pang in his heart. Joe had the heart of an artist and was prone to romantic thoughts. He fell in love as easily as others fell out of it.

"We need to wash her first and shave her too. Hair no good for sushi."

As casually and deftly as if he were preparing sushi, Jiro began scrubbing Selene down with soap and water, careful to get every nook and cranny except what was covered by the duct tape. He then selected one of the many lethal-looking sushi knives and used it to shave her. Selene struggled and the knife cut her.

"We need to knock her out. This no good. We always knock the fish in the head before we cut. Just be careful not to kill her."

Joe grabbed one of the heavy steel pots and whacked Selene over the head. Her eyes rolled and her nose and ears began to bleed.

"No good. She still feel everything. It hard to cut when she squirm. We need drugs. Maybe saki help."

Joe smiled. "I'll be right back. I think I may have something."

He walked back out into the parking lot, to the SUV, and rummaged through Selene's purse. The Rohypnolol was right on top. There were only four tablets left. Selene had been a busy girl. He returned with the package and handed it to Jiro, who dissolved all four of them in saki.

"She need drink it now."

Joe pinched her nose shut and waited until she opened her mouth before pouring the saki down her throat, effectively waterboarding her with it. She jerked her head from side to side. Joe spilled more saki on her than down her throat.

"It's okay. Saki make her taste better. Like drunken shrimp."

Joe knelt down and looked Selene in the eye. "You hear that, Selene? Like drunken shrimp."

The head injury was still bleeding and Selene's eyes had become glassy. The pupils had widened to the size of nickels.

"Good. That's very good. Okay, now we continue."

Jiro never stopped smiling as he and Joseph shaved every inch of hair from Selene's body with filleting knives.

"She very pretty. Very beautiful. Where you find her?"

"She found me."

Jiro smiled and nodded. "That's good. She love you?"

"She said she does."

"Good sushi always made with love. Love make the meat more tender."

Joe didn't doubt that Jiro was right.

"Okay, now we cut. I'll show." Jiro sliced down the center of Selene's torso, peeling the meat and fat from her ribcage and exposing the bones beneath. Selene shrieked, but she didn't squirm nearly as much. The roofies had done their job after all. Either that or it was the concussion.

Jiro lifted off one entire side of her torso, breasts and all. Her heart and lungs were still working.

"That's amazing, Jiro."

Jiro quickly sliced the meat into sushi-thin sections and then dipped them in wasabi and soy sauce. He served them with pickled daikon and ginger.

"You try," he said, handing a small plate to Joe along with a pair of chopsticks.

Joe took the chopsticks and lifted a small slice of meat from the plate. He dipped it in the soy sauce and wasabi and popped it into his mouth. It was amazing. The meat literally melted on his tongue. Joe closed his eyes as bursts of pleasure spread from his taste buds down to the root of his manhood like tiny explosions.

"Incredible, Jiro! You are truly an artist. That was the most incredible thing I've ever experienced."

Jiro beamed with pride.

"Good! Good! I try now."

Jiro, took a piece of meat that had once been part of Selene's breasts and slurped it down. He chased it with a small glass of saki and smiled ebulliently. "Mmmm. I told you. Love make the meat more tender."

Joe nodded. Selene was watching him with eyes full of pain. Tears streamed down her cheeks as she sobbed uncontrollably.

"Mind if I try?" Joe picked up another filleting knife and flensed the muscle tissue and bubbly yellow fat from the other half of Selene's torso. He removed the tape from Selene's mouth first. He wanted to hear her lubricious screams pealing from her throat as he carefully unmade her, taking painstaking care not to injure any of her vital organs. He wanted her to live as long as possible.

The groans and shrieks were like a symphony of pain. The perfect accompaniment to the meal. She was bleeding so heavily it wouldn't be long before she was gone, but Joe wanted her to see as much of her own destruction as possible before she perished. She was trembling, going into shock from the tremendous injury to her body and the overwhelming loss of blood. Joe sliced her thigh down the center and peeled her vastus muscles away from the femur. He sliced up the fatty meat just as he had watched Jiro do moments ago. Selene began to convulse. Joe made eye contact with her as he ate her piece by piece. He kissed her slowly on the lips and she breathed her last and final breath into his mouth, tasting her own blood and flesh on his tongue.

48

Dear Lana,

By now, I'm sure you've learned of my escape. The media has acquired a sudden preoccupation with my case. They have exaggerated a great many things. I hope it has not caused you any sleepless nights. I promise that you are safe. I have done enough harm to your family. I would never harm you. I have not hurt anyone in weeks. I am trying my best to abstain from sexual violence. It is hard. I have to stay away from people as much as possible. Just the sight of bare thighs, or even a bare calf, a neck, the scent of freshly bathed skin, they all make me want to ... act out.

I've read that relapse is normal during any recovery. Let's hope that's not the case. I started attending Sex Addicts Anonymous again. I found a new group right here in—whoops! I guess I shouldn't tell you where I am. It sucks not to be free to be completely honest with you. After your last letter, I felt like we were really coming to understand each other. But staying free has to remain my top priority, that and finding my grandfather. I have located him by the way.

He lives not far from you, actually. I

have considered coming to visit you after I see him, but I'm afraid that would be a recipe for relapse.

I'm still uncertain whether there really is a curse. Selene's behavior has begun to make me suspect I may have been right about it and how it is transmitted. I wanted to clarify what the news has been saying about Selene and I. I was not in love with her. Your sister, Alicia, is the only woman I have ever loved that way, Lana. You have to believe me. Selene was a very sick, very demented woman. She did terrible things to people. She isn't traveling or hiding out with me either. The news got that wrong too. Selene was the last time I acted out. But like I said, I've been good ever since.

I watched you last night through your bedroom window. You are magnificent. As gorgeous as Alicia ever was. No one could ever replace your beautiful sister in my heart, but if anyone could, you would be the one. That's why I have to stay away from you. But it's so hard. It's just so hard.

Sincerely,
Joseph Miles

WRATH JAMES WHITE is the author of *The Resurrectionist, Succulent Prey, Yacob's Curse, Sacrifice, Pure Hate,* and *Prey Drive (Succulent Prey Part II)*. He is also the author of *Voracious, To The Death, Skinzz, The Reaper, Like Porno for Psychos, Everyone Dies Famous In A Small Town, The Book of a Thousand Sins, His Pain,* and *Population Zero*. He is the co-author of *Teratologist* co-written with the king of extreme horror, Edward Lee, *Orgy of Souls* co-written with Maurice Broaddus, *The Killings* and *Hero* co-written with J.F. Gonzalez, *Son of a Bitch* co-written with Andre Duza and *Poisoning Eros I and II* co-written with Monica J. O'Rourke.

His short stories have appeared in several dozen magazines and anthologies. In 2010, his poetry collection, *Vicious Romantic* was nominated for a Bram Stoker Award.

deadite press

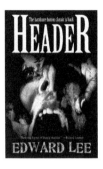

"Header" Edward Lee - In the dark backwoods, where law enforcement doesn't dare tread, there exists a special type of revenge. Something so awful that it is only whispered about. Something so terrible that few believe it is real. Stewart Cummings is a government agent whose life is going to Hell. His wife is ill and to pay for her medication he turns to bootlegging. But things will get much worse when bodies begin showing up in his sleepy small town. Victims of an act known only as "a Header."

"Punk Rock Ghost Story" David Agranoff - In the summer of 1982, legendary Indianapolis hardcore band, The Fuckers, became the victim of a mysterious tragedy. They returned home without their vocalist and the band disappeared. A single record sought by collectors, a band nearly forgotten, and an urban legend passed from punk to punk. What happened to The Fuckers on that tour? Why was their singer never seen again? No one has been able to say. Until now...

"Zombies and Shit" Carlton Mellick III - Twenty people wake to find themselves in a boarded-up building in the middle of the zombie wasteland. They soon discover they have been chosen as contestants on a popular reality show called Zombie Survival. Each contestant is given a backpack of supplies and a unique weapon. Their goal: be the first to make it through the zombie-plagued city to the pick-up zone alive. But because there's only one seat available on the helicopter, the contestants not only have to fight against the hordes of the living dead, they must also fight each other.

"The Book of a Thousand Sins" Wrath James White - Welcome to a world of Zombie nymphomaniacs, psychopathic deities, voodoo surgery, and murderous priests. Where mutilation sex clubs are in vogue and torture machines are sex toys. No one makes it out alive – not even God himself.
"If Wrath James White doesn't make you cringe, you must be riding in the wrong end of a hearse."
    -Jack Ketchum

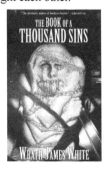

"Like Porno for Psychos" Wrath James White - From a world-ending orgy to home liposuction. From the hidden desires of politicians to a woman with a fetish for lions. This is a place where necrophilia, self-mutilation, and murder are all roads to love. Like Porno for Psychos collects the most extreme erotic horror from the celebrated hardcore horror master. Wrath James White is your guide through sex, death, and the darkest desires of the heart.

"Bigfoot Crank Stomp" Erik Williams - Bigfoot is real and he's addicted to meth! It should have been so easy. Get in, kill everyone, and take all the money and drugs. That was Russell and Mickey's plan. But the drug den they were raiding in the middle of the woods holds a dark secret chained up in the basement. A beast filled with rage and methamphetamine and tonight it will break loose. Nothing can stop Bigfoot's drug-fueled rampage and before the sun rises there is going to be a lot of dead cops and junkies.

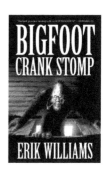

"Survivor" J.F. Gonzalez - Lisa was looking forward to spending time alone with her husband. Instead, it becomes a nightmare when her husband is arrested and Lisa is kidnapped. But the kidnappers aren't asking for ransom. They're going to make her a star-in a snuff film.. They plan to torture and murder her as graphically and brutally as possible, and to capture it all on film. If they have their way, Lisa's death will be truly horrifying...but even more horrifying is what Lisa will do to survive...

"Genital Grinder" Ryan Harding - *"Think you're hardcore? Think again. If you've handled everything Edward Lee, Wrath James White, and Bryan Smith have thrown at you, then put on your rubber parka, spread some plastic across the floor, and get ready for Ryan Harding, the unsung master of hardcore horror. Abandon all hope, ye who enter here. Harding's work is like an acid bath, and pain has never been so sweet."*
- Brian Keene

AVAILABLE FROM AMAZON.COM

deadite
press

"WZMB" Andre Duza - It's the end of the world, but we're not going off the air! Martin Stone was a popular shock jock radio host before the zombie apocalypse. Then for six months the dead destroyed society. Humanity is now slowly rebuilding and Martin Stone is back to doing what he does best-taking to the airwaves. Host of the only radio show in this new world, he helps organize other survivors. But zombies aren't the only threat. There are others that thought humanity needed to end.

"Tribesmen" Adam Cesare - Thirty years ago, cynical sleazeball director Tito Bronze took a tiny cast and crew to a desolate island. His goal: to exploit the local tribes, spray some guts around, cash in on the gore-spattered 80s Italian cannibal craze. But the pissed-off spirits of the island had other ideas. And before long, guts were squirting behind the scenes, as well. While the camera kept rolling...

"Reincarnage" Ryan Harding and Jason Taverner - In the 80's a supernatural killer known as Agent Orange terrorized the United States. No matter how many times he was killed, he kept coming back to spread death and mayhem. With no other choice, the government walled off the small town, woods, and lake that Agent Orange used as his hunting ground. This seemed to contain the killer and his killing sprees ended. Or so the populace thought…

"Suffer the Flesh" Monica J. O'Rourke - Zoey always wished she was thinner. One day she meets a strange woman who informs her of an ultimate weight-loss program, and Zoey is quickly abducted off the streets of Manhattan and forced into this program. Zoey's enrolling whether she wants to or not. Held hostage with many other women, Zoey is forced into degrading acts of perversion for the amusement of her captors. ...

"Answers of Silence" Geoff Cooper - Deadite Press is proud to present the extremely sought after horror stories of Geoff Cooper. Collecting fifteen tales of the weird, the horrific, and the strange. Fans of Brian Keene, Jack Ketchum, and Bryan Smith won't want to miss this collection from one of the unsung masters of modern horror. You won't forget your visit to Geoff Cooper's dark and deranged world.

"Boot Boys of the Wolf Reich" David Agranoff - PIt is the summer of 1989 and they spend their days hanging out and having fun, and their nights fighting the local neo-Nazi gangs. Driven back and badly beaten, the local Nazi contingent finds the strangest of allies - The last survivor of a cult of Nazi werewolf assassins. An army of neo-Nazi werewolves are just what he needs. But first, they have some payback for all those meddling Anti-racist SHARPs...

"White Trash Gothic" Edward Lee - Luntville is not just some bumfuck town in the sticks. It is a place where the locals make extra cash by filming necro porn, a place where vigilantes practice a horrifying form of justice they call deaddickin', a place haunted by the ghosts of serial killers, occult demons, and a monster called the Bighead. And as the writer attempts to make sense of the town and his connection to it, he will be challenged in ways that test the very limit of his sanity.

"Whargoul" Dave Brockie - It is a beast born in bullets and shrapnel, feeding off of pain, misery, and hard drugs. Cursed to wander the Earth without the hope of death, it is reborn again and again to spread the gospel of hate, abuse, and genocide. But what if it's not the only monster out there? What if there's something worse? From Dave Brockie, the twisted genius behind GWAR, comes a novel about the darkest days of the twentieth century.

AVAILABLE FROM AMAZON.COM

deadite press

"Brain Cheese Buffet" Edward Lee - collecting nine of Lee's most sought after tales of violence and body fluids. Featuring the Stoker nominated "Mr. Torso," the legendary gross-out piece "The Dritiphilist," the notorious "The McCrath Model SS40-C, Series S," and six more stories to test your gag reflex.

"Edward Lee's writing is fast and mean as a chain saw revved to full-tilt boogie."
- Jack Ketchum

"Ghoul" Brian Keene - There is something in the local cemetery that comes out at night. Something that is unearthing corpses and killing people. It's the summer of 1984 and Timmy and his friends are looking forward to no school, comic books, and adventure. But instead they will be fighting for their lives. The ghoul has smelled their blood and it is after them. But that's not the only monster they will face this summer . . . From award-winning horror master Brian Keene comes a novel of monsters, murder, and the loss of innocence.

"The Dark Ones" Bryan Smith - They are The Dark Ones. The name began as a self-deprecating joke, but it stuck and now it's a source of pride. They're the one who don't fit in. The misfits who drink and smoke too much and stay out all hours of the night. Everyone knows they're trouble. On the outskirts of Ransom, TN is an abandoned, boarded-up house. Something evil happened there long ago. The evil has been contained there ever since, locked down tight in the basement—until the night The Dark Ones set it free . . .

"His Pain" Wrath James White - Life is pain . . . . . . or at least it is for Jason. Born with a rare central nervous disorder, every sensation is pain. Every sound, scent, texture, flavor, even every breath, brings nothing but mind-numbing pain. Until the arrival of Yogi Arjunda of the Temple of Physical Enlightenment. He claims to be able to help Jason, to be able to give him a life of more than agony. But the treatment leaves Jason changed and he wants to share what he learned. He wants to share his pain . . . A novella of pain, pleasure, and transcendental splatter.

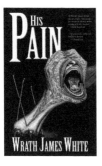

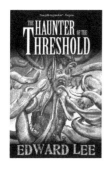

"The Haunter of the Threshold" Edward Lee - There is something very wrong with this backwater town. Suicide notes, magic gems, and haunted cabins await her. Plus the woods are filled with monsters, both human and otherworldly. And then there are the horrible tentacles . . . Soon Hazel is thrown into a battle for her life that will test her sanity and sex drive. The sequel to H.P. Lovecraft's The Haunter of the Dark is Edward Lee's most pornographic novel to date!

"Baby's First Book of Seriously Fucked-Up Shit" Robert Devereaux - From an orgy between God, Satan, Adam and Eve to beauty pageants for fetuses. From a giant human-absorbing tongue to a place where God is in the eyes of the psychopathic. This is a party at the furthest limits of human decency and cruelty. Robert Devereaux is your host but watch out, he's spiked the punch with drugs, sex, and dismemberment. Deadite Press is proud to present nine stories of the strange, the gross, and the just plain fucked up.

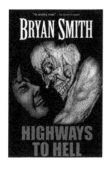

"Highways to Hell" Bryan Smith - The road to hell is paved with angels and demons. Brain worms and dead prostitutes. Serial killers and frustrated writers. Zombies and Rock 'n Roll. And once you start down this path, there is no going back. Collecting thirteen tales of shock and terror from Bryan Smith, Highways to Hell is a non-stop road-trip of cruelty, pain, and death. Grab a seat, Smith has such sights to show you.

"Apeshit" Carlton Mellick III - Friday the 13th meets Visitor Q. Six hipster teens go to a cabin in the woods inhabited by a deformed killer. An incredibly fucked-up parody of B-horror movies with a bizarro slant

"The new gold standard in unstoppable fetus-fucking kill-freakomania . . . Genuine all-meat hardcore horror meets unadulterated Bizarro brainwarp strangeness. The results are beyond jaw-dropping, and fill me with pure, unforgivable joy." - John Skipp

AVAILABLE FROM AMAZON.COM

Lightning Source UK Ltd.
Milton Keynes UK
UKHW021257231122
412711UK00021B/631